THE ABANDONED PRINCESS

THE FOUR KINGDOMS AND BEYOND

THE FOUR KINGDOMS

The Princess Companion: A Retelling of The Princess and the Pea
(Book One)

The Princess Fugitive: A Reimagining of Little Red Riding Hood
(Book Two)

The Coronation Ball: A Four Kingdoms Cinderella Novelette

Happily Every Afters: A Reimagining of Snow White and Rose Red
(Novella)

The Princess Pact: A Twist on Rumpelstiltskin (Book Three)

A Midwinter's Wedding: A Retelling of The Frog Prince (Novella)

The Princess Game: A Reimagining of Sleeping Beauty (Book Four)

The Princess Search: A Retelling of The Ugly Duckling (Book Five)

BEYOND THE FOUR KINGDOMS

A Dance of Silver and Shadow: A Retelling of The Twelve Dancing
Princesses (Book One)

A Tale of Beauty and Beast: A Retelling of Beauty and the Beast
(Book Two)

A Crown of Snow and Ice: A Retelling of The Snow Queen (Book Three)

A Dream of Ebony and White: A Retelling of Snow White (Book Four)

A Captive of Wing and Feather: A Retelling of Swan Lake (Book Five)

A Princess of Wind and Wave: A Retelling of The Little Mermaid
(Book Six)

RETURN TO THE FOUR KINGDOMS

The Secret Princess: A Retelling of The Goose Girl (Book One)

The Mystery Princess: A Retelling of Cinderella (Book Two)

The Desert Princess: A Retelling of Aladdin (Book Three)

The Golden Princess: A Retelling of Ali Baba and the Forty Thieves (Book Four)

The Rogue Princess: A Retelling of Puss in Boots (Book Five)

The Abandoned Princess: A Retelling of Rapunzel (Book Six)

FOUR KINGDOMS DUOLOGY

To Ride the Wind: A Retelling of East of the Sun and West of the Moon (Book One)

To Steal the Sun: A Retelling of East of the Sun and West of the Moon (Book Two)

FOUR KINGDOMS FAIRY TALE NOVELLAS

To Ensnare a Prince: An Entwined Prince and the Pauper Retelling (Book One)

To Entangle a Heart: An Entwined Prince and the Pauper Retelling (Book Two)

THE ABANDONED PRINCESS

A RETELLING OF RAPUNZEL

MELANIE CELLIER

LUMINANT PUBLICATIONS

THE ABANDONED PRINCESS – A RETELLING OF RAPUNZEL

Copyright © 2023 by Melanie Cellier

Return to the Four Kingdoms Book 6
First edition published in 2023 (v1.2)
by Luminant Publications

All rights reserved. Without limiting the rights under copyright reserved above, no part of this publication may be reproduced, distributed, transmitted, stored in, or introduced into a database or retrieval system, in any form, or by any means, without the prior written permission of both the copyright owner and the above publisher of this book.

The characters and events portrayed in this book are fictitious. Any similarity to real persons, living or dead, is coincidental and not intended by the author.

ISBN 978-1-922636-59-1

Luminant Publications
PO Box 305
Greenacres, South Australia 5086

melanie@melaniecellier.com
http://www.melaniecellier.com

Cover Design by Karri Klawiter
Editing by Mary Novak
Proofreading by James Packer

*For anyone who has ever felt overlooked and unseen—
you are known and you are loved*

ROYAL FAMILY TREES

KINGDOM OF ARDASIRA

Sultan Kalmir—Sultana Nadira

Parents of

Prince Zain (Zaid)—Cassandra of Eldon

KINGDOM OF KURALAN

Sultan Khalil—Sultana Rabia

Parents of

Prince Tarek (Rek)—Zaria of Kuralan

Princess Adara—Navid of Kuralan

Prince Xavier—Kalila of Kuralan

Prince Xander

THE FOUR KINGDOMS

KINGDOM OF NORTHHELM

King Richard—Queen Louise

Parents of

Prince William—Princess Celeste of Lanover
    Parents of
    Princess Danielle

Princess Marie—Prince Raphael of Lanover
    Parents of
    Prince Benjamin
    Prince Emmett

KINGDOM OF LANOVER

King Leonardo—Queen Viktoria

Parents of

Prince Frederic—Evangeline (Evie) of Lanover
    Parents of
    Prince Leo
    Princess Beatrice

Princess Clarisse—Charles of Rangmere
    Parents of
    Princess Isabella
    Prince Danton

Prince Cassian—Tillara (Tillie) of the Nomadic Desert Traders
    Parents of
    Prince Luca
    Princess Iris
    Princess Violet

Prince Raphael—Princess Marie of Northhelm

Parents of
Prince Benjamin
Prince Emmett

Princess Celeste—Prince William of Northhelm
Parents of
Princess Danielle

Princess Cordelia—Ferdinand of Northhelm
Parents of
Princess Arabella
Prince Andrew

Princess Celine—Prince Oliver of Eldon
Parents of
Prince Oscar
Prince Otto

BEYOND THE FOUR KINGDOMS

KINGDOM OF TRIONE

King Edward—Queen Juliette

Parents of

Prince Theodore (Teddy)—Princess Isla of Merrita

Princess Millicent (Millie)—Nereus of Merrita

Princess Margaret (Daisy)

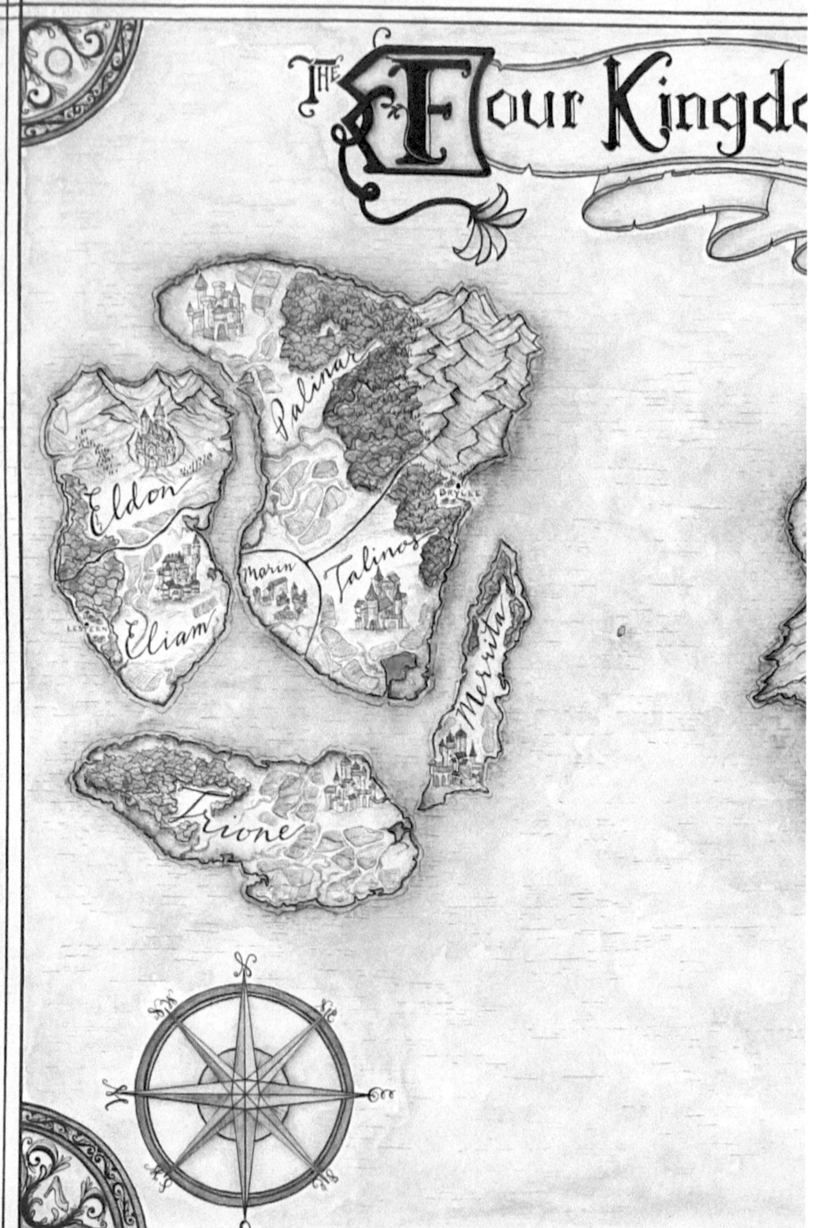
THE FOUR KINGDO
Palinar
Eldon
Brylee
Marin
Talinos
Eliam
Merrita
Trione

OMS
and Beyond
RANOST
RANGMEROS
GREENWOOD
Northhelm
NORTHGATE
Rangmere
Kuralan
BORDER CROSSING
Arcadia
ARCADIE
WINTER CASTLE
The Great Desert
KAREMA
MADDOX
LANARE
Lanover
SIRRALA
CATALIE
INVERNE
Ardasira
LARGO
BANISHMENT
ISLAND

PART I
THE TOWER

CHAPTER 1

The voices of the sailors could be heard from the bowels of the ship, their shouts of alarm punctuated by the slap of the waves against the hull and the uneven tilt of the ship. I had picked up sea legs quickly at the beginning of our voyage, but it was becoming more and more difficult to keep my balance.

"I think we should all head up on deck." Giselle—the oldest of the girls included in our delegation—sounded worried.

"I second that." Cassie joined the Eldonian princess at the cabin door. "I don't fancy being caught below decks if the ship's going down."

"I'm sure it won't come to that." Daria's worried gaze was directed my way.

"Imagine if it did!" I might be three years younger than the youngest of them, but that didn't mean I was scared. "I've never been shipwrecked before. We could all cling to pieces of wreckage and kick our way to shore."

We might need to remove our long dresses to successfully achieve our own rescue, but I didn't mention that since the others already seemed horrified enough.

"Perhaps we could try the longboats before we're reduced to scrounging for flotsam," Giselle said as she hurried us toward the deck.

I sighed as I climbed the steps. What was the point of leaving home on a grand adventure if my companions were just as obsessed with being sensible and responsible as my family back home?

It had seemed like the most marvelous thing when I was invited to join the Eldonian delegation to the Four Kingdoms—the new lands discovered beyond a stretch of previously impassable ocean. I suspected my sister-in-law, Isla, was responsible for the idea, and I had been suitably grateful before my departure. I just hoped my three companions—two Eldonians and one Elamese—would make the most of any adventures we encountered. If our ship going down before we reached our destination didn't rouse a speck of excitement in them, what would?

I certainly couldn't rely on Lori to be anything but sensible. I was fairly certain my parents had chosen a maid three decades my senior and without an ounce of excitement in her blood with studied purpose. Just like Daria, they worried I needed to be *watched*.

I peered around the deck for Lori, hoping she hadn't noticed my arrival. Given our current situation, she would no doubt attach herself to my side the moment she found me.

But my attention was pulled back to my companions when someone suggested the ship might be steadying—a most disappointing possibility. Before I could comment, however, the captain appeared.

"My men have plugged the hole with their hammocks. And now they're hard at work on the pumps." My heart sank until he continued. "But a lot of water got in, and it's only a temporary solution."

I brightened again. Perhaps we were going to have a proper adventure after all.

I stayed quiet as the older royals discussed the situation with the captain, knowing I would do my cause more harm than good by speaking up. I might have been born a princess, but with a nine-year age gap between me and my older siblings, I had always been treated like a baby. The only way I could learn anything interesting was by silent observation—or spying as my brother and sister called it.

It wasn't that I liked creeping around and listening to people —it was just the only option when everyone was determined to overlook and exclude me, always attempting to relegate me to the nursery.

My hopes were rewarded, however, when the decision was made to set some key delegation members ashore on the closest beach. The damaged ship would then follow the wind south to a more accessible port in Lanover with Giselle's older brother and his wife, Celine—originally a princess of Lanover—aboard. Celine was unwell, so she was relieved to head for her parents and leave Princess Giselle as the new delegation head.

Recognizing my moment to speak had arrived, I pounced.

"Naturally I'll accompany you ashore and continue on to our destination, Princess Giselle," I said, in my best formal tones.

Everyone turned to look at me with matching expressions of disapproval.

"As the lone representative from Trione, I couldn't possibly miss the opportunity to greet the Arcadians," I added.

Giselle and Daria exchanged a look, and I could easily read their thoughts from their expressions. They knew perfectly well my real reason for refusing to stay tamely with the ship. But it was true I was the only official delegate from my home kingdom, and while I was only thirteen, I was also a royal. It would be difficult for them to deny my claim.

I grinned in triumph as it was agreed that Cassie, Daria, and I —along with our various attendants—would join Giselle in a haphazard disembarkation onto the closest deserted beach.

I half hoped I would slip while climbing down the rope ladder to the longboat and end up in the ocean. But the process was managed in a disappointingly staid manner, and when the longboat reached the beach, I was swept into the arms of a burly sailor and deposited on the sand before I could protest.

Did they think I would panic if I encountered a drop of water? I might not have the good fortune to be half-merfolk like some of my family, but I had still grown up in a palace by the ocean. I could have swum myself to shore from the ship without the help of a piece of flotsam if it had come to it.

I couldn't stay downcast for long, though. Finally something adventurous was happening to me that didn't revolve around my older brother or sister. And they weren't even here to tell me to be careful or to try to take charge.

Daria was closest to me in age, but she didn't seem to share my excitement. And when I turned to Cassie, she looked more thoughtful than pleased with the unexpected development. Giselle joined us on the sand, but she seemed burdened with the weight of her unexpected new position as head of our delegation. She'd brought her strange horse, Arvin, though, and something about him always made me smile.

The mood of the other girls slowly brightened as I joked, trying to spread my own enthusiasm for our situation. Thankfully Giselle had declared we would walk toward the Arcadian capital rather than waiting tamely for rescue, and the journey would be more pleasant if the other girls were in lighter moods.

The bright spring sunshine helped my cause, the blue sky daring anyone to remain gloomy and downcast. And when we finally set off, we were walking between ordered fields, with a row of trees beside the road to provide shade. Personally I would have preferred a wilder and more intriguing setting, but the other girls calmed as we moved through the pleasant scene.

I positioned myself beside Cassie. Despite our four-year age gap, I felt a sense of kindred with the Eldonian girl. Giselle might be the other royal, but Cassie knew the value of silent observation. She had even grown up in a castle full of secret passages, a place I wished I could visit.

I questioned her on everything she knew about the Arcadian capital and particularly the palace. She had never been there herself, of course—none of us had been in the Four Kingdoms before—but she seemed to know more about it than I did.

"Do you think the Arcadian palace will have hidden doors and secret passageways?" I asked, finally getting to my most burning question. "Will you help me find them, if they do?"

She didn't answer, so I hurried to clarify. "Not that I'm saying I want to spy on the Arcadians!" A wistful note crept into my voice. "I suppose that would be terrible manners and might cause some sort of diplomatic incident. I just want the chance to see the passages themselves. And the clever mechanisms for concealing the doors. Do you think I would be able to find any on my own? I know they can be well-hidden, but you must be an expert. Maybe you could give me some hints at least?"

I looked at her expectantly, and she smiled back but in an absentminded way. I sighed internally. I was familiar with what it looked like when older people had lost interest in my words and were only pretending to listen.

A small wood appeared in the distance, swallowing the road. I examined it with interest, imagining threats lurking beneath the shadow of the canopy. A delicious shiver ran through me, unnoticed by Cassie, but a throat-clearing behind me made me stiffen. Lori had positioned herself behind us, the two ceremonial Trionian guards flanking her. Cassie might not be paying much attention, but my maid had her watchful eye on me as always.

Hit by a steak of rebellion, I spoke again in the same conversational voice I'd been using previously. "I'm planning to strip down to my shift and run screaming through the palace at every opportunity."

Cassie nodded, her eyes on the trees ahead of us, but a strangled cough sounded from behind us. I threw a mischievous look over my shoulder, meeting the eyes of one of the startled guards.

They were both fairly new to my family's service—chosen because they didn't yet have wives or children to hold them back in Trione—so they weren't used to me yet. Most of the guards and servants at the palace back home knew me too well to be shocked by anything I said.

Lori cleared her throat reprovingly, and I sighed aloud this time, turning back toward the fast-approaching trees. As the road plunged us into their midst, I angled my steps to drift slowly away from both Cassie and my looming attendants.

A noise in the trees to one side of the road caught my attention. It had been faint, drawing my notice only because the clink of metal didn't belong to nature. Was there someone there?

I directed my drifting steps even wider, trying to look casual as I stepped off the road in the hope I wouldn't attract the attention of Lori or my guards. Cassie was tense about something, even if I didn't know what, and perhaps the noise in the woods was related. I would just take a little peek and see what I could find.

I peered at the spot where I had heard the noise, the broad trunk of an ancient tree blocking my vision. There seemed to be something caught on its rough bark, so I leaned closer to look.

The small piece of material appeared to have torn off an article of clothing, and if it was still caught on the sharp spur of bark, it must have happened recently. I removed it from the tree and looked back toward the road, feeling triumphant. I had found something.

My eyes met Giselle's, hers full of worry as she hurried toward me, clearly concerned at my small detour. I drew a breath to call to her, but strong hands grabbed me around the middle, expelling the air.

My eyes widened, my gaze still locked on Giselle, as someone jerked me roughly backward. The sound of my name, screamed in Giselle's voice, echoed through the trees as the road disappeared from view.

CHAPTER 2

I flailed, my arms and legs kicking wildly as I tried to squirm out of my captor's grasp. I couldn't imagine who had hold of me, but there was nothing gentle in their grip.

Shouts, screams, and the clang of striking swords reached me through the trees, making me redouble my efforts. Whatever was going on back on the road didn't sound good. I had to get back there.

The man cursed, holding me firmly off the ground and preventing my struggle from gaining any force. Grunting in frustration I leaned down and bit his arm.

It had been many years since I had bit one of my older siblings, but I clamped down now with gusto, not relenting until I tasted the tang of blood.

The man shouted, thrusting me away from him. I fell to the ground, spitting as I landed on hands and knees. I didn't stop to get my breath, though. My attacker would soon recover from his instinctive reaction and attempt to recapture me.

Pushing myself to my feet, I fled into the trees.

As much as I wanted to go back toward the road, the sounds

of battle warned me not to be so foolhardy. Instead I fled deeper into the trees.

Trunks loomed all around me, and bushes and vines caught at my skirts, impeding my progress. I was tall for my age, but my legs were still much shorter than my pursuer, and he wasn't hampered by a dress.

Grunts and the crash of movement sounded behind me. I wanted to turn and look but didn't dare slow down. Someone was definitely pursuing me, and from the sound of it, he had companions who had joined the chase.

I had been acting on nothing but shock and a great spike of energy, but fear bit into me at the sound of the footfalls behind me. Escaping one attacker was challenge enough without facing a whole gang of them.

Who could they be, and what did they want with me? For all my normal curiosity, this was one puzzle I wanted to flee rather than solve.

Despite the continued sounds of pursuit, I managed to stay just ahead of my attacker, weaving between the trees. When a particularly tight knot of trees appeared, I headed straight for it, diving into the middle. Slim as I was, I could still barely squeeze through, my dress catching on the final trunk. I ripped the material free and threw myself back into full flight. With any luck, my pursers would mindlessly follow me and find themselves stuck between the close trees. By the time they realized their mistake and circled back around, I would have finally gained some ground.

The trees in front of me began to thin, and I somehow produced an extra burst of speed, launching into the sunlight of a tilled field. I finally risked a glance over my shoulder as I hit the open ground. My ploy seemed to have succeeded in delaying my pursuers because no one was in sight yet.

I slowed slightly as I looked wildly around for anywhere I might conceal myself. Only one option appeared.

A farmer, blithely unaware of the struggle going on among the trees, was walking some distance away. He had his back to me, moving away from the trees, and was guiding a horse pulling an open wagon full of straw. I had no idea where he was going with it, but his slow pace gave me a chance to catch up.

I returned to full speed, expecting my approach to catch his attention. The man must have either been half deaf or very distracted, however, because he gave no sign of hearing me behind him.

As I reached the back of the wagon, I looked toward the trees once more. The tilled dirt behind me was still clear.

Making a split-second decision, I took a flying leap into the back of the wagon. I nearly didn't make it, clinging to the back of the wagon with both hands, my legs dangling behind me and dragging against the dirt. But with a heave from my wiry muscles, I scrambled up and over the wooden barrier.

Landing face first in the heaped straw, I squirmed forward, trying to bury myself out of sight among the scratchy strands. I had made it halfway to the back of the wagon when it dipped slightly, as if someone else was climbing on board. I squirmed harder, unsure what else to do, but a hand grabbed one of my ankles, pulling me to a stop.

I let myself go slack, allowing them to pull me toward them before suddenly planting both hands and kicking hard with my free leg. I was only guessing at the location of my attacker's head, but my boot collided with something solid. A sickening crunch sounded as the hand holding my ankle let go. Drawing a gasping sob, I pushed my way forward through the straw until my hands hit the wood at the front of the wagon.

I groped my way along it until I reached a corner. Curling myself into it, I sat huddled over, my arms wrapped around my knees. I was trembling uncontrollably, my eyes squeezed shut. My attacker was still in the wagon, and there was nowhere else to run. But I couldn't hear the sound of anyone moving through the straw.

The memory of my foot colliding with a skull made me shudder. Surely I couldn't have killed him with a single kick to the head? Was he perhaps unconscious, lying hidden in the straw on the other side of the wagon?

For several minutes, I debated leaping up and jumping from the wagon. If he really was unconscious, I should take the opportunity to escape.

But I couldn't bring myself to move. The energy that had filled me before had vanished, replaced with the shaking that I still couldn't suppress. And besides, there had been more than one person after me. The rest might even now be lurking behind the wagon, waiting for me to appear.

But as we lumbered on further with no disturbance, the image became harder and harder to maintain. Was it just me and the one pursuer left? And was he even alive?

Slowly, my shudders subsided, eventually stilling completely. My courage rose to take its place. I needed to investigate and find out what was happening.

Shifting to my knees, I rose out of the straw. As soon as my head was free, I paused and looked around. Somehow, the farmer was still oblivious, still plodding along by his horse's head.

I gazed across the field behind us, but there was no one in sight. It really was just me and whoever was in the wagon with me. Gathering my courage even further, I looked around the wagon bed itself.

My eyes immediately met those of someone sitting on the far side of the wagon, watching me. But it wasn't the eyes of my original attacker.

It was Lori.

I gasped aloud, but when I went to say her name, she shook her head, sending a warning glance at the back of the farmer's head. My eyes narrowed, but I remained silent, scrambling inelegantly across the heaped straw toward her.

When I got close enough to see the bruise already starting to bloom from under her hair, I winced.

"I'm sorry," I whispered when I reached her. "I didn't know it was you."

She waved dismissively, pulling me down to sit beside her.

"He seems to be hard of hearing," she murmured, nodding toward the farmer. "And I'd prefer to stay out of his notice if we possibly can."

"Why?" I regarded the back of his head with a creased brow. "Do you think he's a threat?"

She shook her head. "Unlikely. But if he doesn't know we're here, he can't report our presence to anyone later."

I frowned. "But shouldn't we be trying to get back? We need to help the others!"

Lori sighed. "It's too late for that."

"Too late!" I cried, almost forgetting to keep my voice low. "What do you mean? They can't possibly all—"

"I saw a couple of the girls escaping on that pesky horse," she said. "And the others may well have fled also. I was focused on following you."

I groaned. "Don't tell me it was you behind me the whole time! Why didn't you call out and tell me it was you?"

"I didn't know who else might be within hearing range," she said grimly. "As it was, the two of us only got away because your guards stopped the men who were trying to follow you."

"But who were they? Why did they grab me?"

"That I can't say. They weren't on the ship with us and appear to have been lying in wait among the trees. But it was a coordinated attack from our own guards as well. It appears the Eldonians turned on the rest of us."

"What?" I cried. "I don't believe that for a second. Giselle's parents wouldn't do that! And Cassie certainly wouldn't be part of such a betrayal."

Lori refused to budge, however, her face dark. "I only know what I saw."

"Whoever was behind it, you're saying at least some of the guards from the ship attacked us," I clarified, trying to wrap my mind around the possibility. "And what about our two guards? You said they stopped the man who grabbed me. Why didn't they come after us?"

Lori hesitated and then shook her head. I stared at her, not wanting to believe what she seemed to be implying.

"Are you sure?" I whispered.

Her lips tightened, and she put a reassuring arm around me. In normal circumstances, I would have shrugged it off and told her I didn't need to be comforted like a child. But these were far from normal circumstances.

Burying my face in her shoulder, I felt moisture gathering in my eyes. I had wanted an adventure, but not one like this.

CHAPTER 3

*L*ori had us both lie down where the edges of the wagon would keep us out of sight of any passersby. Lying in the straw, gazing up at the blue sky, it all felt unreal. We couldn't possibly have been attacked by our own guards before we reached the first destination of our planned tour of the Four Kingdoms. None of it made any sense.

At the sound of the wheels hitting cobblestones, Lori raised herself up enough to look. After a couple of seconds, she lowered herself again to whisper to me.

"It's a hamlet of sorts. We should get off here. Be ready."

The pace of our progress slowed, the wagon eventually stopping as the farmer called cheerful greetings to someone we couldn't see.

"Now," Lori whispered, climbing over the back of the wagon and reaching up to help me down.

She whisked us both between two small buildings, immediately getting to work picking straw off my hair and clothing. I performed the same service in return until we were both clear of the tell-tale signs of our hiding place.

Lori regarded me with a critical air. "You can't go around in that dress," she eventually said. "You stay here."

Before I could protest, she disappeared into the single street that seemed to run through the tiny village. I watched her go with dismay, but one glance at my gown told me she was right. If we were trying to avoid notice, then I couldn't walk through a village like this wearing such a dress. I was supposed to be greeting royalty today, not traveling through the countryside.

Thankfully Lori returned quickly, having managed to procure a simple dress in roughly my size.

"Don't tell me you have coins with you!" I exclaimed as she helped me strip down and change.

"Your parents entrusted a purse to me, so naturally I carry it with me at all times," she said stiffly.

"While everything of value I have with me is back in my trunk," I said ruefully. "And let that be a lesson to me."

"It doesn't matter," she said. "I believe I have enough to cover our needs."

"And what exactly are our needs?" I asked, growing more and more curious about her plan. "Are you sure we shouldn't go back to the road to look for survivors? Or do you think the Arcadians will have arrived to help any injured by now?"

Lori sniffed. "*If* they aren't in on it themselves."

I raised an eyebrow. "Now you think it was a conspiracy between the Arcadians and the Eldonians? That seems far-fetched. Trione has good relations with both kingdoms, especially Eldon, and we've had no reason to expect anything but a warm welcome in Arcadia."

"Warm is not how I would describe the situation," Lori said.

I put my hands on my hips. "You can't be planning for us to walk home just the two of us. Sadly, neither of us are among the Trionians fortunate enough to receive a mer-tail, and while I've always longed for adventure, I haven't yet learned how to walk on water."

"Thankfully your parents had the foresight to send sufficient coin," she said. "We will head back toward the coast and then continue north until we find a ship heading for our own kingdoms. There is no need for us to determine who is truly at fault in the attack—all we need to do is get safely home. Your parents can manage what happens after that."

"You want us to get on a ship and go home?" I cried horrified. "But what about the other girls? We don't even know if they're alive."

"While I hope they may have escaped harm, they are not my responsibility. You are. And since I cannot hope to protect you if we put our trust in the wrong people, we will trust no one and remain concealed."

"You're serious." I stared at her. "We can't possibly just turn around and go home!"

"I see no reason why we cannot," she said frostily.

"I—" I stopped myself before I could express any more rebellion.

Lori would be watching me closely enough already without giving her more reason to restrict my movements. It wasn't as if she was attempting to bustle me onto a ship this very moment. She planned for us to move northward, and the Arcadian capital lay in that direction. Who knew what might happen before we managed to secure two berths on a ship? It would be better to stay quiet for now.

Lori regarded me suspiciously, clearly mistrusting my silent acceptance, but after a moment she decided to let the matter go. Despite her confident manner, she had to be beyond anxious about our situation.

I threw my arms around her waist and squeezed, taking her by surprise.

"Your Highness," she said, disapprovingly, but I grinned up at her, unapologetic.

"You have to stop calling me that if you want us to travel in disguise. Just Daisy is fine. And thank you. For everything."

Her face softened slightly. "Enough of that nonsense now. We need to get moving. One of the locals is heading north in an hour and was willing to give us a ride in his wagon. I said we've been traveling for days and have just arrived from the next town. Everyone I encountered took one look at my face and offered assistance without asking prying questions." She lightly brushed the burgeoning bruise. "Apparently the locals are disposed to help anyone fleeing from harm. So as long as we don't say anything to raise suspicions, we should be able to pass through largely unnoticed."

"My lips are sealed," I said primly, ignoring her look of disbelief. "But do you think we could find some food before we climb into another wagon?"

She immediately softened even further, hustling me out of the shadow between the buildings and into the sunlight.

"Of course we can. If we go now, we might even be able to find something hot."

Lori was right about leaving the hamlet without attracting any particular notice. Unfortunately I was less accurate in pinning my blithe hopes on the capital. The wagon she had found for us was an enclosed one, like those used by the trader caravans, and we were shut away in the back. Lori was delighted to have us out of sight, but it also meant we could see nothing.

I had to rely on the change in the wagon's movements, the increased noises filtering through the wooden walls, and the feel of cobblestones beneath the wheels to announce our arrival in the capital. There could be no doubt about the change, though, and I waited in eager anticipation for the wagon to stop.

But every time it did, Lori put a cautionary hand on my arm

and moments later we started moving again. We were only navigating the increased traffic rather than reaching journey's end. And as more and more time passed, a horrible suspicion crept over me.

"He's not traveling straight through the capital and heading further north, is he?" I asked Lori.

Her pleased smile sent my heart all the way into my boots.

"Yes, that's right. Finding him was an excellent chance. He isn't even a local but was only passing through that village on his way to his home in northern Arcadia. With any luck, our enemies will find we have vanished into thin air."

"Lori!" I cried, horrified. "I thought we were looking for a ship in the capital?"

She gave me an equally horrified look in response. "Of course we aren't going to look for one in the Arcadian capital! Must I remind you that we still don't know the extent of the conspiracy against you? If we can find a large enough ship heading west in the northern part of the kingdom, I will consider it. But I would far prefer we found berths in Northgate."

When I stared at her, dumbfounded, she frowned.

"Northgate—the capital of Northhelm, Arcadia's northern neighbor? Weren't you always poring over your family's maps of these kingdoms? Surely you remember the names of the capitals at least?"

"Of course I know what Northgate is!" I said. "I just thought…"

I didn't finish the thought, a new one taking its place. I had wanted an adventure, and wasn't that exactly what this was? The thought of tamely hopping on a ship to head straight back home had been crushing, but a wild flight across two kingdoms was another thing altogether. After all, in the original plan I was only the youngest princess in a large royal delegation, so how much freedom would that have allowed?

I sat back. "I can see you're right," I said placidly. "I quite agree."

Lori's expression only grew more concerned, her sharp eyes narrowing as she examined my innocent smile.

"We will not be leaving this wagon for as long as it remains in the Arcadian capital," she clarified, and I nodded sagely.

"A very wise plan."

Lori cocked her head, falling silent, although her suspicions had clearly not been allayed. I suppressed a smile. She knew me well but not quite well enough.

I continued to play a compliant and dutiful role for the next few days, lulling her into enough complacency that when we parted ways with the covered wagon in the northern part of Arcadia, she purchased the next leg of our journey in an open one. Seeing the countryside passing by was a great relief and worth the earlier careful good behavior.

But even with a view, sore muscles and boredom soon replaced my initial worry over my missing companions. Even the fascinating glimpse of life among commoners couldn't make up for the long stretches filled with only fields.

In the villages and towns we passed my eyes darted everywhere, taking it all in, but they were too few compared to the endless hours on the road. At least the only town large enough to have a sufficient harbor had no ocean-crossing ships in berth. But it also offered no sign of anything that might distract Lori from our endless journey and her goal of returning home.

When we passed the first squad of royal guards on the road, Lori returned to her previous state of unease and started looking for covered wagons again. Thankfully our first ride had been an unusual find, and she was unsuccessful in replicating the feat. While there was always someone willing to accept coin in exchange for taking a couple of unassuming passengers along on their northward journey, the vehicles varied widely.

However, it soon became clear that the various guards passing in both directions weren't interested in us. From bits of chatter, we gathered they were searching for a missing squad of guards that had disappeared on this road—news that sent Lori into a state of further anxiety and me into a state of suppressed excitement. Neither of our emotions proved to be founded, however. We saw no sign of the missing guards or of whatever threat had caused their disappearance.

Arcadia might be in some sort of turmoil, but our own journey was disappointingly free of any obvious danger. The most notable feature of our travel was the mountain range that loomed before us, growing larger every day. By the time we reached it, I had formulated a new plan.

My hopes now lay in Northgate. Lori didn't intend to hustle us through that capital, and I could only hope that with an entire mountain range between us and whoever had attacked us, she would finally relax. There was no reason to suspect Northhelm of having been involved in an attack far south in Arcadia. And none of our own group would have made it this far north yet since the delegation had planned an extended visit in Arcadia.

I hoped the journey through the mountains might prove more interesting than the road thus far, and at first I was awed by the vastness of the peaks and the wild feel that lingered even on the well-traveled pass. We had no mountain ranges back home in Trione.

But the beauty of the mountains was offset by Lori's increasing discomfort. I had thought she would relax as we left Arcadia behind, but instead she seemed even more on edge.

"Don't talk to anyone!" she snapped one night after I exchanged brief and meaningless pleasantries with a fellow traveler.

I pulled her aside. "What is it? You weren't like this before. I thought you were worried about the Arcadians?"

"I doubted the Arcadians," she said, "but we can't trust anyone we meet in Northhelm."

I stared at her. "Why ever not? What are you talking about?"

She lowered her voice even further. "Don't pretend you don't know who lives here! I'm well aware you loved Celine's stories about her older sister almost as much as that Cassandra did."

"Princess Celeste?" I bit my lip, not quite able to meet her eyes.

I hadn't realized Lori had overheard the stories or knew the true identity of Aurora, the infamous spymaster whose network spanned the length of these new kingdoms. She had started as Celine's sister—a princess of Lanover—but was now crown princess of Northhelm, where she lived along with another one of the Lanoverian sisters who had also married a Northhelmian.

Cordelia or possibly Cecilia. Or had it been Celandine? Someone really needed to talk to those Lanoverians about their naming traditions because how anyone was supposed to keep track of all the sisters was beyond me.

At least the Lanoverian brother who'd married the younger Northhelmian princess had a more distinct name. From the stories, Raphael was just the right sort of person.

I suddenly remembered he had also assumed the guise of a commoner and traveled these kingdoms, just as I was doing. And he had ended with a highly exciting adventure. Did Northhelm hold the same future for me?

"We never know who might be her agents," Lori whispered, recalling me from my fantasies.

"Surely you can't think Aurora's in league with whoever attacked us!" I said aghast, and she shushed me again.

"I think that I'm not going to trust anyone until I deliver you safely home to your parents."

I groaned. "You're being ridiculous! Aurora is the very one to give us some answers. By now, she probably knows who was really behind the attacks as well as what has become of the others. We should be running to her instead of trying to hide from her."

Lori narrowed her eyes. "Don't go getting any ideas. Just because you took a liking to Princess Celine doesn't mean we can trust an unknown relative of hers. Don't forget Celine is now a princess of Eldon, and they were the ones in charge of our delegation. It was also their boat that so mysteriously sprung a leak."

I groaned again. "I didn't think you were really serious about suspecting the Eldonians! They've been allies with Trione for generations."

"I suspect everyone," she reiterated. "And if you had a better sense of self-preservation, you would too." She gave me a long-suffering look. "But then, you never were too worried on that front. I knew what I was getting myself into when I agreed to accompany you—I just don't know what came over me that I agreed to take the post."

I grinned at her. "I'm a trying ward, aren't I?" I slipped my arm through hers and gave her a coaxing smile. "But you'll come to like me eventually. Everyone does."

She snorted. "Brat!"

She whacked me lightly, extracting her arm, and I grinned. After so many days traveling incognito, she had lost any formality in her manner toward me, and I much preferred it that way.

But by the time we emerged from the mountains, I was desperate for something to happen—anything other than the constant monotony of silent travel.

The first proper Northhelmian town was different from the Arcadian ones in subtle ways. Its layout was more ordered, and the people more formal, for a start. Arcadia stood in the middle of the Four Kingdoms, a central point for travelers, which helped explain its more relaxed and easygoing populace. Within minutes I could tell we were going to stand out more in this new kingdom.

The formal manner of the Northhelmians put up a barrier between us and other travelers, meaning I didn't initially take any note of the lone traveler we met on our second night out of the mountains. Several groups had set up camp for the night beneath one of the open wooden shelters provided for the purpose, but there was little chatter or mingling between the groups. So the woman who kept to herself drew little attention.

However when she suddenly displayed the opposite behavior, it caught my eye immediately. Her interest was clearly caught by Lori's conversation with one of the groups of travelers. Our current benefactors were about to turn eastward toward their home village, so Lori was attempting to negotiate a new ride for us. Given the woman's lack of attention to anyone else thus far, I couldn't help but be concerned about her sudden interest in our plans. Especially since she was trying very hard not to appear as if she was paying attention.

I had grown up eavesdropping on adult conversations—it was the only way for me to learn anything of interest—so I recognized the signs easily. This woman wasn't a complete novice at the task, but she lacked the skill of one trained since childhood.

Standing up, I pretended to stretch and shuffle away from the fire as if the flames were proving too hot in the comfortable spring night. No one took any notice of me, and I slipped further back into the shadows.

Lori would no doubt tell me to stay put and do nothing but watch the woman, but I had never liked doing nothing. And after days and days of sitting quietly, I was about to go stir-crazy.

With a final glance, I ascertained that the woman was still locked in place by her small fire, her ear turned toward Lori and the small group of merchants she was negotiating with.

As a lone woman, it seemed unlikely the eavesdropper was thinking of attacking us or trying to steal Lori's preciously guarded purse. So why was she so interested in the conversation?

The woman's small wagon had been positioned on the northern side of the shelter, next to the one we had arrived in. It was a simple matter for me to slip between the two vehicles, putting their solid bulks between me and the gathered campfires.

The darkness outside the shelter felt reassuring rather than frightening, the light from the moon and the distant flames enough for my purpose. I hadn't realized how stifled I felt under Lori's constant watchful eye.

Thoughts of my maid sent me scurrying for the traveler's wagon. Lori might conclude her business and come looking for me at any moment. If that happened, I wouldn't have long to poke around.

At first glance, the wagon—more cart than wagon—looked perfectly ordinary. But I scrambled into the back anyway, determined to get a closer look at the various bags and boxes inside. If the woman had anything to hide, it wouldn't be sitting out in the open for anyone to see.

I moved methodically through each bag, checking the contents without dislodging anything. The cart possessed the usual paraphernalia of a long-term traveler, and nothing more. When I finished with the last bag, I sat back, my brow creased as I gazed unseeing across the dark fields beside the shelter.

The items in her cart might not be suspicious in themselves, but they still left me concerned. If the woman lived out of this cart, as it appeared, what business sustained her? She didn't appear to be a woman of wealth, and neither was she transporting trading supplies of any kind. Everything I had discovered appeared to be for her own personal use.

Perhaps she was traveling between kingdoms in order to take up a new position with distant relatives or something of the sort. It was a possibility, although something about the situation still felt off. My older siblings might have scoffed at me, but I had honed my instinct over years, and I trusted it now. Something about this woman was untrustworthy, and I wanted to know why she was so interested in my and Lori's plans.

"Well, hello there," a soft voice said from the back of the wagon, making me start violently.

I whipped around to stare at the woman who had approached in absolute silence.

"I must say, I didn't expect it to be quite this easy," she said with an amused smile.

I swallowed, a feeling of foreboding seizing me.

"I'm sorry. I got confused in the darkness," I said quickly. "I thought this was our wagon and was looking for my bag."

The woman tipped her head to the side, regarding me with interest. "No, I don't think you did."

"I get confused more often than I should," I said in my brightest and most childish voice. "My family are always scolding me for it."

The woman's eyebrows rose. "Are they? That's funny since I had the impression you don't have a family."

I swallowed. "Of course I do!" My bright tone sounded forced this time, and I glanced toward the half hidden glow of the campfires.

The woman followed my gaze, her eyes too knowing for my comfort. "I don't think your travel companion is your mother, somehow. You needn't worry about her."

"I should be getting back to her," I said quickly, moving toward the woman since it was also the way out of the wagon. "She will be worrying about me."

"Not at all." The woman gave me a smile that made me feel even more ill at ease. "She's already asleep, and sleeping quite peacefully from the looks of it."

"Impossible," I said flatly, giving up the attempt of maintaining a childish facade.

"I think you'll find far more things are possible than you could dream," the woman said, sounding pleased with herself.

I tensed my muscles and rushed toward her, determined to shoulder my way out of the wagon if necessary. The woman moved, however, turning slightly to give me just enough room to squeeze past.

The bare skin of my arm brushed against something hard and sharp on her clothing, but it didn't scratch deep enough to draw blood, so I didn't bother to look back. Jumping down from the wagon, I dashed toward the scattered fires.

I came to a sudden halt when I saw ours, my mouth dropping open. Just as the woman had said, Lori lay beside it, fast asleep.

Impossible! There was no way she had returned from her conversation, found me gone, and just lain down to sleep. I rushed toward her, taking in the details I had missed at first.

She lay awkwardly across her bedroll, still fully dressed including her boots. It was less like she'd prepared for sleep and more like she'd been knocked unconscious. But despite the formal air of the locals, they couldn't possibly have missed someone attacking Lori in their midst. And while the North-helmians might not be the friendliest of people, they had so far seemed scrupulously honest and law-abiding. I couldn't believe all these groups were part of some elaborate scheme against us.

"Lori! Lori!" I cried loudly, but she didn't stir. Neither did anyone else even look up from their fires.

I knelt over Lori, attempting to shake her by the shoulder. My hand kept slipping off however, my fingers unable to get a proper grip although I could see nothing unusual about her clothing.

I sat back on my heels, frustrated and confused. At least I had managed to ascertain that she was still breathing.

Clambering to my feet, I marched up to the next fire and faced them down, hands on my hips.

"Excuse me, but did you see what happened to my companion?" I pointed back toward Lori, but I needn't have bothered. Not one of them even looked my way. "Excuse me!" I repeated more loudly. "What is going on here?"

Again, none of them looked up. I gazed around the shelter.

Not a single person was looking my way despite my loud tone. No one had even broken off their conversations.

Taking a deep breath, I let out a blood-curdling scream. I usually saved it only for special occasions, and my siblings both swore it was enough to give its listeners a heart attack.

No one flinched or started. No one gave any indication of hearing me at all.

I stared around at them, utterly at a loss.

"So it works regardless of age," the lone traveler said. "That's good."

CHAPTER 4

I turned slowly to face her. "What is going on here? Are you all in league together? What have you done to Lori?"

"Relax, child, she's just sleeping. It seemed the least messy way."

"Least messy?" My voice rose. "Why are you doing this? And why are all these people helping you?"

I glanced around, looking for the tell-tale signs of people watching while pretending not to. But either these people were the best actors I'd ever encountered, or they genuinely couldn't hear a word I was saying.

"Oh no, they're not involved," she said. "They just can't see you. Or hear you. Or sense you." She paused, frowning slightly. "At least, they shouldn't be able to sense you. Why don't you try grabbing one of them? You could give them a good shake."

I stared at her, increasingly sure I must be lying beside the fire myself, trapped in a dream.

"Go on," she prompted. "Give it a try."

I wanted to refuse—just on principle because it was what she wanted me to do. But I had to try something.

I reached for the closest person, attempting to grab his shoulder and shake it. But as with Lori, I couldn't get a proper grip. Just as my fingers were about to grasp his shoulder, they swerved, skimming just over the top of it. I tried holding my wrist with my other hand and forcing my fingers forward, but it was no use. While I never made the conscious decision to pull back, my fingers acted of their own accord each time, preventing me from making proper contact with him.

So I tried the cup in his hand instead, intending to wrench it free and dash the water over his face. I couldn't pry it loose, however. He didn't appear to be holding on tightly, but his fingers might as well have been pincers of steel.

A wild, terrified feeling was growing inside me, sending panicked thoughts racing through my mind. I scanned our surroundings and spotted another cup sitting on the floor nearby. Some of my fear eased when my fingers closed around it and lifted it with ease. But no sooner had I got it to waist height, than the person closest to me reached out and took it from me.

I was powerless to stop him, my fingers turning weak and useless. I still felt a surge of hope at the interaction, however, but the other person gave no indication of having noticed it. He simply reached out, took the cup, and replaced it on the ground, all the while never ceasing his quiet conversation. It was as if the action had been done entirely without conscious awareness.

Growling in frustration, I strode toward our own small fire. Picking up my water skin, I downed several messy gulps, relieved to find that when no one else was nearby or paying attention, my hands still worked like normal.

A new idea struck me. Digging through my bag, I found a piece of paper and pen and scrawled a few messy words across the parchment's surface. But when I hurried back to the other fire and thrust it in the man's face, there was no response.

When I positioned it to entirely block his vision, he reached up a hand and pushed it down, my hand giving way at the lightest touch on the paper. Once again, he gave no sign of noticing any of our bizarre interaction.

"How utterly fascinating," the lone traveler said brightly. "The others never got as far as trying something like that. It's a neat arrangement, all told. I approve."

"What have you done to me?" I asked, hearing fear in my voice for the first time.

The woman held up her right hand, allowing me a clear view of the enormous ring on her third finger. The jewel at its center was black, a dull, ominous shade that reflected no light, although it somehow didn't dim the brilliance of the elaborate gold setting that held it in place.

"Is that a godmother object?" I asked, horrified. I had heard plenty of stories about how they could have their purposes twisted by those with ill intent.

The woman gazed down at it and shrugged. "I suppose it must be. I know of no other source of power. I didn't pry it from the hands of some deserving woodcutter's son, though. I got it from my brother."

"Your brother?" Even with my mind panicking, I couldn't turn off the spark of curiosity. Being in danger only made me want a better understanding of my situation.

"That is not the point, however," the woman said briskly, disappointing me. "The important point is that the blinding enchantment works just as well on you as it did on the others."

"But why?" I asked, honestly bewildered. "Why would you want to enchant me?"

"I don't," she said.

I stared at her. The whole interaction seemed to be descending further and further from clarity or sense.

"Well, not you specifically," she clarified. "Except that you seemed like as good a target as any."

"You attacked me because you think I'm alone in the world and virtually friendless?" I asked, incensed. "Do you make a habit of kidnapping youths with no one to defend them?"

"Not at all." She smiled, apparently amused by my outrage. "I hope I have more discernment than to think you alone in the world."

I glanced down at Lori, still deep in an unnatural slumber.

"Our fellow travelers might be deceived," the woman continued, "but it's obvious to me that you're fleeing someone. I didn't choose you because no one is looking for you. I chose you because someone clearly is."

I gaped at her. "You're that confident in your enchantment?" I shook my head. "You may find you've bitten off more than you intended." I hoped my words didn't come off like the bravado they were. "Half of Arcadia must be looking for me by now. And other kingdoms will soon join them."

To my consternation, the woman's eyes lit up. "Truly? You're truly someone of that much importance? What excellent good fortune."

Sudden and infuriating understanding bloomed. "I'm a test? You're doing all this to test your enchantment?"

The woman nodded. "You're quick! I like that."

"You like…" My words trailed off as I stared at her.

My siblings had always regarded me as the wildest person they knew, but even I couldn't wrap my head around the bizarre audacity of this woman.

I stepped toward her, anger filling me. "I see the enchantment doesn't work against you."

She realized my intention a moment before I reached her. Trapped in the slender frame of a thirteen-year-old, I had no chance of getting the ring off by physical force. Not without the element of surprise.

I reached for my hidden dagger. But as I pulled it out, she also drew something from a pouch at her waist. I expected to see a weapon, but she appeared to be holding a glass vial.

I drew back abruptly, but it was too late. She had already unstoppered it, waving it toward my face.

"We can't have any of that now," she said, as I staggered backward.

I tried to tighten my grip on my knife hilt, but my fingers were already weakening and growing slack. The world faded as I felt my body lower toward the ground.

I came back to my senses to jolting movement and discomfort in my arms and legs. As more of my awareness returned, I realized there was discomfort almost everywhere.

It only took me a moment to understand why. I was sprawled awkwardly in the back of a cart, my arms and legs twisted because of the ropes securing me to the bed of the cart.

I had been first enchanted and now abducted by a woman with unknown intentions. I had thought Lori was being overly anxious, but it turns out she had wildly underestimated the potential danger.

"This," I muttered in a thick, groggy voice, "is not the adventure I was hoping for."

I could almost hear Millie and Teddy in my head, saying *I told you so!*, so I forced myself to shake my head and sit up, taking better stock of my surroundings.

I was no longer in or near the rest shelter. My thoughts flew to Lori, my heart contracting. But if I'd woken up, she must have as well. She would be frantic with worry, but at least she wouldn't be dead.

I pushed myself up far enough to see my abductor sitting in the front of the cart, driving. But even without attempting it, I could see that the ropes tying me wouldn't stretch far enough for me to reach her.

I turned my attention to the ropes themselves, but with my

hands firmly tied together, I couldn't get the right grip to undo any of the knots. And there were many knots.

I sighed loudly enough that the woman glanced back at me. When she saw me awake, she had the audacity to smile, as if she was a friend, greeting me after an ordinary nap.

I was used to observing people—as a princess, I'd had the opportunity to observe a great many—but I'd never encountered anyone like her. I tried to assess what I knew or had guessed of her, but there was little to go on.

She appeared around thirty, although it was possible she was older. And she was attractive enough in a generic sort of way that didn't draw especial attention.

The perfect person for a spy, my brain supplied unhelpfully. *Pleasant enough to make people want to assist her, but not beautiful enough they'd remember her.*

"What's your name?" I asked, needing an anchor to pin my thoughts around.

"Eulalie," she replied after a second's pause. "It's old-fashioned, I know. My parents had a taste for unusual names." She paused again. "And what's your name?"

"You don't know it?" I asked, still not quite able to believe she'd really picked me at random after a chance meeting on the road.

She shrugged. "Your companion never mentioned it in her conversation."

"It's Daisy," I said after my own pause for consideration.

"Daisy?" Eulalie rolled it around on her tongue. "When you said there would be multiple kingdoms looking for you, I thought you must be royalty. I've never heard of a Princess Daisy, though."

I bit my tongue, unwilling to tell her my true identity. Those who knew me might call me Daisy, but in the official records I was Princess Margaret. That's assuming she even knew the royal trees of the kingdoms across the water.

"Oh, look," she said suddenly. "Another test."

I stretched higher so I could see what had caught her attention over the horse's head. Ahead of us, a cluster of buildings had appeared on the road. We were approaching a town.

"How long have I been asleep?" I asked, not expecting her to answer.

"Only a few hours," she said with surprising candor.

I looked instinctively behind us, wondering if Lori had woken up as well.

"There's no one there." Eulalie sounded amused. "But feel free to try to escape while we're stopped in the town. We can linger there for a few hours to give you a good chance."

I stared at her.

She glanced back at me again and laughed. "I really mean it. I honestly want you to try your best."

"Because this is a test," I said slowly, and she nodded.

I wanted to spite her—to tell her I was going to lie silent and unnoticed in the back of the wagon. But I couldn't bring myself to do it.

Determination filled me instead. She was taunting me because she thought I couldn't escape. I would just have to prove her wrong.

I didn't prove her wrong.

Even when she walked away, leaving me alone in the back of the cart, I still didn't manage to get anyone's attention. And alone, I couldn't even untie myself.

The more time passed, the angrier I became with my failure. But the heightened emotions did nothing to make me more effective. I shouted, screamed, even threw myself back and forth, making the wagon rock and the things inside it bounce around. No response.

I eventually gave way to the most humiliating thing of all. Tears.

I sobbed quietly, aware of being alone in a way I had never been alone in my life before.

"Are you all right?" The soft voice took me entirely off guard.

My tears stopped instantly, and I looked up, eyes wide.

The frowning face of a young boy filled my vision, his eyes concerned as they traveled from my tear-stained face to my bound hands. "Did someone tie you up?"

"You…you can see me?" I asked, sounding tear-logged and hesitant, utterly unlike my usual self.

"Of course." The boy frowned. "Why wouldn't I?"

I got onto my knees, inching as far toward him as I could. "Can you go and get help? Tell your parents I'm tied up here and need rescuing? You should hurry!"

His eyes grew rounder, his expression hovering somewhere between anxious and excited.

"Hurry!" I repeated, gesturing with my bound hands for him to leave.

He hesitated only a second longer before fleeing at full pace. I watched him go, torn between hope and tension.

Would he follow through or get distracted? And if he did bring his parents, would they make it back before Eulalie?

Each second seemed like a minute, and every set of footsteps made my heart rate increase. Was it the boy and his family or Eulalie returning?

After three random people wandered past, playing havoc with my blood pressure, I finally heard the sound of multiple hurrying feet.

"There!" a proud, childish voice announced. "There she is!"

"Thank you," I gasped out. "Thank you for coming back."

He smiled at me, but both his parents were frowning.

"Please help me," I said. "I'm under an enchantment. It must have finally worn off, but my captor could be back any minute."

"An enchantment?" the boy asked with interest. Now that his parents were beside him, the excitement seemed to have won over the nerves.

"Enchantment?" The boy's mother looked at him with an exasperated sigh. "You mean this is just another one of your games? You had me genuinely worried!"

The boy gave her an offended look. "It's not a game! She's right there. Look!" He pointed at me again.

"Yes, I'm right here," I said, breathlessly. "I need your help. If you could just untie me." I held out my bound hands, but already my tight nerves were unwinding, crushing disappointment settling in to take their place.

The child had been a fluke. It wasn't that the enchantment had expired, but that he was somehow immune from it.

"That's enough," the father said sternly to his son. "You should know better than to worry your mother and me like that."

"But Father!" the boy protested, his voice turning whiny. "I *didn't* make it up! She's really there!"

"I said, *that's enough!*" The father glared so sternly that the boy subsided with a petulant look.

"No, please! I really am here!" I called, tears running down my cheeks again.

I used to fancy myself unseen and overlooked, but it was nothing to the horror of being truly invisible.

The boy threw me a look that was half resentful, half regretful. I wasn't sure if he was annoyed at me for getting him in trouble or sorry he hadn't been able to help.

"Maybe you could try untying me yourself?" I asked him in desperation, but his parents were already dragging him away.

"Wait!" I shouted, giving way to my desperation. "Wait!"

But they were already halfway down the street, disappearing far too quickly. The last of my earlier hope popped, leaving me even more discouraged than before the boy's appearance. I barely even registered the other flickers of movement on the street. I was fairly sure the unfamiliar wagon was being surreptitiously watched, but that didn't do me any good if the observers couldn't see me.

I suspected a local was contemplating robbing the apparently unattended vehicle since someone had been lurking half out of sight in nearby shadows for several minutes. But even if they came and riffled through every bag, it wouldn't do me any good. Or perhaps it was Eulalie herself, observing the success of her test.

"That's an unexpected development." Eulalie's displeased voice made me whirl around to stare at where she was emerging from behind a different building altogether.

"You were watching the whole time?" I muttered, more statement than question. The hope I'd briefly held really had been nothing but an illusion. "What if I'd escaped?"

"I told you to try, didn't I?" She stared down the street where the family had now disappeared. "But I didn't expect that. Was the boy special somehow? Or was it his age?" Her voice dropped to a murmur, as if she was talking to herself. "Did either of the others ever come in contact with a child?"

"Others?" I lunged over to the side of the wagon closest to her, gripping the edge. "What others?"

"There's no need to get so excited," she said coldly. "There aren't any others anymore."

"You killed them!?" I cried, genuinely horrified, but also wanting to see her response to my bald accusation.

She stiffened and frowned. "They shouldn't have caused trouble. I told them…" She trailed off with a glance at me, apparently not wanting me to know what she'd told them.

Had they attacked her? I glanced down at the thick ropes and copious knots. If so, Eulalie wasn't taking any risks this time. Was that why she'd chosen a thirteen-year-old girl? If I was an experiment, it sounded like I wasn't the first. If her previous victims had been adults and had attacked her, she must have decided to go for a weaker test subject this time.

"Did I go too far?" she asked, as if I'd spoken aloud. "Is it because you're a child yourself? Does that affect the enchantment somehow? I'm sure that previously..." She frowned, lost in thought.

"You might as well free me, then," I said. "I have no idea who you are, so I can't cause any trouble for you."

Eulalie grinned in response, the expression sending a chill down my spine.

"I like you, Daisy. You have spunk."

I suppressed a shiver. It had been beyond a long shot, but I was getting desperate.

"What are you going to do with me?" I asked.

She glanced down at her ring, taking my eyes with her. I immediately wanted to look away but couldn't. Like before, the deadness of the black trapped my eyes, making me shiver in discomfort.

"Did you know it used to be blue?" she asked conversationally. "It's been getting darker with each use. If I'd known when I started that I had limited test opportunities, I would have been more careful with the first ones. But it's too late for that. You're my last chance, so we'll just have to see this test through." She smiled.

I gulped. "What does that mean?"

"I need to work out why children can apparently see you. It must have something to do with you being a child yourself. The others were adults, and I'm sure I remember one of them encountering a child without issue." She shook her head. "There may be another way around it, or the effect may disappear with time. But if not, your age may be the key. Perhaps when you become an adult, we'll no longer have the issue with children."

"When I become an adult?" I asked, my mouth dry.

She smiled brightly. "Like I said, we'll just have to take our time with this test."

CHAPTER 5

I leaned as far out the tower window as I could without plummeting to my death. It was a fine line, but I had honed the skill over five long years.

"Charli!" I shouted, gesturing wildly for the petite girl to approach closer.

She looked up at my cry, her expression remaining calm despite my exuberance. But the slightly taller girl next to her didn't respond at all.

Instead Jayda gaped around the clearing, her eyes sweeping the space without latching onto anything. My stone tower was far too tall and prominent not to draw the eye, but she gave no appearance of seeing it at all. Her response was expected, but it still made my insides twist.

I looked down at the boy sitting at the base of the tower, consuming the last of an apple core.

"Was Jayda's birthday today, Barnaby?"

"Yesterday." He paused to spit out a seed. "But she was busy with her parents all morning, and then there was that spring storm in the afternoon. She couldn't get away until now."

I slumped against the stone, looking back at the two girls. "So it's still the same."

It had been two years since the next oldest of the local children had turned thirteen, and I hadn't been able to help the creeping hope that the enchantment might have faded in that time.

Charli took Jayda's arm and pulled her closer to the tower before gazing up at me, her face twisted into a sympathetic expression that made my gut churn.

"Sorry, Daisy," she called. "We were hoping, but…"

"Can you really still see her?" Jayda asked with wide eyes. "I know the others said they couldn't anymore after their birthday, but I wondered…"

She didn't finish the thought, but I knew what she was thinking. The younger children openly suspected their old playmates of only pretending to no longer see me or my tower once they turned thirteen. They thought the youths wanted to mark themselves as too grownup for the *childish games* they had previously indulged in with the younger children.

As a result, the youngsters branded the youths heartless, but I'd never been convinced. I recognized their expressions well enough to know they truly didn't see me, and I suspected the enchantment had a hand in making them brush off their old reality so easily.

"You'll have to apologize to your brother for doubting him," I called down, but of course she didn't react.

Charli gave a small grin. "She says you'll need to apologize to Simon."

Jayda stared upward, missing my location and glaring angrily at empty air to my left. "You might be invisible now, but I can see you haven't lost your sense of humor!"

She faltered, looking at Charli. "She really is still there?"

Charli nodded, and Jayda looked upward again. I hoped she wouldn't promise to still come and see me anyway. Charli was good-natured enough to agree to act as interpreter, but I could already see the discomfort on Jayda's face. And I knew from experience that the discomfort would only grow. At best she would come a few times, with longer and longer breaks between them until eventually she disappeared altogether. It was better if she made a clean break now.

"I can't believe the whole tower is just...gone!" Jayda waved her hands in front of her, as if she expected them to hit the stone.

I wished they would. It would have been much easier for the children to convince their parents of my existence if the adults could have felt the invisible tower. But just as with everyone else over thirteen, Jayda's hands didn't quite make it to the tower wall. Instead they swerved, waving back and forth just in front of the stone instead of pressing forward, although she didn't seem to notice the awkward movement. I had no idea how the enchantment managed to redirect her movements without her noticing, but it had never yet failed.

I looked from Jayda to Charli. "How long is it until your birthday again?" I tried to keep the panic from my voice.

She hesitated before replying more quietly, "Three weeks."

I groaned as Barnaby tossed the stem of the apple and stood up.

"No need to worry about losing Charli. You'll still have me." He grinned up at me, displaying two missing teeth.

Charli echoed my groan. "Are you trying to make her more depressed? What good are you?"

"Hey!" He turned wounded eyes on her. "I'm extremely useful!"

"Are you?" She pinned him with a look. "What's the last useful thing you did?"

"Well...I..." He spluttered, clearly unable to think of anything.

"That's not fair!" he cried at last. "I just can't think of anything on the spot. Tell her, Daisy!"

He looked up at me, and I smiled sweetly down at him. "There was that time you taught Otis how to use a slingshot to shoot stones through my window. One of them even hit me on the head."

"You can't count that! I'm older now!"

"Oh?" Charli asked mercilessly. "So much older that you wouldn't dream of blaming Otis for stealing the cakes I sent for Daisy?"

"He really did take them!" Barnaby cried.

"Yes—because you volunteered the two of you to make the delivery and then told him we would never notice if all the nicest ones were missing."

Barnaby glanced up the tower, finally looking guilty. "Sorry, Daisy."

I rolled my eyes. "You should have just asked. I would have been happy to share. It's not like I did anything to bake the cakes. Eulalie would never let me have anything as dangerous—or useful—as an oven up here."

I ran a hand along my excessively long hair. "I can't even cut my hair since I'm pretending not to have any sharp blades."

"Don't worry, Daisy," Charli said quickly. "I know how much you love cakes. I can keep baking them for you even after I turn thirteen. I'll get Anaya and Arlo to deliver them since Barnaby and Otis can't be trusted."

I managed to smile my thanks, although I hardly felt like smiling. When Eulalie stuck me in the abandoned tower and extended my enchantment to cover the building, I had been terrified of the loneliness stretching before me.

Charli's arrival in the clearing had been like a burst of light in deepest darkness. She had brought the other village children soon enough, but even at eight years old, she had proved to be the most sensible of the lot. I had barely even felt the loss of her two older sisters after they'd each turned thirteen and been excluded by the enchantment.

Charli's humorous quips, sharp mind, and excellent baking skills had been a lifeline. But soon she would be gone.

"Don't you turn eighteen soon, though?" Barnaby asked. "I thought you were going to get out when you turned eighteen?"

I grimaced. The end date of Eulalie's test period was approaching. I knew that much. She mentioned it sometimes when she visited. She always avoided talking specifics, but I knew from the timing what she meant.

And when I was feeling hopeful, I liked to imagine that once she was finished her test she would release me. I had built all my plans and strategies around trying to convince her to do so when the time came.

But there were other possibilities. Eulalie's previous test subjects had met a different kind of end.

Not that their deaths had been linked to the completion of her tests. She had let drop enough information about them for me to know they never made it that far. They had become too dangerous for her to keep around. It was the reason I put so much effort into appearing harmless to my largely absent captor.

But Eulalie didn't have to kill me when the test ended. She didn't have to free me either. She could just leave me. Walk away after I turned eighteen and never look back. And I would never be free. Worse than that even. It was entirely likely that after I turned eighteen I would stop being seen by children. The adults she'd enchanted had been invisible to everyone except Eulalie herself.

If that happened, I would be trapped forever—alone except for one person. But how could I take comfort in the presence of Lori, my friend and protector, when she would be condemned to the same cage of invisibility as me? How could I be anything but sorry when I knew she had only become trapped because of me?

Lori had followed me—even when she couldn't see me, she

had followed the lone, fleeing traveler, convinced Eulalie knew something about my disappearance. And she had been touching the tower, hiding behind it, when Eulalie stretched her enchantment to cover the building. Lori's loyalty had trapped her.

Lori had been here for five years just like me, but we had different roles in our careful charade. I played the submissive and weak captive who stayed dutifully in her cage. Lori stayed out of sight altogether. Even after all this time, Eulalie didn't know she was part of the enchantment. The children didn't even know—with the exception of Charli—so Lori couldn't spend much time in the clearing.

Lori was the one who sustained me—the source of much of my food and practical necessities. Of course Eulalie had never bothered to question how I maintained myself on her sporadic gifts. She didn't care about those sorts of details. Or perhaps she assumed the children were supplying me.

But even if no one else knew, I knew how much I owed to Lori. So I could take no comfort in the thought that if I was trapped in the enchantment forever, then at least I would be trapped with her. She didn't deserve such repayment for her loyal service.

I drew a long breath. One way or another, the end date was approaching. My birthday was nearly here. And that meant Eulalie would soon be returning for one of her unpredictable visits.

I glared up at the blue spring sky. The specter of Eulalie's presence was enough to sour even the brightest weather.

Charli shook her head, her expression exasperated. "Daisy doesn't know what will happen when she turns eighteen. Not even her enchanter knows if Daisy will still be able to see us then or not."

"Probably not," I said glumly, unable to drum up the necessary hope that was required to envision a different ending.

"I suppose you can't come down today?" Charli asked.

I shook my head vigorously. "There's no saying when Eulalie will show up. You know that. And now is more dangerous than ever, since she's sure to be on her way back for my birthday."

"You should lie in wait and conk her over the head the minute she appears." Barnaby brandished a stick threateningly, probably imagining he looked like a noble knight.

He waved it too close to Charli's face, and she snatched it out of his hand. "Are you trying to put my eye out?" She rolled her eyes. "Thank goodness Daisy is more sensible than you! If she kills her captor, the enchantment will never be lifted and she'll be stuck like this forever!"

"I think it would be fun to be invisible. I could spy on my brothers and take all the best pies before they get to them."

Charli turned her back on the younger boy, clearly out of patience with his nonsense.

"It's in a week, right?" she asked, looking up in concern. "Your birthday, I mean."

I nodded, running my fingers lightly over the vines that curled near the tower window. "But I hear something exciting will be happening in the village before then."

I had never visited the nearby village, but after five years of observing its inhabitants, I felt like I knew it well.

Charli raised her eyebrows. "I came here on purpose to tell you about the royal tour. But you already know about it?"

"Apparently not everyone was put off by the storm's mud," I said with a glance at Jayda. "After the rain died down, the moon came out, and I had quite the stream of visitors."

I gazed around the lush greenery that surrounded my tower. The clearing was enclosed by dense forest, but the small haven was beautiful, the soft grass dotted with colorful wildflowers, and a burbling stream feeding the small pond. The clearing gave a sense of privacy without being too far from the village, and while it was the haunt of the children during the day time, it had become a favorite with some of the adults at night.

There must once have been paths that led to the tower—back when it was first built, at least. But any such paths had long since become overgrown, and the village had forgotten the tower's existence until several of the children had stumbled on it shortly after my arrival. I suspected one of them had been following Eulalie, spying on the stranger in the forest, although none of them had admitted to it. Once they discovered both the tower and me, it had become their favorite place to play during the day, and they had long ago worn a new path from the village to the clearing.

They had brought the adults along their path, of course, attempting to convince them of my existence. The adults had found no sign of me but had instead noticed the beauty and peace of the location. During the day they were busy with their own pursuits and left the children to their discovery. But nights were another story.

I had witnessed two marriage proposals and several betrayals, as well as an untold number of sensitive conversations. Trapped in my tower, I couldn't help overhearing their words, but I was honest enough to admit I didn't try to avoid it. I observed their interactions as assiduously as I had watched the various negotiations in the palace of my childhood. And I was pathetically grateful for the mental stimulation they provided. I might be trapped on the outside, always in the role of observer, but at least I wasn't cut off from the world entirely.

Charli grimaced at my mention of visitors. "I suppose they were all plotting and planning how to win favor over their rivals in the eyes of the royals. As if the royals care about the activities of a small village's worth of their subjects!"

"So it really is true?" I asked. "It seems hard to believe the king and crown prince will be coming here of all places."

"They're touring the whole kingdom apparently." She shrugged. "In preparation for King Richard stepping down and handing the throne to Prince William."

"Is Princess Celeste coming too?" Eagerness seeped into my voice. "Can you find an excuse to bring her to the tower? I've heard she's the most beautiful princess in all the kingdoms, even the new ones." I'd heard more interesting things about her, too, but I didn't mention those.

Barnaby rolled his eyes. "Who cares about that? I'm hoping Prince Raphael comes. He's won the annual archery competition in the capital every year since he married Princess Marie."

"If he comes, he'll bring his wife as well, won't he?" Jayda asked, joining in on the half of the conversation she could hear. Her face lit up as if she was imparting a scandalous secret. "I heard she's not even a real princess."

Charli sighed. "That sort of nonsense is exactly why King Richard and Prince William are touring the kingdom. So everyone can see for themselves that they're the true rulers."

Jayda sniffed and turned up her nose. "Let's go back. It's boring here now, and it's kind of creepy to hear you both talking to no one."

"Daisy isn't no one!" Charli looked up at me, worry in her eyes.

I smiled back and waved them away. "Head back like she says. Don't worry about me."

I knew what she was thinking, though, because it was the same thing I was thinking. Even if I could still see children after my own birthday, Charli would soon be in the same situation as Jayda, and then I would have lost the one child who was an actual friend.

I could see the weight on her shoulders as she walked away, so I rallied enough to call after them.

"Do think of a way to bring at least one of the royal visitors here! I'll die of curiosity if you can't!"

Charli looked back and waved, her amused smile providing a reward for my efforts. But as soon as she turned away again, I slid inside the tower and slumped to the floor.

CHAPTER 6

A familiar black cloud settled over me. In a week I would turn eighteen. I was about to become an adult, and I had spent my entire youth locked in a tower. When the villagers turned thirteen, they left behind the childish games of this clearing and exchanged them for real life in the village. But I had done exactly the opposite.

A small, bitter laugh slipped out. How juvenile my old longing for adventure seemed now. I had gotten exactly what I wished for, and it had robbed me of five precious years.

I forced myself to take a deep breath, placing a hand on my stomach to make sure it was expanding as I breathed in. My longest-lasting governess had been the one to teach me the breathing technique—insisting I use it whenever I needed to refocus. Repeating the old exercise always made me think of home, but that didn't stop it from working. As always, the longer I focused on the movement of my body, the more the cloud lifted.

I had missed many things in the last five years, but I had also learned some—chief among them how to regulate my emotions. Otherwise I would have been completely lost to the black cloud.

Once I felt clarity in my thoughts again, I stood up and forced myself to walk briskly up and down the large room that filled the top of the tower. Physical activity could also help drive away the cloud, as did directing my thoughts in more helpful directions.

I stopped beside the chest that stood at the foot of my bed. It was a large one, big enough to fit all my extra blankets and bedding, as well as my full collection of clothing.

Pulling back the lid, I took out each of the dresses and laid them across my bed. I handled them with affection since I had made each of them myself after a great deal of trial and error. My parents had allowed me to learn many skills outside the normal scope of a princess—usually because I badgered them into permitting lessons—but dress creation hadn't been one of my interests.

Charli and the other girls would have helped me, but since they didn't know of my royal background, I hadn't wanted to admit my ignorance to them. Charli at least suspected me of coming from a wealthy or even noble family, but I didn't think she'd guessed the full truth.

Thankfully she had been quite willing to smuggle me one of her sister's old dresses—a specimen that was too worn to be passed down after her sister outgrew it. And Eulalie had left a basic sewing kit and some lengths of material in the chest. After carefully taking the dress apart, I was able to use it as a pattern for future dresses and was inordinately proud of some of the resulting creations.

And since I had plenty of time and a proper princess's skill at embroidery, the gowns had no lack of ornamentation. That embroidery was the reason for laying out the dresses when I needed a happier direction for my thoughts.

I ran my fingers over the symbols and scenes that I had worked into the skirts, bodices, and sometimes even sleeves. Eulalie knew I needed something to fill my time in the tower, and she seemed to accept embroidery as a suitable occupation. But while she delivered large batches of thread, I didn't have enough material to make decorative wall hangings. So my dresses had become the canvas for the pictures I created with my needle and thread.

Over time, I had decorated a dress for each of the princesses I had known growing up—the ones I had looked up to, the fortunate recipients of thrilling adventures. I saw their lives differently now, but the dresses still felt like an echo of my old friends.

My fingers swept over a group of dancing figures in bright, cheerful colors, my fingers lingering on the leaves of a large potted plant. A potted plant was a strange thing to embroider on a dress, but I hadn't been able to help myself. I had often watched the balls of Lily's Princess Tourney from behind sheltering leaves, wishing I could join the older princesses as they left the ballroom for secret adventures underground.

At the time I had thought it wildly unfair that I was too young to be caught up in the enchantment, but after five years under an enchantment of my own, I saw it differently. How terrified had the other girls been at the start of each new event? Were there times they had despaired of completing the Tourney alive? Did they still wake up in their sleep, gasping with dread from frightening memories that haunted their rest?

My fingers skipped onto the next dress, a stark white creation that was unsuited to life in a forest clearing. I had been unable to resist the pristine material, though, or the desire to decorate it with wild green stems, and deep crimson roses. I had never seen the now-fabled snowy rose garden of beastly Prince Dominic's cursed castle, but seeing the dress always reminded me of Sophie. I wasn't the only princess who had found herself a prisoner, alone and far from home. How foolish that I had once considered her situation romantic.

I always laid the dresses out in chronological order, and my lips curved upward at the fire motif on the next one. Celine's fireballs were a godmother gift desired by adventurous children everywhere, and I was no exception. But she had received her fire in order to fight a cold so great it had nearly consumed an entire kingdom. As a child, my lack of experience with physical discomfort had led me to skim over that part of the story, believing it merely a necessary prequel to glorious triumph. Living that discomfort turned out to be far less glorious than hearing tales about it.

The apples decorating Snow's dress made my stomach twinge. How long had it been since I ate? I couldn't remember, but I didn't stop my progress down the line of dresses. There would be plenty of time to eat later. There was always plenty of time.

Snow reminded me of myself as much as Sophie did—she had lost her family and been offered refuge by a clan of children. Charli and the others hadn't given me physical haven, but they had provided me refuge all the same. They saw me and heard my voice, and I now understood what a great gift that was. Back home I had thought myself alone and unseen, but that had never really been the case. I had been loved and protected—my mind full of dreams of adventure because of the deep security of my actual life.

I didn't resent my past self's foolishness, though. Childhood was supposed to be full of protected innocence.

The next dress was made of the softest material Eulalie had ever left me and was decorated with embroidered feathers. Addie —my favorite of the older princesses—at least had a flock of swans to keep her company. Would a single animal companion have been too much for me to ask for? Perhaps a cute owl? I was desperate enough that I would have even accepted some sort of lizard, but the few who had found their way up the side of my tower had never shown the least interest in me.

I sighed and moved on to the sea-green dress that represented both my sister and my sister-in-law. I had gotten ambitious with this one and attempted a trumpet skirt because the shape reminded me of a mermaid's tail. I had failed miserably, of course, but I kept the dress because I couldn't bear to abandon the reminder of my sisters. Did they worry about me? Did they think I was dead?

I skipped quickly to the next one before I could become too distracted by thoughts of my family. The remaining five gowns also depicted the adventures of girls like me, but these ones were products of my imagination—or rather of the vivid dreams that seemed to be a consolation prize for the lack of entertainment in my tower.

The dress for Giselle showed a princess with a blonde braid riding a magnificent horse at full gallop. The detailed depiction of the horse had taken me several attempts and finishing it had filled me with so much pride I had worn the dress for nearly a month straight.

I liked the dreams of Giselle in the guise of a goose girl, whiling away her days in a vast royal park. They were peaceful, and I always woke up from them in a good mood. As far-fetched as it was to think that the Eldonian princess could have ended up caring for geese, I liked to pretend it was true.

Daria's dress had strings of tiny wagons along all the hems, a decorative caravan that resembled one Lori and I had passed during our journey north. Of course Snow's old friend couldn't have ended up with a caravan of traveling merchants, but the dreams of their bonfires and dances were so much fun that I never fought the fancy.

Given her preferred occupation, Cassie's dress should have been a simple creation, designed for fitting into a crowd. But instead it was one of my most elaborate. Almost the entire surface was covered in bright flowers and vines—some of which I had never seen outside my dreams. I knew my dream version of Cassie couldn't be real since my friend had apparently spent the years of my captivity discovering new kingdoms across the Great Desert. It made no sense to imagine her surrounded by startlingly verdant gardens. But at least my subconscious sometimes threw out a more realistic story—one where Cassie hunted for treasure through the dusty and abandoned corridors of a city carved into a cliff.

The last two dresses were for girls who existed only in my dreams, inhabitants my imagination had created to populate the new kingdoms. But after five years disconnected from reality, they felt no less real than the others.

I touched the long sleeves of Zaria's dress, admiring the embroidered effect that emulated a row of bracelets. I couldn't be surprised my imagination had created a girl who discovered hidden treasure caves full of thieves—it was exactly the sort of adventure I had dreamed of as a child. But I had learned from bitter experience that the reality of such an adventure would have been far from my imagining. The fictional Zaria could have her treasure. I just wanted to be free from my tower.

The last dress kept my attention the longest. I had worked hard on it, but it still didn't look right.

"What if I moved the seam that way?" I traced my finger over a line of stitching with narrowed eyes. If Zaria was the embodiment of my childish dreams, Kali came from a deeper, more wild part of my imagination. She didn't just have the animal companion I desired—her cat actually talked. And the dresses she wore in my dreams bore no resemblance to anything I had seen while awake. I still hadn't quite worked out how to mimic the creations of my imagination, and my current project wasn't ready to be worn.

A gurgle from my stomach reminded me that I needed to eat. I stepped back and ran my eye down the line of dresses.

"I thought you were all living my dream," I said to the gowns, although in actuality I was speaking to the distant women they represented. "But you must have all been frightened and lonely and uncomfortable, just like me. And yet, you endured. You conquered the enchantments that threatened your lives and your kingdoms. And I will endure as well. No matter how many years

I'm trapped here, I will one day shatter my enchantment and find my happy ending."

The last of the black cloud lifted as it always did after the reminder that I wasn't the first to face pain, difficulty, and despair. I would never admit to anyone, even Charli, that I talked to my dresses. But I had once been a thirteen-year-old locked alone in a tower. I could have come up with sillier ways to ground myself and fight back the darkness.

The hours I spent embroidering those scenes were spent reminding myself that the girls of my past memory and my current dreams had overcome their trials. After so many hours of repetition, those thoughts had become sufficiently ingrained that just seeing the dresses let me step out of the cloud and back into a place of hope.

I moved to the small section of my room that acted as a kitchen, preparing a simple meal that I ate at my sturdy wooden table and chair. The two pieces of furniture formed the center of my ever-more-elaborate exercise routines—routines I should practice once I finished eating.

But even without the black cloud fogging my thoughts, it was hard to muster the energy for it. My eyes strayed to my shelf of books, but I knew they would be equally unable to hold my attention. I had read every volume more than once—both the titles Eulalie begrudgingly supplied and those smuggled up by Charli and carefully concealed among the others.

But my thoughts were too busy focusing on a princess who didn't feature among my dresses—one whose stories I had only heard about from Celine. I had claimed to be interested in Celeste's godmother-gifted beauty, but I only had the mildest curiosity about her looks. My true interest lay in her other gift-ings. The village children didn't know about Princess Celeste's alter ego as the spymaster Aurora, but I couldn't help pinning some hope in it.

Everyone said Celeste was not only the most beautiful but

also the most intelligent of all the royals. In the first year of my imprisonment, I had been sure her network would hear the rumors of me, and she would find a way to see through the enchantment.

That hope had proved to be unfounded, but it might be different if Celeste herself ended up in the village. The possibility of such an eventuality had always been too small to even consider, but the tour changed everything.

From the conversations the night before, the royal guard were keeping the king's itinerary a closely guarded secret. The honored towns and villages were only being notified of the royal arrival just before it happened. There must have been rumors it might come this way, but I suspected Charli had kept those from me on purpose. She wouldn't have wanted to get my hopes up until it was confirmed the royals would be coming to our remote corner of the kingdom.

I finished my food and started striding up and down the room. I could sit around doing nothing, just waiting to see if Charli would be able to lure a royal to the clearing, and holding onto the foolish hope that royal might be Celeste. Or I could climb down and do what I'd never done before—go as far as the village and see the tour's arrival for myself.

I stopped my thoughts there. I couldn't let my jittery impatience get the better of me. Now, of all times, I couldn't afford any self-indulgent escapes, even of the shortest duration. With my birthday fast approaching, Eulalie might reappear at any time, and I couldn't let her catch me out of the tower. I had long ago imagined every possible nightmare scenario that might happen if she did, and it wasn't worth the risk.

It was the same risk that meant I hadn't seen even a glimpse of Lori in days. I couldn't allow a moment's impatience to ruin the sacrifices we had both made.

I groaned and paced faster. After all this time, I had grown used to my situation, but sometimes the desperate desire to be free of the tower hit me as strongly as it had in the first few weeks. But I couldn't lose focus now.

I had accepted my captivity for five long years for a number of reasons. Many of them were purely self-interested, of course. It might give me immediate relief to go striding off into the village and beyond, but there wasn't a lot of point to escaping when no one would be able to see or hear me. Food I ate would have to be stolen, as would clothes and any other necessities. And I wouldn't even be able to interact with the objects around me unless I was somewhere out of sight. Written notes left in an obvious place or delivered by a child would appear blank. In short, I would have to live in the world as a ghost.

And worse than that, I would have to always be on the look out over my shoulder because there was one adult who could see me. One adult who had killed her previous, unruly test subjects.

As long as I appeared to stay meekly in my tower, Eulalie would supply food, material, books, even information on occasion. But if I showed any rebellion…I shivered.

I had felt guilty enough just convincing the eight-year-old Charli to bring me a rope. Could I really be sure there would be no ramifications for her or her family if she assisted me? But I had only been thirteen myself back then and desperate to be free.

Even after she had found a rope with enough length, it had taken a painfully long time for any of the children to succeed at getting it to me. They had tied one end to a rock, but getting it through my window had been a challenge. In the end Simon had managed it, spinning the rope quickly enough to get the necessary height and releasing it at the right moment to send it shooting upward at the correct angle.

I closed my eyes and relived the magical feeling of grass beneath my feet and warm arms hugging me tightly. Spurred on by Lori's concerns—called up to me at night, after the children had left—I had planned to keep my time out of the tower short. I had intended it as merely the prelude to more elaborate trips and an eventual escape. But it had proved much more difficult to climb up than to climb down.

After two hours, much sweating, and a great deal of grunting, I had finally scraped myself back up over the lip of the window. I don't know how long I had stayed sprawled on my back on that occasion, but thankfully I had roused myself enough to pull up the rope, detach it from the beam I had used as an anchor, and conceal it in the chest.

In retrospect, I should have hidden it somewhere craftier. But at the time I was just relieved Eulalie hadn't appeared an hour earlier. When she discovered the rope, she was furious, recognizing instantly that I was plotting an escape. But it didn't seem to occur to her that I might have already managed a brief stretch of freedom only to return to my cage.

She had confiscated the rope, of course, and threatened many dire consequences on the nearby village if she ever found me with such a thing again. After that, my brief excursions from the tower had been achieved by tying together my sheets, blankets, and most of my dresses. I had ripped more than one in the process, and gotten a nasty bump on my rear end when one of my knots failed mid-climb.

Such excursions happened only on occasions when I was certain Eulalie was far from the tower, and now was hardly an opportune time for one. Clearly she knew about the children and allowed our interactions—monitoring when they lost the ability to see me was part of her testing. But that acceptance had limits.

The children had helped me with open hearts, and I had to protect them and their families. Even if I could have made a proper escape, I wouldn't have saved myself and Lori and left them to Eulalie's vengeance. It certainly wasn't worth taking the risk just so I could live as a ghost.

My goal had to be freeing myself of the enchantment and then taking Eulalie down. And playing along with her was my best hope of convincing her to set me free at the end of the test. If she thought I had been a help rather than a hindrance during these years, it was possible she'd balk at killing me and release me instead. Especially since I had been preparing a convincing argument of why it would benefit her.

I gave up striding back and forth in favor of lying on the floor and staring at the tower's rafters. I wasn't sure how long I lay there, but eventually I roused myself to eat again. After that, the normal routines took over. I tidied, cleaned, and prepared myself for the evening as usual.

The skies had cleared after the storm, and the moon was large in the sky, so even when night fell, the darkness was far from complete. I packed away the extra blankets I had dragged out during the rain, rejoicing in the warmer weather. I had always loved nights that remained mild even after the sun's departure.

"Daisy!"

The shout made me drop the blankets and rush for the window. It sounded like Charli, but she never came to visit me after dark.

I had left the wooden shutters open to enjoy the night air, so I leaned out to peer down at the ground. Charli stood there, squinting up at the light that must have been pouring from my window.

It took my eyes a moment to adjust to the softer moonlight as I took in the slim girl and the stranger standing beside her. Not only was he clearly well over thirteen, but I had never seen him before. If he was from the village, he had already been over thirteen when I first arrived, and he had never been among those who visited the clearing at night for a secret rendezvous.

A current of excitement ran through me. Had Charli already succeeded? Had she brought me a royal?

CHAPTER 7

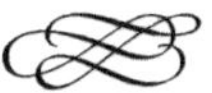

The young man gazed around the clearing with keen interest, his gaze skirting over the tower in a way that had become familiar. He couldn't see me.

"You're sure she's here?" the man asked Charli, his deep voice pleasant although the slight accent was unfamiliar.

Charli laughed, looking up at him with a slightly dazed expression that I recognized. I used to wear it myself whenever I looked at Gabe, the Talinosian prince who had spent years as a ward of my family. I had been a child during his stay, so he had always regarded me in the light of a young sister, but that hadn't stopped my crush. I had outgrown it years before my imprisonment in the tower and had been delighted when he married Addie, the nicest of the royals his own age. But I remembered the feeling well enough to recognize it on Charli's face. I only hoped he hadn't goaded her into bringing him here just so he could mock her.

"Of course she's here," Charli said. "She's always here. She's stuck in a tower, remember?"

"And you can see this tower?"

I tensed, but the man sounded intrigued rather than mocking.

Charli nodded. "It's right there." She pointed straight at me. "It's made of stone and has a large window up the top facing in this direction. There are no doors, though, and no stairs."

He followed her pointing finger, his eyes looking right at me, although his gaze remained unfocused.

"And she's there, in the window? Did she come when you called?"

Charli looked at me and nodded. "Daisy, this is Prince Xander of Kuralan. The tour arrived in the village this evening, and he was accompanying them. He started asking around about the girl in the tower immediately, and everyone told him I'm the oldest of the children who still believe. So he asked me to bring him here. He wouldn't even wait for daylight tomorrow."

"I traveled a long way to get here." He grinned. "I don't like waiting, and I won't be hurt by a little darkness."

"Kuralan?" I asked, preoccupied by the beginning of her introduction. "What's that? It's not one of the Four Kingdoms."

The name sounded familiar, though, as if it was an old companion I had merely forgotten for a moment.

"Oh wait!" I cried before Charli could answer. It was a name from my dreams, although I had heard it once in real life as well. "Isn't that one of the new kingdoms? The ones Cassie discovered across the desert?"

I stared down at the supposed prince with even greater interest. Had he really come from across the vast desert that bordered all the maps of these lands? How had no one known there were kingdoms on the other side of the sand?

"She wants to know where Kuralan is," Charli diligently repeated. "She's asking if it's one of the new kingdoms Cassie discovered across the desert." She paused and looked back at me. "Who's Cassie?"

"I think she means Princess Cassandra of Ardasira," the prince said.

"Cassie really is a princess now?" I gasped, remembering the elaborate wedding I had dreamed up for her, the one where she had married a handsome prince.

Charli opened her mouth to repeat my question, and I called for her to stop.

"Never mind, don't tell him I said that."

She obediently subsided, looking confused, while I bit my lip and stared down at the young man in my clearing. Revealing my connection with Giselle's delegation might give away my identity. My astonishment at the situation had nearly overpowered my good sense.

But should I be hiding who I was? Five years ago, his family and mine hadn't even known each other existed, but if he was really a royal, they might have established dealings in my absence. He might have connections to all the kingdoms. If he knew that Princess Margaret was missing, might he have come here to see if the children's claims were true and I was the missing princess?

Fresh excitement gripped me.

"Wait there! I'm coming down!" I dove back inside and snatched up the dresses that were conveniently still lying across my bed, pulling the blankets and sheets up with them.

"You're coming down?" Charli called up. "Right now? In the dark? You never come down in the dark."

"It's not that dark," I shouted back, not bothering to return to the window.

My fingers moved feverishly as I secured knots, tugging and re-tugging them to check they were holding firm. Despite my excitement, I knew better than to make a sloppy chain. If a knot failed too high up, I would have to send Charli back for a grappling hook and rope before I'd manage to get back inside. Something I knew from bitter experience.

"What do you mean she's coming down?" the prince asked, still appearing to accept Charli's claims of my existence without a second thought. "I thought she was trapped in the tower."

I snorted as I imagined Charli's eye roll.

"We may be children, but we're not useless," I heard her say. "And Daisy herself isn't a child. She's been in there for *five years*. Do you really think we couldn't find a way for her to climb down in all that time?"

"Not a child…" the prince repeated in eager tones, ignoring the implied insult in her words. "You said she's turning eighteen next week, right? And she says her name is Daisy?"

The significance he placed on my age, birthday, and name made my heart beat even faster. Did he know the nickname of the missing princess? Had my family provided information about me?

I abandoned my checking and double-checking and started tying the anchoring sheet around the beam. Scooping up armfuls of material, I tossed it blindly through the window. Once it was all outside, I leaned over to check it was stretched out properly against the stone.

I could hear Charli giving the prince a running commentary on what was happening, but I wasn't paying attention. My full focus was on reaching the ground as quickly as possible.

As soon as I was sure my makeshift rope was secured, I bundled up my skirts and tucked them out of my way. Gripping the material, I rested both feet against the stone, my back toward the ground, and started lowering myself hand over hand, my feet walking backward down the wall as I went.

The further down I got, the faster I moved, my impatience impossible to contain. Eventually my hands fumbled over a knot, and I lost my grip.

I dropped through the air, barely managing to get my feet under me in time to land.

"Oof!" I ended in a crouch but quickly straightened to glare up at the dress whose knot had betrayed me. "Thanks a lot, Snow. Keep a better hold of me next time."

"She's here," Charli told the prince, making me flush with

embarrassment and relief that the prince couldn't hear me muttering to myself like I'd lost my mind.

"Really?" He sounded excited. "Where exactly? Can you position me right in front of her?"

"It won't make a difference," Charli said. "It doesn't matter how close you get, you won't be able to see or hear her, and you won't be able to touch her either."

He gave her a grin that was far too charming. Now that I could see him close up, I could see why Charli was so affected. He was dangerously handsome, with golden skin and dark hair, and his brown eyes sparkled with a familiar mix of sincerity and mischief that reminded me of the distant Prince Gabe.

"Please?" he pleaded with Charli. "Humor me just this once?"

Charli sighed and looked at me. When I shrugged, she took the prince's arm and maneuvered him until he stood almost toe to toe with me.

My breath caught at his nearness, and I reminded myself firmly that he wasn't Gabe, and I was no longer eight years old. There was absolutely no reason for my heart to be beating faster.

"How tall is she?" the prince asked, drawing my attention to his own height and the broad shoulders that went with it.

"The top of her head is about at your chin. Why?"

The prince didn't answer, and I didn't have time to ponder the question before he leaned forward, aiming his face remarkably accurately toward mine.

My brain sputtered to a stop, my body freezing in shock. Was he trying to—?

As his lips approached mine, the enchantment kicked in and his head began to sway away from me. But the awkward backward movement was interrupted by an abrupt lurch forward, as if he had been shoved hard from behind.

His lips collided with mine, the impact rocking me backward as I received the most awkward first kiss in history.

CHAPTER 8

I jumped backward, my hand responding without conscious thought. Flashing up, it slapped him across the cheek.

He fell back a step from the force of my attack, and my stinging hand flew to my mouth. I wasn't sure if it was my hand or my lips that was tingling more from the unexpected and shocking series of events.

What had just happened? How had he kissed me? And how had my hand made contact with his cheek?

I stared at him, so overloaded with shock that it took me a moment to realize he was staring straight back at me. His left cheek was red from my blow, but he didn't seem aware of any pain. His mouth was hanging open, and there was no mistaking the way his eyes were locked on mine.

Something sparked inside me, and I rallied.

"What are you doing?" I demanded. "You can't kiss a stranger you've only just met!"

His expression immediately grew sheepish. "Sorry about that. I was trying to break the enchantment."

"With a surprise kiss?" I asked, my outrage not ebbing.

He rubbed the back of his neck, his other cheek now flushed almost as dark as the abused one. "Well, lots of the tales suggest…"

"A kiss of true love?" I raised an eyebrow. "I see you have a high opinion of yourself. Did you expect me to fall in love with you at first sight?"

"No, no, I…" He stopped, his grimace dissolving into a laugh. "It was rather arrogant of me, wasn't it?"

The open admission disarmed me, but I managed to keep my stern expression in place.

"How about this?" he asked meekly. "I'll promise no more surprise kisses, and you promise that if you really have to hit me again, you'll avoid the face."

"Excuse me?" It came out sounding more amused and less offended than I'd intended.

"I'm sure you understand," he said earnestly, gesturing at his face. "I have a responsibility to preserve a national treasure like this."

I gaped at him until I caught the wicked twinkle in his eyes that belied his earnest expression.

I snorted. "Fine. As long as you keep your lips to yourself, I'll refrain from any further physical abuse."

Charli made a strangled noise, reminding me that we weren't alone. When I glanced at her, her eyes were fixed on the prince, and she looked like she was about to faint.

"You…you can hear her?" she gasped.

A strange sensation swept through my body as her words sunk in, and I realized what should have been the first thought on my mind. What did my first kiss matter beside the enormity of what had just occurred?

"Did it work?" I asked urgently. "Did your kiss break the enchantment?"

It seemed beyond far-fetched, but how else could I explain it?

The prince's eyes traveled up and down my body before slipping sideways to stare at the tower.

"I can see you and the tower clearly," he said in amazement. "And I can hear you as easily as I can hear her." He gestured toward Charli without turning to look at her. "And I certainly felt that slap. You seem completely real, but I'm equally sure I couldn't see you when I first arrived."

"The enchantment is broken." I said the words slowly, trying to make myself believe them. It felt too wonderful to be real. "I'm free. I can't believe a plan that foolish actually worked!"

"Thanks," the prince said wryly.

I grinned at him, too elated to be annoyed at his methods any longer.

He smiled back, looking bemused but happy.

He held out his hand in a more standard greeting. "Good evening, Princess Daisy. I'm Prince Xander of Kuralan, and I can't tell you how good it is to meet you after all this time."

I put my hand into his and dropped into my most stately curtsy.

"The honor is all mine, Your Highness."

"Please call me Xander." There was a look in his eyes I couldn't name.

"Daisy isn't a princess," Charli cut in, staring between us. "Are you, Daisy?"

"Actually…" I bit my lip. "Sorry. I didn't want Eulalie to find out my true identity, and I know you guys can't recognize her since she enchanted herself. I didn't want to risk one of you saying something and her overhearing you…"

"A princess…" She shook her head, looking dazed. "But there aren't any Princess Daisys. They made us study the new kingdoms in school—the ones across the ocean and the ones across the desert—and I would have noticed a Daisy."

"Officially I'm Princess Margaret," I admitted.

"A lovely name," Xander said, earning a glare.

"Don't even think about trying to use it. I don't answer to Margaret, and I never have."

"Duly noted," he said in such deceptively meek tones that I continued to eye him suspiciously.

"I can't believe you're a princess!" Charli cried. "No wonder people kept coming to the village and asking about our claims there was a girl locked in a tower. There must be so many people looking for you."

"People asked about me?" I cried. "Why didn't you say anything? I thought all the adults who came to check the clearing were from the village."

"Because I didn't want to disappoint you. You know the village adults think you're an elaborate game their children like to play, and the visitors always quickly came to the same conclusion." She sighed. "No one believes children." She glanced sideways at Xander. "Except for him."

"I've followed far less substantial rumors in my search for the missing princess," he said cheerfully. "I would have made it here sooner if you weren't so remote."

He looked at me apologetically. "You're a long way away from where you were taken, and even further from my home across the desert. Since Lanover has become my home in the Four Kingdoms, and my search has been centered around Arcadia, this is my first time in Northhelm."

I nodded, willing to forgive anything from the person who'd saved me—especially if he'd come all this way specifically to look for me.

"You're a twin, aren't you?" Charli asked abashedly. "I remember that from the royal trees. And your brother married a Lanoverian? Is that why you live there?"

"It's…complicated," Xander said with an easy smile. "But my new sister-in-law certainly has strong ties to Lanover. And all the Lanoverians have been very welcoming—even the ones living in Northhelm." He looked back at me. "One in particular has a great interest in you. She'll be very pleased to hear I've succeeded in finding you—and will be unimpressed at her own people's failure."

"Aurora," I whispered breathlessly, and one of his eyebrows rose in response.

Those sporadic visitors Charli had mentioned must have been her agents. So she really had been looking for me all these years.

"Is she here?" I asked, but he shook his head.

"She remained back in the palace with her daughter. We should travel there immediately, though. King Richard and William have to finish the tour, of course, but I was only ever a tag-along, so I can leave whenever I want. Once they hear I've found you, they'll understand completely. They'll probably order us to go, in fact. Everyone has been worried about you. Only the assurances of the wise women have kept your family and friends from revealing the news of your disappearance to the entire population of all the kingdoms."

"The wise women?" I asked.

"Godmothers, I should say. We call them wise women in my kingdom."

"The godmothers made assurances about me?" I asked, frowning.

He nodded. "I'm afraid Princess Giselle got swept up in some awkwardness after the attack on your delegation, but the godmothers helped straighten it out, and they assured everyone that the other three of you were under their eye, busy in your own adventures. And Daria and Cassandra proved them right. But as soon as I heard you were still missing after so long, I knew I couldn't sit around and do nothing waiting for you to reappear."

"The godmothers said I was busily occupied and everyone should stop worrying?" I asked, my voice rising until I almost exploded in fury. "They just left me sitting doing nothing in a tower for FIVE YEARS!"

If I could have ignited fires with my glare like Princess Celine, the whole clearing would be burning. Had they really told everyone I was safe and then just abandoned me? Just wait until I got my hands on one of their smug, superior—

"Charli? What are you doing here on your own?" The disapproving voice cut through my thoughts.

I spun to stare at the new arrival. His face was still recognizable as Simon, but the boy I had known had been replaced with a young man. Jayda's older brother looked disapprovingly at Charli, as if there were more than just a couple of years between them. He wore his extra years in the officious way of youth who liked to think of themselves as adults, and Charli and I rolled our eyes simultaneously.

"I'm not alone," she said caustically. "And I notice you aren't either." She gave a heavy look at the young woman on his arm. The older girl was carefully not looking at Charli, and although she looked quite different from how I remembered, I was fairly sure it was one of Charli's older sisters.

Simon gave Charli a superior look. "You're getting too old to keep up this nonsense with Daisy. Real or not, how is she going to help you if you run into trouble wandering the forest at night? You know you all promised the adults not to come out here after dark."

"That's my fault, I'm afraid," Xander said with his charming smile.

He looked relaxed, and almost friendly, but his voice carried a note of something else—a reminder, however subtle, that he was not only capable of dealing with trouble in any form but also outranked Simon in every possible way.

"I didn't mean Daisy…" Charli's voice trailed off as a crease appeared between her eyes. She looked from Xander's confident presence to Simon and then back again.

She swallowed at the same moment as a terrifying possibility occurred to me.

"Can't you see him?" she asked.

"Him?" Simon sounded impatient. "No wonder no one believes you're telling the truth if you keep adding people to the story."

"I'm not adding..." Charli swallowed, her voice wobbling slightly. "Are you seriously saying you can't see Prince Xander?"

"Prince Xander?" Charli's sister finally spoke, sounding incredulous. "You should at least try to make your stories believable. Why would the prince want to come here with a child like you?"

I gaped at her. She must have been jealous of her younger sister to make such a ridiculous assumption. Charli wasn't pretending she was on some sort of romantic stroll with a prince.

For the millionth time, I had to swallow my outrage at being rendered silent and invisible. There was nothing I could do to stand up for my friend. I used to think I was the unnoticed younger sister at home, but I had been clueless about what it was truly like to be powerless.

"Is this some sort of game?" Xander asked, sounding tense. "I'm standing right here."

"Regardless of what you've been fancying, this is dangerous, Charli." Simon stepped forward and took Charli's elbow in a firm grip. "Your sister and I will escort you home right now—and don't even think about arguing."

It was Charli's sister who looked like she wanted to argue, her expression furious. But she could hardly say anything. She would look ridiculous and desperate if she said anything else to expose her jealousy of her younger sister.

But she didn't need to say anything for me to be well aware that Charli wasn't actually much younger than these two, and that her sister was well aware of it. Romance had always been far from Charli's mind, but it was impossible not to notice her golden beauty. Her older sisters were all pretty, and together they made an impressive sight, but even as a child Charli had stood out.

I had always suspected Charli spent so much time in my clearing because her sisters resented her—it was probably the same reason they had spent so little time around me. In fact, I had long suspected them of being part of the reason the adults were so firmly convinced the children were only playing a game. I could too easily imagine them taking any opportunity to undermine the way others saw Charli, encouraging them to think her flighty and childish.

Xander couldn't possibly know the various dynamics between the village's children and youth, but he bristled at Simon's behavior all the same. He stepped forward, clearly meaning to free Charli from the older boy's grasp.

But when he reached for them, his hand veered away, failing to make contact. Growling, he tried again, his face tensed in concentration. It made no difference, though. No matter how hard he focused, he couldn't force his hand into contact with them.

Charli looked back at him, her face pale. "That's why I shoved you before," she said in a quiet voice. "You won't manage it on your own. I'm surprised even that worked. Nothing we tried ever worked before."

"No." I dropped back a step, shaking my head. "No, no, no." It couldn't be possible.

I'd been stubbornly ignoring the implications of Simon's words, pretending it was just a game on the part of the two youths, because I didn't want to acknowledge the truth. But I couldn't hide from it any longer. For one brief, shining moment, I had thought myself free from the enchantment. But it had just been an illusion.

"Stop muttering nonsense, Charlotte!" Charli's sister snapped as Simon began to drag the younger girl away.

Charli cast an anxious, apologetic look over her shoulder. "What should I say? Who should I tell…?"

Xander lunged after them, but his efforts were pointless. I

already knew that. Hurrying after him, I grabbed his shoulder and gave it a slight shake.

"Answer her questions! You're a prince, and you've just disappeared. Do you want to get her in trouble?"

Xander stopped, frowning down at me. When he looked up at Charli, nearly at the tree line, his face tightened.

"Don't say anything!" he called after her. "I told them I was going looking for Princess Daisy, but no one knew I was going with you. There's no reason for you to get yourself involved with this."

I nodded urgently. "And we really don't want Eulalie to know what's happened! So you can't spread this story around. There's no point anyway when she's the only one who'll believe it."

Charli had time to nod once before she was tugged out of sight. Xander and I remained silent and motionless, staring at the trees where she had disappeared.

"I'm sorry," I said after a moment, not even trying to hide my miserable tone. "It was never my intention to drag anyone else into this with me. "

Xander started and looked at me. "Of course it's not your fault. You didn't ask me to kiss you."

My eyes narrowed. "No, now that you mention it, I certainly did not. I retract my apology. This is entirely your fault."

Xander laughed, the sound unexpected. "Duly noted." He looked around the clearing. "So what now?"

I stared at him. "That's it? You're just accepting it that easily?"

"Would it help if I ranted and raved or insisted it couldn't be true? I'm happy to oblige if you'd like it." He frowned after the disappeared youth. "You must know those two better than me. Might they have been faking the whole thing? It would be good acting for two youths from a remote village, but I suppose it might be possible."

I shook my head. "I know what it looks like when someone

can't see and hear you. I have plenty of experience with that. Those two definitely had no idea you were standing there."

Xander nodded. "Then somehow your enchantment has extended to me. So back to my question. What happens now? Perhaps you could start by explaining exactly how the enchantment works? It was the strangest feeling when my hand kept veering away from where I was telling it to go."

I looked around at the moonlit clearing, trying to wrap my head around this unbelievable new reality.

"You said you could see the tower now, too?"

He nodded.

"In that case, I have to assume you're fully in the same bubble as me. In which case the most important thing to remember is that we aren't the only ones in here."

His eyebrows shot upward. "We're not?"

"No. And Eulalie is extra dangerous because she exists in both our bubble and the real world."

"Eulalie is the one who enchanted you? Charli mentioned something about her. Who is she?"

I grimaced. "I have no idea, although I'd dearly love to know. And, even more importantly, I'd love to know what she's searching for—and what she's going to do once she finds it."

"Searching?" Xander's interest peaked. "Charli didn't say anything about your enchanter searching for something."

I shrugged. "It's not something I talk about with the village children. But Eulalie is clearly working on something else than just my test—something that has prevented her from making a move sooner. She spends most of her time away from here, and from what I can gather, she's searching for something. She wants Northhelm for herself—I've picked up that much from her comments—and the ring that controls her enchantment is central to her plan to get it. But she needs something else as well. Something she doesn't already own."

Xander glanced around at the dark trees. "What does she look like?"

"There's no point trying to describe her—" I stopped. "Actually, I suppose now you're part of the bubble, you might see her real self like I do."

"Doesn't she look the same to everyone?"

I shook my head. "It wasn't always the case—she looked quite normal when I first met her. But when we reached the tower, she stretched the enchantment to cover the tower as well, and the ring changed. It might not sound like much of a change because it was black before and it still is. But it used to be a strange, dull black and now it seems to actively suck in the light around it."

I shivered. "It's hard to explain, but you'll understand if you ever see it. It's an utterly unnerving effect. And after it happened, her skin became strange—almost leathery looking, although it's hard to describe exactly. I think it was a side effect of overusing the ring's magic. It means she can't just go strolling around the kingdom unnoticed anymore. She still looks that way to me, but Charli says she looks normal to her. Normal but different every time she sees her, and none of the children can pull up a mental image of her appearance after she's gone. So they can't be lookouts watching for her arrival. They never realize it's her until I point it out after she's gone."

"If she's overused the ring, does that mean its power is gone?" Xander asked. "Did she find a different enchantment to conceal her identity?"

"She must have found a different one because I don't think the ring could do that, even when it was at full strength. And it's certainly not at full strength now. I'm not sure it has anything left in it."

"But how can she use it in her plans against Northhelm then?"

I winced. "That's another of the things that worries me. If she's right and the ring does still have one more use in it, she may well succeed in her plan—whatever that might be. But if I'm right and the ring is emptied of power, then when she attempts to use the ring, the entire enchantment might blow up in her face."

"Would that free you?" Xander asked, sounding eager.

"Free *us*, you mean," I said, reminding him he was now in this with me. "That would be the most optimistic option. But if you'd seen this ring, I don't think you'd be so hopeful. Apparently it started as blue, but now it's black as tar, and seriously, the way it sucks the light in from around it…" I shivered again. "I think it's far more likely that when she uses it, anyone attached to the enchantment will be destroyed along with the ring itself."

"Destroyed?" His hand went to his sword hilt, a defensive instinct that would do no good against an enchantment. "We can't let that happen! If you're capable of getting out of her tower, why have you just been sitting up there for so long? We have to find out her plan!"

CHAPTER 9

"Oh, wow," I said sarcastically, "why did I never think of that?"

Xander winced, giving me an apologetic look. "Sorry. But can you explain it to me? Why haven't you gone after her?"

"Because I knew I had time," I replied. "Don't think it's been easy, making myself wait and do nothing. It's been the hardest challenge I ever took on. But if there's one thing I have ample time for, it's thinking. And no matter how I thought it through, I always came to the same conclusion. The best way of keeping myself and the villagers safe was to wait. I want to live, but I also want to be free of this enchantment, and there's only one way that's going to happen—if Eulalie chooses to reverse it."

I put my hands on my hips, staring him down. "So no, I don't think trying to creep around the kingdom after her is the best way to achieve my goals. I don't need to follow her anyway. She always comes back to me eventually. And when she visits, I can ask her questions, as long as I'm not too obvious about it. That's how I know she's looking for something. Waiting gets me answers, just more slowly, and it keeps everyone safe in the meantime. She's a dangerous person—she killed her previous test subjects and has already made threats against the children and their families. I was a child when I was first captured, and she had the advantage over me in every way."

"I'm sorry," he said again, sounding even more guilty.

I relaxed my stance, realizing that despite my irritation at his simplistic response, it felt good to talk this out with someone my own age. "I may have been a child back then, but every year, I've gotten taller and stronger, and I can finally match Eulalie in size. I can't attack her before she lifts the enchantment since I don't know what that would do to the enchantment itself, but once I'm free…"

Xander put his hand on my shoulder. "I'm in this with you now, and I won't abandon you. You won't have to face her alone."

I tried to ignore the warm feeling spreading through me at his words. "She's waiting for my birthday to finish the test, since I'll be eighteen this year. She's mentioned it often enough that I know it's her end point. However, she's been less forthcoming about what she intends for me after that. But I'm hoping I can convince her to free me."

Xander raised his eyebrows. "Is that really a likely option?"

I shrugged. "Likely or not, I have to try. I've been playing the role of docile captor for years now to help sell my claim that I'll never be a threat to her. I'm not foolish enough to think that would be enough on its own, though. The crucial argument is the ring. She knows it's running low on power. She keeps insisting it has enough power left for a final use, but I think she's nervous. That's what I'm going to push on. I'm going to try to convince her that her best chance of succeeding at her plan is to reverse my enchantment and send its power back into the ring."

"Does it work like that?" he asked.

"I have no idea. But I don't think she does either. Since the power is draining out of it, she hasn't had the chance to do a lot of tests. It doesn't matter if it actually works—I just have to convince her it might."

Xander frowned. "And if she isn't convinced by your theory? You're pinning a lot on hopes of what *might* happen."

"And that hope has kept me going for five years!" I stepped away from his hand, glaring at him again. "If you knew me at all, you'd know how hard it's been for me to wait. It's not a decision I made lightly or easily. Maybe in my position, you would have handled the situation entirely differently—but you were never put in my position, and you haven't endured everything I've endured for the last five years."

Xander winced and ran a hand through his hair. "I'm handling this very badly, aren't I?"

"Yes," I said with open hostility, "you are."

"Then let me apologize again."

As soon as he said the words, I felt myself softening. Xander had apparently come here to rescue me, and in exchange, he'd been pulled into my nightmare. It was only fair to give him some grace while he adjusted to the situation. After all, I'd had five years and he'd barely had five minutes.

"We seem to have circled back to my original question," he said after a moment's silence. "What do we do now? Having me trapped in this so-called bubble with you wasn't part of Eulalie's plan or yours."

"I can't imagine it was part of your plan either." I sighed. "At least you're inside my bubble and not an enchantment of your own. That's the reason Charli can still see and hear you. If Eulalie had enchanted you directly, you'd be completely cut off." I sighed again. "Not that being seen by children helps when it comes to the other tour members. How do you think they'll react to your disappearance?"

He grimaced. "I'm not sure I know them well enough to say. They won't take it lightly, though. Northhelm is still forging ties with Kuralan, and they'll be worried about what my father will do if I disappear into thin air while in their kingdom."

"Are you the crown prince?" I asked, wondering for the first time about his family and his place within it.

He laughed. "Thankfully not!"

"Your twin is older, then?"

"Actually we have a highly responsible and respectable older brother and a slightly less responsible older sister, so we both escaped that terrible fate."

"I always wondered what it would be like to be the oldest," I said, a little wistfully. "No one would ignore you or tell you to disappear off to the nursery then."

A smile spread across his face, his eyes twinkling in the moonlight. "But what fun would there be in that? The best mischief is always had when there aren't too many people watching. At least for us royals."

I blinked, struck by his words. I had always felt constrained by my family's insistence on seeing me as a baby, but how many of my various escapades would I have managed if I had been the oldest?

"That is a surprisingly good point," I said slowly. "And maybe it applies here as well."

Xander raised a single eyebrow. "My entire family might die of shock if they ever heard me saying this, but I'm not sure this is the right moment to be thinking about fun."

I laughed. "You're making me more and more curious about what you and your twin used to get up to back in Kuralan. But I didn't mean fun, exactly. I meant that maybe we can use our current invisibility to our advantage."

"I thought you said Eulalie could still see us?"

I nodded. "She can, of course, which is a pity. But it will still make it easier to investigate her. We won't need to worry about anyone else."

"Does that mean you're planning to leave the tower?"

I looked all the way up his tall frame. "Somehow I'm not sure the hiding and waiting strategy is going to be viable any longer. I think Eulalie might just notice you."

"I'm not sure whether to be flattered or insulted," he said with a wry smile.

"Never mind that," I said. "We need to work out a plan."

"Do you have something in mind?" he asked, sounding impressed.

I waved a hand dismissively. "Of course. Didn't I tell you I've had a lot of time to think? Just because I chose not to action any of my plans, doesn't mean I never made them."

He gave me an odd look. "You're not how I imagined."

I gave him an unimpressed look of my own. "Were you picturing a poor, innocent damsel in need of your strong manly shoulders to lean on?"

"They are impressive shoulders, aren't they?" he said with a shameless grin. "I'm not surprised you noticed them. Back home they've been known to make girls swoon."

I humphed and rolled my eyes, turning toward the tower in a pointed show of rejection. He just laughed and leaned close, his breath brushing against the skin near my ear.

"I didn't say I was disappointed in the reality. Quite the opposite."

I flushed, glad I was facing away from him, and strode off toward the tower at my fastest walk. He chuckled again and easily kept pace a step behind me.

When we reached the foot of the tower, he stared at my makeshift rope. Closest to the ground was a particularly frilly dress I had made for the sake of a challenge and rarely wore.

"You climb down using your dresses?" he asked.

I rolled my eyes. "What were you expecting me to use? My hair?"

He looked at me with a grin. "It is rather long."

I groaned. "That's because my parents always insisted I wear it long so that it could be put up in elaborate styles for formal occasions. Of course, it was still a manageable length back then, but after five years without a cut, it's practically at my feet."

"Couldn't you cut it yourself?" he asked. "Don't you have scissors or a knife?"

"Of course I do. I have various sharp items concealed all over the tower, but that doesn't mean I want Eulalie to know I have them. And I couldn't bring myself to butcher my hair with my one official pair of blunt sewing scissors. When I get free of Eulalie, I'm chopping it all off," I added fiercely.

"That would be a pity," Xander said softly, reaching out to run the lightest of fingers along a strand of my hair.

"Feel free to grow your own hair out if you like long hair," I muttered.

"Maybe I should." He grinned. "At least then everyone would be able to tell me apart from Xavier."

"Are you identical?" I asked, distracted by curiosity. "My brother and sister are twins, but obviously not identical. I always felt a little lonely, wishing I had a twin of my own. Especially since I was nine years younger than them."

"But it wasn't just the three of you growing up in your palace by the sea, though, was it? Didn't your parents have a ward?"

I threw him a surprised look, and he shrugged. "There's a desert and an ocean between our kingdoms, but delegations have been sent back and forth, and I believe an alliance is in progress. I've studied maps of Trione and heard stories. I especially asked for details about you that might help me identify you, but I heard stories about all your family. I would love to visit sometime. Despite the months I've spent in the Four Kingdoms, I'm still fascinated by the ocean. The nomads and desert traders call the Great Desert the Sea of Sand, but growing up in a kingdom bordering on the desert didn't prepare me for the actual ocean."

"I miss the ocean," I said wistfully. "Our palace was on the shore, and the sea is so all encompassing. Even when you can't see it, you can smell it and hear it. It gets so quiet here without the sound of the waves in the background."

"You must miss your home and family," he said softly.

His sympathy nearly undid me, so I shook myself and adopted a dismissive manner.

"Since I would like to see them again one day, there's no time to be standing around reminiscing."

"What do you suggest we do?" he asked. "I'm ready and willing to hear about any number of your well-thought-out-but-unactioned plans."

"We need to find out exactly what Eulalie is planning to do after my birthday. My first step will be to question her directly. I know she's due back here in the next few days, and it might be my last chance to talk to her face to face. I'll find out everything I can and make my case for her to reverse the enchantment. If she does, then we can arrest her." I glanced at his sword. "Mainly, you can arrest her."

He laughed, but there was a hard glint in his eyes. "I would be more than happy to assist in such a matter."

"I need to maintain my fiction of being a compliant captive at least until that conversation, so I need to go back in the tower." I eyed his well-muscled frame, trying to guess how much he weighed. "It will be better if you stay down here. You can hide among the trees—even if Eulalie happens to see you in passing, she won't know you're connected to me or the enchantment."

"Not a chance," he said cheerfully. "I didn't come all this way so I could spend days cowering in the forest. And I'm certainly not going to leave you to have that conversation with Eulalie alone. I need to arrest her, remember?"

I raised an eyebrow. "I'm hardly going to look like a compliant prisoner if I have a prince in the middle of my prison."

"Obviously I'll hide when she appears," he said.

"There aren't a lot of hiding places in the tower," I said doubtfully.

"How about I judge that for myself?" He smiled disarmingly. "I'm better at hiding than you might think."

"Fine," I said. "Suit yourself. Just don't start climbing until I'm safely inside the tower."

"Noted," he said. "If I'm going to plummet to my death mid-climb, I'll make sure to plummet alone."

"That would be appreciated," I said dryly, "but I would prefer you avoided the plummeting altogether. When I eventually get out of this enchantment, I would rather not have to explain to your parents that I was forced to abandon your invisible body in a clearing on the other side of the kingdoms."

"I'm overwhelmed by your thoughtful care."

I snorted and took hold of the dress at the bottom of the chain. But Xander kept talking, making me pause.

"If Eulalie releases us from the enchantment, and I arrest her, excellent. If, however, she tries to kill you instead because your usefulness is past, then I will intervene, of course, and I can't guarantee her safety. What exactly do you think will happen to us if she dies?"

"I would rather not find out," I said shortly. "So be careful with that sword of yours. If you're going to skewer her, do it somewhere expendable. Like an arm or a leg."

"Got it." He looked amused. "I will do my best." He hesitated. "But what about a third option? What if she refuses to lift the enchantment and tries to leave you as a captive?"

I grinned. "That's when the hiding and following comes into play. If she won't give us answers, we'll have to find them for ourselves."

"We're going to go jaunting off across the kingdom together? Just the two of us?" Xander sounded entirely too pleased about that prospect.

I narrowed my eyes, about to set him straight when another voice spoke.

"Absolutely not!" Lori stepped into view around the tower. "I hope I don't need to remind you that my charge is not only a young lady but a princess. She doesn't go *jaunting* off alone with strange men." She sniffed disapprovingly, eyeing the prince from head to toe as if he was a scruffy young schoolboy in need of a good wash and better manners. "Claimed rescuer or not."

I suppressed a laugh, adopting a demure air.

"May I introduce my lady-in-waiting, Lori? Lori, this is Prince Xander of Kuralan who has crossed many kingdoms to rescue us from this tower."

Lori snorted. "That'll be an impressive feat since I've never so much as set foot in the tower."

"Lori?" Xander looked from the older woman to me, his eyes lighting up. "Your maid? The one who disappeared with you? We were all hoping you were still together! Has she been with you the whole time?" He turned to Lori. "I assume you must be under the enchantment as well since you can see and hear us both."

"We've been together nearly the whole time. Eulalie put us both to sleep initially and tried to carry me off without anyone noticing. But Lori woke up quickly, and she was convinced it was no coincidence that not only had I disappeared but one of our fellow travelers as well. She doggedly tracked Eulalie the whole time, even though she couldn't see me, of course. She said Eulalie kept acting strangely, and she was sure she knew something about my whereabouts."

"Impressive loyalty and dedication." Xander gave a respectful nod in Lori's direction.

She shrugged. "I was entrusted with the princess, and I wasn't going to lose her."

I smiled affectionately at her. "When Eulalie reached this clearing and the old tower—both of which had been long forgotten by the nearest village—she extended my enchantment to cover the tower. Unbeknownst to her, Lori was touching the tower at the time and also got included in the enchantment. She's successfully hidden herself from Eulalie in all the years since. She maintains a vegetable garden, hunts, and does all sorts of other things to provide for herself and me. She does far more than me, in fact, and I would be lost without her. I have great affection for the children, but Lori is the one who kept me going for five years." A hint of pride entered my voice. "I did make that dress she's wearing, though."

"I'm just doing my duty," Lori said before a small smile curved the corners of her mouth. "Plus, there's all that gold to think of."

"Gold?" Xander looked between us.

I laughed. "Yes, indeed, and I have no intention of going back on my word. When we make it home to Trione, she'll have her body weight in gold—if I have to give her my own dowry to achieve it."

Lori smiled fully, her eyes radiating affection. I knew perfectly well she hadn't stuck by me because of the promise of reward. We had never resumed the formality we dropped during our desperate flight, and I knew Lori regarded me as family more than royalty or employer. But from the way she was looking disapprovingly at Xander, she hadn't entirely forgotten her old duties.

"So it will be the three of us on a quest to save the kingdom and free ourselves from this enchantment?" Xander smiled charmingly. "The more, the merrier!"

I frowned at him, worried he was mocking her, but he genuinely seemed to mean it.

"After you, ladies." He stepped back with a half-bow.

"Oh, I don't go up the tower," Lori said. "I live in the nearby forest."

"You've really never been up once?" Xander asked, as if unable to believe anyone could show so little curiosity.

She chuckled. "I may be strong, but I'm not young and spry anymore. You won't catch me clambering up and down dresses."

"Besides, didn't you hear me before?" I added. "Eulalie doesn't know Lori is here, and there's nowhere in the tower she could easily hide herself. We've taken so much care to keep her secret that even the children don't know about her, aside from Charli. Are you sure you don't want to go into the forest with her?"

"Positive." He smiled at me with such certainty, I turned quickly for the tower.

Taking hold of the dress at the bottom of the chain, I began pulling myself upward. I used the same method as when I'd climbed down, walking up the wall with my feet while I pulled myself upward with my hands.

When I was halfway up, I allowed myself one quick glance down, secretly pleased to see an impressed look on Xander's face. I had made sure to build my strength since the days of my first escape, and I could now handle the climb with relative ease.

When I reached the top and maneuvered through the window, I leaned back out to let him know he was clear to start climbing.

"Now I really am afraid I'm going to look a fool," he called up at me in a delighted tone. "You made that look far too easy."

I smiled with self-satisfaction. "If you're going to fall, try and do it low enough that you don't break any bones, please. I may not need you to rescue me, but I'd rather not have to rescue you."

As tempting as it was to watch his ascent, it was far more pressing for me to dash around the tower and tidy up from the mess I'd left. As soon as I finished shoving the last piece of dirty clothing into the small washroom, I rushed back to the window.

I stuck my head out only to quickly pull it back in after it nearly collided with the prince's head. Stumbling back several steps, I watched as he pulled himself effortlessly over the window ledge, the muscles on his arms straining.

"It held," he said with a grin. "But I think only just."

"We need to pull it up," I said, trying not to show how conscious I was of his presence.

It had been one thing to be near him in the large, open clearing, but seeing him here, in my space, felt unexpectedly different. Had he always been this tall and broad?

He responded to my words, hauling up the makeshift rope and depositing it on the floor of the tower room. Once it was all inside, he began working on the knot holding it to the beam. I watched him for several seconds before giving myself a shake and hurrying into action.

Grabbing the length of the rope, I started on the first knot I could find, detaching the various items from each other. Xander did his best to help, but when I saw him giving the unusual dress that was my current project a very odd look, I snatched it out of his hands and shoved it into the chest along with the rest of my crumpled dresses. I'd just finished folding the last of the blankets and sheets when the whistling call of one of the local birds pierced the night air.

My head shot up, my eyes growing wide.

"Is that a nocturnal bird?" Xander asked, his brow creased.

I leaped across the distance between us, slapping my hand across his mouth. His eyes widened, but he didn't push me away. Instead he went still, his eyes flying to the window.

"That's Lori," I hissed in a whisper. "She's warning us."

CHAPTER 10

*X*ander's eyes lit up with understanding. I didn't have to tell him what Lori was warning us about.

I cast a despairing look around the circular room at the top of the tower before looking back at Xander. I'd expected to have more time to come up with a hiding place for him.

He glanced toward the door to the washroom, but I shook my head. It was a tiny space inside, and Eulalie sometimes used it on her visits.

Xander gripped my wrist, lowering the hand I'd forgotten was still clasped over his mouth.

"It will have to be that, then." He pointed to the chest at the foot of the bed.

I gazed at it in concern. It was a large chest, but could it possibly fit Xander?

He didn't hesitate, though, pulling out the dresses I'd just put inside. He threw them to me, and I shoved them under my mattress.

"Daisy!" Eulalie called in a displeased voice. "Daisy!"

Xander stepped into the chest, and I was distracted for a moment as I watched him somehow fold himself into it, although he had to remove his sword and scabbard and lay them at the bottom of the chest first. When I didn't move, he gave a shake of his head, and I rushed over to carefully close the lid.

"Sorry," I whispered as the final crack was closing. Hopefully he didn't have any issues with claustrophobia.

Glancing around, my eyes fell on the neatly folded sheets and blankets, and I sucked in a breath. Snatching at them, I shook them out with fumbling fingers, throwing first the sheets and then the blankets over my bed.

By the time I was finished, Eulalie was calling me again in a tone of even less patience. I ran to the window, trying to control my breathing as I blinked down at her.

A rock flew past my head, clattering noisily on the stone floor of the room. I swooped to snatch up the rope that trailed behind it. As I secured it to the beam, I called down at her. "Sorry! I was sleeping."

I leaned out the window and attempted what I hoped was a convincing yawn. She looked out of temper which wasn't ideal for the conversation I was planning.

She pulled herself up the rope quickly, nearly as practiced as me. I stepped back, my mind racing as I tried to think of the most natural way to question her about her recent movements.

When she stood in front of me, she frowned suspiciously. "You were sleeping with your lantern burning?"

I shrugged. "I didn't feel like being in the dark tonight."

Her eyes narrowed, but she said nothing, merely gazing around the tower. I held my breath as her eyes rested on the bed which was piled abnormally high, but she passed on after a moment and I breathed again.

"I didn't expect you so many days before my birthday," I said. "Were you passing through the ar—"

"Did you think I wouldn't feel it?" she asked sharply, cutting me off.

I faltered, trying to work out what she was talking about. "Feel what? I don't know what you—"

Once again she didn't let me finish. Thrusting out her hand, she held her ring under my nose.

I blinked at it. It was the same light-sucking well of blackness I remembered, but now there was a hairline fracture running down the middle of it.

"You really thought I wouldn't notice this?" she hissed. "You've been messing with the enchantment! But how? What have you done?"

"I..." I stumbled over my words. The conversation wasn't going anything like I'd planned. I had hoped to keep her in a good mood and get her talking about her travels before we got anywhere near talking about the enchantment.

"I don't know how to change the enchantment," I managed. "If I did, do you think I'd still be here after five years?"

Her eyes narrowed to slits as she examined my face. I did my best to look innocent—an expression I had practiced often in my childhood and perfected on Eulalie's many visits.

"It shouldn't be possible for you to change it," she admitted at last, conceding the point.

I breathed a little easier, making a drastic decision. There was no salvaging a casual conversation. I just had to dive in.

"You're the one who controls the enchantment," I said. "So you should remove it now, while you still can."

She laughed. "You got bold! Tell me, why would I do that?"

I leaned forward, widening my eyes and trying to look earnest. "Look what's happened to the ring! It must be completely drained. It's going to be useless for further enchantments—it may even end up hurting you. You need to put some of the power you've used back into the ring. If you reverse the enchantment on me and my tower, you'll get back the power you need, and I'll get what I want as well."

"You think I should just let you go?" she asked incredulously.

I gripped her arm with both my hands. "I'm not a threat to you! You've seen that over five years. Whatever you do next has nothing to do with me." I let a tear slip out of one eye. "I just want to go home and see my family again."

"And you don't think your family will be interested in me?" she asked in a mocking tone.

"So what if they are? I don't know anything about you except your first name, and that might not even be your true name. I don't know where you live, I don't know what you're planning to do next, and I can't even describe your appearance. Once the enchantment that ties us together is lifted, I wouldn't even be able to recognize you if I passed you on the street. I can't imagine you'll be hanging around this tower if I'm not here."

Her expression changed slightly as she absorbed my words. They weren't even lies. After five years, I knew almost nothing about her and had no idea where she lived—if she even had a settled home.

"There's no need for anyone to lose here," I added into the lengthening silence. "Don't you think it's worth a try?"

She looked down at her ring, running a finger across its cracked surface. I suppressed a shudder. The last thing I wanted to do was touch the awful blackness of the twisted gem.

"It's true that I need the ring for one final enchantment," she murmured softly, as if to herself. "I haven't waited and planned for so long to fail now. But would the power really go back inside? It hasn't cracked all the way yet. I'm sure there must be more power left inside it."

"But how do you know what will happen if you try to use more power than it has?" I tried to fight the desperate edge creeping into my voice. "It might destroy itself and both of us too. That wouldn't fit with your plan, surely?"

She frowned, almost looking swayed by my words.

"I have waited and waited, and I only have one chance," she

muttered again. "It has to be now for this to work. One small enchantment to take a kingdom. But what if it does fail?"

"Exactly!" I latched onto her words. "It's not worth taking a risk like that. You should take back my test enchantment before it's too late."

She frowned at me, but she hardly seemed to see my face, her thoughts caught up in a heavy struggle. Slowly her expression lightened, and I could barely breathe from the hope. My words had swayed her. She was going to lift the enchantment.

Her eyes roamed over the room with the same unseeing glaze as when they'd looked at me. Except her gaze once again caught on the bed. It looked sufficiently rumpled to have been slept in, but there was no denying the blankets were piled much higher than usual, despite the warmth of the night.

Something changed in Eulalie's manner, her back straightening, and her eyebrows drawing together.

"They're pretty words, Daisy." Her eyes met mine. "But how can I trust someone who's deceiving me?"

I felt my face pale despite my effort to remain calm. "What do you mean?"

She launched into sudden movement, striding across the tower toward my bed. But at the last moment, she veered toward its foot, stopping in front of the chest. In one fluid motion, she wrenched open the lid.

"This is what I mean, Daisy."

CHAPTER 11

*E*ulalie's smug expression faltered, her eyebrows shooting up as Xander exploded upward. She clearly hadn't known who was inside and must have thought it was one of the village children.

"A man?" She fell backward, out of his reach.

As soon as he straightened to his full height, her eyes latched onto his face. "A prince! How do you have a prince in your tower?!"

She had clearly expected to have the upper hand and was thrown dangerously off balance by the surprise of Xander's identity.

He stood weaponless before her, his sword still at the bottom of the chest, but he met her gaze fearlessly, his muscles taut as he held himself ready to move.

Lightning fast, his gaze flicked sideways to me. "Are you all right?"

"You can see this place and her?" Eulalie asked sharply. "The enchantment is still active, so how is that possible?" She gasped and looked down at her ring. "Are you somehow inside the enchantment as well? Is that what cracked the ring?"

"I have no idea," Xander said evenly. "You're the one who controls it."

I shifted anxiously. I didn't like how quickly Eulalie had leaped to the correct conclusion. I didn't like anything about this situation. I should never have allowed Xander to climb into the tower. I had agreed to his claim I needed protection, but in truth I had just been excited at the idea of company after all this time. I had wanted him beside me, and now it had ruined everything. I had been working toward this conversation with Eulalie for years, and now my chance of convincing her was gone in one moment.

Eulalie took a step toward Xander. "I can't free Daisy—she belongs to me now. But you should not be here. You need to be removed."

Xander bristled, although he should have been hopeful at her words. Even if we couldn't convince Eulalie to free me, maybe we'd succeed at getting her to free him.

"You'll remove him from the enchantment?" I asked breathlessly.

She threw me a contemptuous look. "I'm not touching this enchantment. But that's not the only way to get rid of him."

"What? No!" I cried, my mind instantly leaping to what she had done to the adult men previously caught by her ring.

Xander didn't look afraid, though. Instead he stepped toward her, all towering menace.

She took one look at him and her hand flew to the ring, as if she feared he was about to rip it from her finger. I wished he would.

But instead he fell back a step. And then another. Eulalie advanced forward instead, keeping pace with his retreat.

Xander's face was creased now, confusion in his expression. Something about his bearing was off, his leg muscles straining hard despite his faltering steps. Was he trying to advance and being driven back? Eulalie extended the hand wearing the ring, and he stumbled back another step.

Was the ring somehow repelling him?

"What are you doing?" I shouted.

She glanced sideways at me. "I've learned a few things about this ring in the last couple of years. It turns out it has more abilities than I initially realized." She stepped forward and forward again.

Panic filled me as I saw her intention.

"No!" I screamed, lunging forward.

But Eulalie was positioned between me and the prince. As I approached her, an invisible force drove me off course, forcing me away from her, just as it was pushing Xander.

I redirected my steps, running toward Xander instead. He didn't appear to see me, his focus so intensely on Eulalie that he was oblivious to everything, including the approaching danger.

Three steps before I reached him, the back of his legs hit the window ledge. He started, twisting to look at the gaping hole behind him, but the movement only made him more vulnerable.

As I lunged across the remaining distance, Eulalie also stepped forward. Pushed by the force of her ring, he toppled backward through the window.

Screaming, I thrust my upper body after him, reaching with my right hand. To my shock, my reaching fingers found flesh, and I instinctively closed my fingers around his wrist.

I felt his hand close around mine in return just as his weight hit me, nearly pulling me out the window after him. I braced myself against the windowsill, straining to hold us both in place.

But a futile sense of horror was growing inside me as I felt his hand slowly slipping through mine. His weight was too much for me to have any hope of pulling him back inside. It was too much for me to even hold him in place.

Hands grasped my shoulders, shaking me and causing my grip to slip even further. Whatever effect Eulalie had managed from the ring earlier, it was gone now, no barrier preventing her from wresting me away from the window.

"Now, now," she said. "I can't have you go over as well. I don't like intruders and thieves, but I take care of my things."

I shivered at her words, but I was in no position to fend her off. She shook me again, pulling me backward as she did so, and Xander's fingers slipped the rest of the way out of my grasp. I screamed, but it was too late. He was gone, and I was being dragged back into the tower room.

I thrashed around, successfully managing to pull myself out of Eulalie's grip. I whirled to face her, too enraged to think clearly. Throwing myself at her, I clawed at her with outstretched arms and curled fingers.

She dodged around me, shaking her head and tutting. "Now that the influence of that unpleasant prince has been removed, I think it's time you went back to being the old Daisy."

She gave no appearance of realizing how deranged her words sounded, making it even more obvious how much her mental state had deteriorated since I first met her. Was this also an effect of overusing the ring, a companion to the strange, leathered skin?

My attack faltered, and it gave her time to whip something out of her satchel. My eyes widened as I caught a whiff of a scent I had only smelled once before but would never forget.

I tried to pull back, but it was too late. I had inhaled the gas and the world was already fading away.

I woke up to find myself laid out on the bed, resting on top of all the layers of sheets and blankets. I sat up so abruptly my head spun, and I had to wait a moment for my vision to settle.

My first thought was of Xander and my second of Eulalie. There was no sign of either in the still, silent room. Only the open chest and the lumps beneath me gave any sign it wasn't a perfectly ordinary morning.

I jumped out of bed and rushed to the chest to peer inside. Xander's sword lay at the bottom, apparently missed by Eulalie in the rapid sequence of events. It hadn't all been one of my strangely realistic dreams, then.

I hesitated by the chest for a moment longer, not wanting to face what came next. But I forced myself to shake off the cowardice and cross to my window. Bracing myself, I peered down at the distant ground.

It was clear.

I frowned and leaned further out the window, ignoring the beautiful day and clear blue sky. On more careful inspection, the grass at the base of the tower wasn't quite as clear as I had initially thought.

It didn't hold a motionless body as I had feared, but small twigs and branches were scattered across the ground. Had there been a storm overnight? I couldn't remember the sound of wind, but I had been drugged, so that didn't mean anything.

I scanned the rest of the clearing. There was no sign of anything out of place, and even the delicate spring flowers that dotted the grass were intact. Whatever had happened had been limited to the base of the tower, but I couldn't think what it might have been.

Could Xander have survived the fall? If so, he couldn't have taken himself to a doctor for treatment, not while he was still under the enchantment. Had the worst happened, then, and Eulalie had dragged his body away?

I whirled back to the bed and started frantically tying together the layers of blankets and sheets. I needed to get down to the ground and find out what had happened.

But as my brain caught up with my movements, absorbing the full impact of everything that had happened, I slowed down. My entire time in captivity had been building to that conversation with Eulalie. Nothing about it had gone as planned, but apparently my years of compliance had achieved one positive effect at least. Eulalie had bought the image of me as a quiet, non-rebellious captive. Even after the appearance of Xander, she had still left me here, believing I would meekly wait for her return.

But I couldn't stay in the tower any longer. I had played my final card and failed. She wasn't going to voluntarily free me from the enchantment, and my visions of physically defending myself against her had been shown to be a fantasy. Whatever effect she had temporarily activated in the ring would be as effective against me as it had been against Xander. If he had been helpless to reach her, I would be even more so.

I wasn't safe in the tower. And I would never be free if I stayed here. The time had come to leave for good. When I climbed down this time, I wouldn't be coming back up. My only hope was to track Eulalie and find a different way to free us all.

I just hoped Xander would still be able to join me. I refused to believe Eulalie had dragged him away. If I thought too much about that option, I wouldn't be able to get myself safely out of the tower.

Despite my racing thoughts, I still moved quickly, driven by images of Xander injured and alone in the forest somewhere. I selected a couple of dresses I hadn't yet embroidered and bundled them up with some basic necessities. But I hesitated in front of the shelf of books. Some of them had become like old friends, but it would be foolish to take the extra weight.

I did add Xander's sword, scabbard, and belt, though. He would want them returned to him.

When I was finished, I added the remaining dresses to my rope and secured it to the beam. I threw my bundle out the window first, followed by the blanket rope. Taking a final deep breath, I looked around the tower room. It had been my prison, my refuge, my home, and my cage for five years. It was difficult to imagine never seeing it again.

Turning my back on it, I faced the window and the world outside. Blue sky, green grass, and the vast openness of possibility was before me. This was my future.

I gripped the top dress—Sophie's mix of snow and red roses—and lowered myself out the window.

"Thank you," I whispered, although there was no one to hear my foolishness this time. "I'll free myself just like you did."

I worked my hands down the rope, crossing to Lily's dress and then Snow's. Step by step, I walked down the tower, passing each of my old friends. I knew it was only my fanciful imagination, but I felt like I was being handed from friend to friend, their silent voices giving encouragement and support. It was time for me to break my enchantment.

I reached the last dress—the sea-green that made me think of home. My breath caught, tears springing to my eyes and a lump forming in my throat. How I wished I could feel the real arms of my family around me.

My hands slipped, and I fell the length of the final blanket, landing with enough force that I had to stop and catch my breath. As soon as I was able, I stretched onto my toes and started working to undo the last knot. It took longer than I liked given the awkward angle, but I finally managed to free the bottom blanket.

With a grunt of satisfaction, I folded it up and added it to my bundle. The days had warmed up significantly, but I would still want a blanket for the nights to come.

Now that I had my feet on the ground, I could confirm that the litter of sticks and twigs covered only a small area at the bottom of the tower. But what I hadn't been able to see from my window was that a light trail of them led off into the trees. I followed it, my heart rate increasing.

I had only risked venturing out of the clearing to Lori's makeshift home once, but it had been in this direction. Had she been the one to find and assist an injured Xander?

My pace increased until I was running, my steps barely slowing as I broke through the tree line and into the cool shade of the canopy. The trees grew closely enough to earn the title of forest, but not so close as to make a hurried passage impossible.

I strained my memory to remember the path to Lori's shelter. I veered toward the left, passing a large bush that was already covered in small berries.

As I rounded it, still moving quickly, I collided with a tall body. I gasped, rocking off balance as strong hands caught my arms to steady me. Looking up, I gasped again. Xander.

PART II
THE JOURNEY

CHAPTER 12

"**Y**ou're alive!" I cried and promptly burst into tears.

His hands, which had been falling away from my arms, reached for me again. He pulled me against his chest and wrapped me in a comforting embrace.

"It's all right," he murmured. "I'm all right. I promise."

Embarrassment swept over me, and I pulled back, mopping at my face. He let me go, his expression warm as if he was touched by my emotions. I felt like a fool, though, blubbering all over him when he was practically a stranger.

"How are you here?" I asked. "Aren't you injured at least?" I examined him from head to foot, pulling his arm to make him turn so I could examine his back. "You should be injured."

He raised an eyebrow even while his eyes laughed at me. "Are you disappointed?"

"What? No! Of course not! I just can't believe…" I trailed off.

"I definitely thought it was all over while I was falling through the air," he said, relenting. "But it turns out someone was watching over me."

He smiled over his shoulder, and I half expected a godmother to appear from the trees, wings glinting. He was a prince, after all.

But the figure that appeared was far more familiar.

"Lori!" I ran over and threw my arms around her.

She embraced me back briefly before picking up the bundle I had abandoned on the ground. "So you've finally left that place for good?"

I nodded. "There's no reason to stay now. I assume Xander told you what happened with Eulalie?"

Lori nodded, and I frowned.

"How did he escape injury, though? Don't try to tell me you caught him because I won't believe it."

"Naturally not," Lori said in disapproving tones. "I'm not fool enough to try such a thing."

"She was ready before I fell," Xander said. "She got to work as soon as Eulalie climbed into the tower."

"I always worried about that window," Lori said. "I didn't say anything in case you hadn't thought of it, but it occurred to me early on that it would be an easy way for that woman to dispose of someone she no longer had a use for." Her dark expression told me she hadn't expected me to last in the tower so long.

"She had gathered a large pile of thin branches just inside the trees," Xander explained. "Just in case. When Eulalie arrived so soon after we climbed up, Lori guessed we wouldn't be ready for her and that everything would go wrong. So she dragged the branches out and piled them below the window."

"It was the best I could do to cushion the fall," Lori said. "I never thought it would be comfortable, but I'm pleased it prevented any broken bones."

"I can assure you that I'm more than grateful to be left with nothing but bruises," Xander said fervently.

"That explains all the twigs!" I cried. "But where are the branches now?"

"You noticed those, did you?" Lori nodded. "You were always

observant. Thankfully Eulalie wasn't so attentive and missed them in the moonlight."

"She was well and truly shaken to come down and find no sign of me," Xander said with a satisfied smile. "It was worth the effort we took dragging the branches away so quickly. I just wish I'd dared to attack her. But from her manner, she was afraid of exactly that, which meant she likely had the ring activated. If I'd realized she had that ability, I would have moved more quickly up in the tower!"

"I'm sorry I didn't warn you," I said miserably. "I didn't know about it myself. But at least it's not active all the time. She turned it off as soon as you fell so that she could pull me back. That's part of the reason I lost my grip."

"Thank you for trying," he said. "Your efforts helped slow my fall and gave me the chance to position myself for landing."

He paused, his face darkening as he considered my words. "If she'd turned the ring off, I should have arrested her the second she touched the ground," he growled.

Lori shook her head. "She probably turned it back on the second she saw you were gone. And besides, we couldn't risk provoking her before we knew what had happened to Daisy. What if she'd put her under a further enchantment? She might have been able to hurt her from the ground for all we knew." She looked at me inquisitively. "She didn't enchant you further, did she?"

I grimaced, examining my limbs. "Not as far as I can tell? She knocked me out like she did to us both on the road. I've never heard of a gas like the one she uses, but there's no fighting it."

"Gas?" Xander frowned. "It sounds like nayera."

We both turned to stare at him.

"What's that now?" Lori asked. "Neyara?"

"Nayera," he repeated. "It's a gas that can render someone unconscious. Back home its creation is highly controlled and only doctors are permitted to possess it. But I know some vials were secretly distributed in the Four Kingdoms. I don't know how Eulalie got her hands on any of them, though. I thought Aurora tracked them all down."

The last sentence had been murmured quietly, as if to himself. But as soon as he'd finished speaking, his expression froze, as if he'd realized his mistake. He looked at Lori, worried.

"Don't worry," I said breezily. "Lori already knows all about Aurora and her true identity. She was on the boat with us when Celine was telling stories about her sister."

Xander grinned. "I can imagine what Celeste will think of that. I gather Celine has never been the most circumspect."

I laughed. "Celine is amazing."

"Of course you would think so," Lori muttered, and Xander grinned again, making me glare at him.

"The important question is where is Eulalie now?" I asked, getting us back on track. "If she left the clearing early in the night, she might be anywhere by now!"

"Not quite anywhere, I shouldn't think," Xander said thoughtfully. "Traveling at night isn't comfortable, and while her fear of me sent her scurrying out of the clearing, I don't think she was scared enough to go fleeing across the kingdom in the middle of the night."

"What if she's searching the forest for you right now?" I looked around in sudden alarm.

"She was definitely moving toward the village," Lori said confidently.

"You've said all along that she has some other objective than just your test," Xander said. "Something that she's searching for. I could hear your conversation from inside the chest, and she was saying something about how long she'd waited and about only having one chance."

"Yes," I said slowly, remembering the words I'd barely noticed at the time. "She's mentioned the end of the test several times— that's how I knew she was waiting for my birthday. But she said it differently this time. It was less like waiting for something to finish and more like a deadline."

"Did she specifically mention your birthday?" Lori asked. "On any of those past occasions, I mean."

I frowned, dismay spreading through me like spilled tea. "Nooo," I drew out the word, embarrassed to admit the truth. "It just seemed obvious from the timing. At the very beginning she mentioned finding out what happened when I became an adult, and then she kept mentioning an end point to the test that aligned perfectly with my birthday, so I assumed…" I broke off and bit my lip, flushing.

"But now we have more information," Xander said, making it sound like my crucial mistake was completely reasonable. "She's not waiting for the end of something but for a specific event. She must have planned everything around this event, and if that one perfect moment is finally approaching and she still doesn't have all the elements she needs, then she'll be growing desperate. She didn't come to the tower because she had everything ready, she rushed there in response to the ring cracking."

"So what was she doing in the area, then?" I asked. "Lori's certain she usually leaves the region entirely on her searches, but she got here quickly after you were enchanted."

"Why, indeed…" Xander said slowly, his brow creased in thought. "Unless…" He looked up, his eyes wide. "I think I might have an idea about that. It would explain the timing of this mysterious opportunity as well."

He fell silent, and I looked at him impatiently. "Well?"

He hesitated. "I want to check something before I say anything. If I'm wrong…Let's just say, I hope I'm wrong."

"What do you need to check? Not anything here in the forest, I'm guessing." Lori produced a proper bag and started transferring my bundle of belongings into it.

"We need to go to the village," Xander said. "And if I'm right, we'll likely find Eulalie there as well as what I need to check."

"That sounds ominous." I took the bag from Lori, and she picked up another one of her own. Her bag was already packed, a saucepan and frying pan hanging from the outside.

"Going to the town makes sense," Lori said. "We need to find Eulalie as soon as possible."

Xander and I nodded agreement, so Lori took off into the forest. We followed behind her, in silence. She didn't hesitate at any point, so I guessed she had walked this route many times. Unlike me, she had never been bound to the clearing.

With each step I took away from the tower, a sense of elation rose inside me. I had longed for so many years to be free, and now I was finally leaving my clearing forever. I now knew the hard reality of my old foolish dreams, but it didn't stop a familiar thrill from creeping through me. It felt good to take action again.

When we reached the outskirts of the village, I stopped instinctively. There were so many people! Lori strode on without checking, however, walking straight down the middle of the main street.

Shaking myself, I followed her. She didn't even bother to avoid the other pedestrians, letting the enchantment prompt a strange dance as it pushed both her and the villagers' steps away from each other. I tried to move with the same confidence although it felt unnatural to walk straight at another person without flinching.

Seeing her operate in the village environment made me realize my earlier impression of Lori's freedom had been an illusion. She had been free to wander a much larger prison than me, but she was still cut off from the rest of the world just as surely as I was. How strange it must have been for her every time she came to the village.

Xander, who was new to the enchantment and didn't have the same emotional scars as Lori and me, regarded the situation with wonder. He laughed as he strode into a small knot of people and watched them scatter outward away from him before coming back together. None of them gave the appearance of having noticed their odd movement.

"This is the strangest thing!" he exclaimed. "It would be very handy in a large crowd!"

"Let's hope we're not enchanted long enough to encounter such a situation," Lori said prosaically.

I nodded fervently but couldn't help taking a sideways step to place myself in the path of an oncoming cart. I might be hiding it better, but I felt some of the same excitement as Xander. I had never had the freedom to experiment with the enchantment in a crowded place before.

The horse veered sideways, just avoiding me, while the driver called cheery greetings to some people in the doorway of a building opposite.

"As entertaining as this is, we should probably be more cautious," Xander said. "Eulalie can see us, even if no one else can."

My insides twisted at his words. I thought I'd changed in my five years, but had I learned nothing? I should know better than to chase risks for the sake of excitement.

"Daisy?" called an incredulous voice from between two houses.

"Eulalie isn't the only one who can see us!" I said, groaning. "We forgot about the children!"

A girl and boy, clearly brother and sister, raced into the street, their mouths hanging open.

I put my finger to lips, gesturing for them to retreat back between the buildings, the three of us following them.

"Anaya. Arlo." I nodded a greeting to them both. "Please keep your voices down. And can you spread the word to the others? We're hunting Eulalie, and we think she might be in the village, so we don't want her to find out we're here."

They both stared wide-eyed from me to Xander before exchanging a look.

"So it was the truth!" Arlo exclaimed.

Anaya grimaced. "I told you Charli wouldn't make something like that up."

"But you said it sounded far-fetched," he protested.

"Charli told you about the prince?" I asked, surprised, remembering our instructions to keep it quiet.

"Don't worry," Anaya said. "She knows we'd never go blabbing about it. We learned our lesson on that years ago."

She looked angry, sparking a twinge of guilt in me. All the children who visited my clearing had been forced to put up with their families' disbelief.

"Obviously she didn't tell Barnaby or Otis." Anaya rolled her eyes.

"Is there lots of trouble over my disappearance?" Xander asked. "I don't want any of you children getting caught up in that."

"If the visitors have noticed, they're keeping quiet about it for now," Anaya said. "No one in the village is talking about it, at least. That's part of why we thought maybe Charli had been mistaken somehow…" Her words trailed off as she looked at the evidence in front of her eyes.

"Well, there's a blow to my pride," Xander said with a laugh in his voice. "I thought they would have at least noticed my disappearance."

I gave him a repressive look. "It hasn't actually been that long yet. And it makes sense they wouldn't start making a fuss about it immediately anyway. They'll want to be sure you aren't going to —" I broke off, turning to Anaya. "Where's Charli right now?"

She blinked. "I'm not sure?" She looked at Arlo.

"She's at her house," he said. "You know how her sisters are. They've been conspiring to give her all the at-home chores while the visitors are here so they can be the ones parading themselves around the village."

Anaya rolled her eyes again. "That sounds right. Especially

since her sister was one of the ones to catch her in the clearing." She looked back at me. "Do you know where her house is?"

"I do," Lori said, surprising me.

Both children looked at her in surprise, appearing to notice her for the first time.

"Are you in the enchantment, too?" Anaya asked at the same moment as Arlo said, "Who are you?"

Lori ignored them both and addressed herself to me. "Charli has helped me often enough. She tells me who has useful items they'd be happy to sell, and when those items will be unattended. Then I take the item and leave coin in its place."

"Does that work?" Xander asked. "The enchantment allows it?"

I nodded. "We can interact with anything in our environment as long as there isn't an adult there to see something floating around or moving on its own."

"It's odd behavior, taking something secretly," Lori said. "But I'm sure no one suspects an invisible person is behind it. And no one has seemed to mind, given I leave the coin."

"That is excellent news!" Xander said. "I was afraid I was going to be limited to eating things we could hunt or forage for ourselves. Thankfully, I always carry my coins on my person, so I have them with me."

"That is admirable forethought indeed," I exclaimed with a sweet smile. "Since our coin has recently run out."

I batted my lashes at him, and he laughed. "Since you ask so politely, how could I say no to sharing my wealth with you?"

"Are you really leaving the tower and hunting Eulalie?" Arlo looked impressed. "So there's no point us going to the clearing anymore?"

I nodded. "I'm glad I ran into you, so I could say goodbye. I don't know—" I paused, finding it hard to say now that the moment had come. "I don't know if I'll ever be back."

"We'll miss you!" Anaya cried, throwing her arms around me.

I hugged her back. "I don't know if I ever mentioned that I'm from across the ocean. I'll invite you to visit me once I'm free from this enchantment."

"Will you really?" Arlo asked, wide-eyed. "Promise?"

"Don't get excited," Anaya said glumly. "Our parents will never let us go."

"They might if a prince invites us." He gave Xander a calculating look.

The prince laughed. "I promise to do my duty if your parents prove recalcitrant."

I smiled gratefully at him. I still didn't want to reveal my true identity—not when Eulalie might be in the village somewhere.

We managed to detach from the children so we could follow Lori to Charli's house, only barely convincing Anaya and Arlo not to accompany us. Thankfully, when we reached the spacious house, we found Charli alone.

She glanced up as the door opened, exclaiming in shock when she saw who was entering.

"Sorry," I said, as soon as the door closed behind us. "But it looked like you were alone from what we could see through the windows, and we're trying to stay out of sight since Eulalie is lurking around the village."

"Eu...Eulalie?" she stuttered, clearly still too shocked to properly respond.

"She came to the tower after you left the clearing," Xander explained. "So now everything has changed."

I quickly explained the situation to Charli, glossing over a few of the details.

"You're leaving?" she asked, looking devastated.

"I'm sorry." This time I was the one to initiate the hug. "I'll miss you, of course. But we have to find out what Eulalie's planning."

She nodded, managing a weak smile. "I always knew you

wouldn't stay forever. It's just that you always felt more like a true older sister than my actual sisters."

I tried to surreptitiously wipe the moisture leaking out of my eyes. I felt affection for all the children, but it was different with Charli. She hadn't been the only one to feel like she had gained a sister. It had been nice to experience being the older sibling for once—even if I was stuck in a tower most of the time—and I wished we could take her with us. But she was much too young to leave her family.

"We should keep this short," Lori said briskly, ending the emotional moment.

"Yes, why did you come here?" Charli asked, pulling herself together. "I hope you didn't put yourself at risk just to say goodbye! You could have left me a message."

"Actually, that's exactly why we came," I said. "We need to leave a message, so we need you to write it for us."

She raised her eyebrows. "A message? For who?"

"The king," I said triumphantly.

"The king!" she sounded horrified. "You want me to write a message for the king?"

"Obviously you won't sign it from yourself. And you'll have to do your best to disguise your handwriting." I turned to Xander. "Please tell me you don't have distinctive handwriting."

"I don't think so." He looked taken aback. "Is Charli going to write a letter from me?"

I nodded. "If you write it yourself, no one will be able to read it. But as long as no one realizes the handwriting is wrong, they should believe Charli's message is from you. Which it is," I added. "Just not from your hand."

"You want to give an excuse for my disappearance," Xander said, catching up with my plan. "So they don't start searching the kingdom for me."

I nodded. "It will just be a waste of time for them. They won't be able to help us. So there's no point causing them unnecessary stress."

Xander smiled slowly. "You're more thoughtful than you appear, Daisy."

I narrowed my eyes. "Is that a compliment or an insult?"

His lips twitched. "Always a compliment, of course."

Charli still looked reluctant, but she fetched a piece of paper and a pen. Pausing with her hand above the page, she looked questioningly at me.

I looked at Xander expectantly. "What should she write in the note?"

"That's easy," he said. "Charli, you can just write that I discovered a time-sensitive clue about the missing princess and have gone to investigate. It's even true, for the most part."

"You can't say that!" I protested. "Even if King Richard believes it, I'm sure he'll feel obligated to inform your family of your disappearance and message, and your family would never believe such a ridiculous tale. We're trying to avoid trouble, not create a diplomatic incident."

"Actually…" He coughed uncomfortably. "There's nothing my family would believe more."

I stared at him. "You can't mean you've done that before?!"

He grimaced. "I didn't leave a note last time, so they'll probably consider this evidence of my personal growth."

I shook my head. "I would be flattered if I didn't already know you've been searching for a meek damsel in distress who doesn't exist."

"I don't believe I ever used the word meek," he said in a falsely dignified manner.

"No, you just thought it," I muttered.

"So should I write it?" Charli asked, looking between us.

We both nodded, but she still hesitated, so Xander began to dictate the exact wording. It was better for him to do it, anyway, since it would sound more realistic. He instructed her on how to form the letters as well. It took them several tries until he declared himself happy with the hand writing, but the final letter looked believable to me.

We stayed long enough to see the previous attempts burned and to complete a final round of farewells. Charli and I clung to each other for an especially long time before Lori finally pulled me away and we faced the harder task: working out where to leave the letter.

CHAPTER 13

"Where were you staying?" I asked Xander as we lingered in the shadows behind another house.

"Many of the tour members are in tents to the south of the village," he said, "but I had a room in the inn along with the other royals."

"Your room is the obvious place to leave the letter, but it might also be risky," Lori said thoughtfully. "If they've already searched it and not found anything, it will look strange for a letter to suddenly appear now."

"Where else would he be likely to leave a note, though?" I asked. "Surely it would be in his room. Maybe we can put it somewhere that's not immediately obvious and hope they assume they missed it the first time?"

"And what if they miss it the second time as well?" Lori asked.

I frowned, unable to give an answer to that.

"I think we're overthinking it," Xander said cheerfully. "Even if they have searched it before, who's to say I haven't returned?"

"What?" I stared at him.

"Just briefly, I mean. I'd rather not go wandering across the kingdom with nothing more than the clothes on my back, so I want to take the opportunity to pack some of my belongings as well. Let them assume I was chasing down this clue, I came back to get my things and leave a note, and then slipped away again."

"If we want to make that believable, we'll need to leave the note there overnight," Lori said. "Otherwise why wouldn't you talk to them in person?"

"I was in a rush, of course, and didn't want to be caught in conversations and protests." He winked.

I snorted. "I get the impression you don't usually let objections weigh with you."

He chuckled. "Xavier and I would never have had any fun growing up if we had."

I rolled my eyes but couldn't help smiling. I had also spent my childhood ignoring a constant stream of objections.

"We'll go now, then?" I asked.

Xander nodded. "It's even possible they haven't checked my room yet. I only disappeared yesterday evening, so they may still be waiting to see if I return on my own. It would explain why the villagers haven't heard anything."

I looked at Lori. "Do you know the way to the inn?"

She nodded. "It's not a very big village. I'll lead us the back way. Everyone keep an eye out for leathery skin." Contempt oozed from her voice at the mention of Eulalie.

"There was a lot happening at the time, but I was shocked by her appearance in the tower," Xander said. "She barely looks human."

"That's what happens when you mess around with godmother objects you were never supposed to have," Lori said in ominous tones.

Xander paused for a moment, looking struck, and then quickly resumed walking. "That reminds me of one of the stories I heard from Rafe back in Northgate. Fifteen or so years ago, Northhelm was under attack from a rebel, an ancient creature, twisted by magic, whom he described as looking inhuman. I think he even said something about leathery skin. This man believed he had some sort of birthright to rule—something about being the older brother of a previous king."

"I've heard that story, or one like it," I said. "It's why the children all hero worship the young royals. But I hadn't heard anything about his skin."

Xander shrugged. "Maybe that didn't make it into the stories, but Rafe was there and saw this man himself. Supposedly he had collected a treasure trove of godmother objects over the centuries."

"You think Eulalie somehow got her hands on some of them after he died?" I asked slowly. "I suppose it's possible. But she obviously didn't expect them to change her appearance to be like his."

"There's the inn." Lori pointed at a larger building set back from the main road. It wasn't fenced, but the area in front of the door looked like a courtyard of sorts, with room for a carriage to pull up in.

I hesitated, examining our surroundings as closely as I could.

"I can't see any sign of Eulalie," I said hesitantly. "Do we just walk in?"

"I, for one, don't want to stand around here doing nothing." Xander smiled a challenge before walking confidently toward a side door.

Lori gave a long-suffering sigh and strode after him. She paused after a couple of steps and looked back at me with raised eyebrows.

I sighed as well and moved toward her. What was wrong with me? Had I become cautious in my years of forced inactivity? Or did I just resent Xander taking the lead?

Once inside, we moved easily through the corridors, but it felt strange to stride invisibly through a crowded building. I kept flinching whenever anyone entered our hall. Xander seemed to have no trouble with it, however, even chuckling to himself at random intervals.

After his second chuckle, I wondered if I had it wrong. Maybe it wasn't the strangeness of the enchantment affecting me, after all, but was instead the effect of my lengthy isolation. Once upon a time I had enjoyed immersing myself in crowds and would plunge into a crowded marketplace without a second thought. Now I flinched away from strangers as if I didn't know how to exist around others.

It was a painful realization, and I forced myself to stop flinching, even if it took my full concentration to achieve it. Xander turned up the stairs toward the guest rooms, but I lingered in the door that led to the front rooms of the inn. I needed to overcome my new hesitancy, and exposure seemed the best way to do it.

I pulled the door open and stepped into the tap room. It was crowded full of people, despite being the middle of the day. With the royal tour in the village, no one was following their usual routines.

Afraid of setting off a chain reaction of people bumping into each other, I wedged myself in a corner. Safely out of the way, I watched the people coming and going. Some stopped just to talk, while others ate and drank, but there was a clear center to the room.

A distinguished man with silver hair drew all eyes, not so much for his commanding presence as for the bright jewel he wore around his neck. It was a large sapphire in an ornate gold setting suspended on a gold chain. It would have been an impressive gem regardless, but its most distinctive feature was the way it glowed with its own internal light. Everyone in the room kept glancing at it with the lone exception of the younger man at the silver-haired man's side. He was deeply immersed in a conversation with the other people at their table and didn't appear to notice it at all.

The younger man had golden hair and blue eyes and was

strikingly handsome for someone in his thirties. He also bore enough resemblance to the man beside him for me to recognize them as father and son.

My eyes passed back and forth between them, but in the process, my gaze caught on someone sitting at a table behind them. I straightened to full height, going stiff. Eulalie was sitting there, right in the open, eating a midday meal.

My instinct was to run out of the room, but thankfully my shock held me motionless. She didn't appear to have noticed me, and I didn't want to draw her attention with sudden rapid movement.

The door to the back stairs—which I had left ajar—opened more widely, and Lori poked her head in. When she saw me in the corner, she gave me a confused look. Her expression slowly changed to one of concern when she took in my face.

I opened my eyes as wide as I could, tipping my head toward Eulalie. Lori frowned, still staring at me, so I jerked my head in my captor's direction more vigorously. She finally looked across the room, letting out a soft exclamation when she saw Eulalie.

Horrified, I finally launched into movement, sliding across the room and through the open door. Tugging Lori with me, I closed it firmly behind us.

"We don't want to draw her attention!" I said, painfully aware I had been the first one to make a mistake.

I should never have gone into the room in the first place. Once again I was proving that I still leaped thoughtlessly into action like the child I had once been.

"Whose attention?" Xander asked from behind us, making me jump.

"Don't scare me like that!" I scolded.

He frowned instead of teasing me as I had expected.

"What happened?" he sounded concerned. "You look spooked."

"Eulalie is in there." I indicated the closed door. "It shocked me, but I don't think she saw me. So now we won't have to go searching for her, at least."

Xander went to open the door, but I grabbed his arm, pulling him back.

"What are you doing?" I hissed. "We don't want her to notice us."

"I'd say she was far too distracted by the king to pay any attention to this side of the room," Lori said.

"The king?" I asked at the same moment as Xander said, "King Richard is here right now?"

He slipped out of my grip and eased the door slowly open. Peering through the gap, he was silent for an extended period. When he closed the door again, he looked thoughtful.

"He doesn't look worried, so I'm guessing they think I returned to my room late last night and just haven't emerged yet. It didn't look disturbed as far as I can tell, so they probably haven't checked it yet." He hoisted his pack higher on his shoulder. "Hopefully that means everything will go smoothly with finding the note."

"I can't believe I didn't consider that Eulalie might be in there," I said bitterly, still thinking about my foolhardiness. "Her individual enchantment makes her look like a stranger to everyone but us, and what more logical place would there be for a stranger than the inn?"

"And more importantly, this is where King Richard and Prince William are," Xander said with so much weight that I frowned at him.

"Do you think she's here for them?"

"It certainly looked like it," Lori said.

The door to the tap room opened, making us all startle. Lori and I moved back to flatten ourselves against the wall, but Xander looked frantically around as if trying to find somewhere to hide.

I grabbed his arm and pulled him against the wall with us.

"We don't have to worry about that, remember?" I said at normal volume. "It's those advantages I was talking about."

He blinked, a slow smile growing on his face as two men in the uniform of royal guards left the tap room and started up the stairs. They looked mildly concerned, but I caught a brief glimpse of the tap room as the door swung shut again, and everyone else looked calm. Nothing alarming could have occurred in the short time since I'd left the room.

"Can't they see my pack?" Xander asked, shifting it on his shoulder.

"As long as you're holding it when they encounter you, they can't see it," Lori said. "You can't conceal a whole building by touching it or anything, but it seems to work on anything small enough to be picked up."

"Fascinating," Xander said.

"It gets a lot less interesting after five years," I said sourly, only to immediately brighten. "But this is a lot more fun than being stuck in my tower. Think of the places we could go! We could walk straight into the royal vault." I cackled, and Xander laughed at me, although he looked so genuinely amused, I couldn't take offense.

"There might be a few thick, locked doors in the way of that particular goal," he said.

"Just don't goad her into strutting into the throne room and plonking herself down on Northhelm's throne." Lori gave me a long-suffering look. "She would do it—and wilder things besides, I'm sure—and knowing our luck, that would be the exact moment the enchantment lifted."

I gurgled. "If it did, I would be nothing but grateful!"

The clattering sounds of rushed feet interrupted our lighthearted conversation. We all turned to see the two guards hurrying back down the stairs, their earlier mild concern amplified to far higher levels.

They stopped at the base of the steps, and the younger one

looked to the older. The older hesitated for a moment and then jerked his head toward the door. The younger one seemed to understand his unspoken message, hurrying into the tap room alone.

"He's the most senior of the guards along on the tour," Xander said, indicating the man who still stood near us.

"Is that our letter?" I pointed at the paper gripped in the man's hand. "They must have gone upstairs to check what had happened to you."

"That confirms they thought I was in there," Xander said. "It's a good thing we brought the letter straight away. The timing was perfect."

The door opened again, this time letting the younger guard and four other men out of the tap room. We all flattened ourselves further against the walls since the space was starting to feel crowded. Neither the king, the prince, nor either of the new guards noticed us, though, the enchantment holding firm.

"What's all this?" King Richard asked. "Is there something wrong with the prince?"

The senior guard silently handed over the letter. Prince William stood calmly and quietly beside his father, waiting for the king to finish reading. His manner was that of a soldier at attention, but something subtle in his bearing told me he was having to restrain himself from leaning forward to read over his father's shoulder.

When the king finished, he silently handed the paper to his son. William read more quickly, his eyes quickly jumping back to his father's face.

"When did he leave? Last night?" he asked.

The king looked to the senior guard who looked pained. "I'm afraid I don't know, Your Majesty. His Royal Highness has proved...resistant to close surveillance, even for the sake of his own protection."

Xander grinned. "The Northhelmians are good people, but

they're so formal and proper. I couldn't bear having two people watching my every move with disapproving eyes."

"Naturally you couldn't go against the wishes of a foreign prince," William said quickly, earning a grateful look from the guard.

King Richard seemed about to speak, but instead he paused and looked to his son. "How would you like to handle this, William? Whatever consequences there are with Kuralan will be yours to manage."

"Is he really going to abdicate soon, then?" I asked.

It had seemed a distant, abstract fact back in my tower, where the rest of the world had been a distant place. But now that the king and prince in question were standing in front of me, it seemed a far more interesting development. Watching them brought back memories of listening in on official meetings and spying from hidden corners as the business of kingdoms was conducted.

"The necessary ceremonies will happen as soon as the tour finishes and they return to the capital," Xander said. "King Richard says that his stamina and faculties aren't what they once were, and the time has come for him to retire and allow his son to take his turn at ruling. He'll still be around to advise him, though."

"It's a good ruler who knows when the time has come to let go of power," Lori said approvingly. "Far too few pass that big test."

"We'll have to send word to Sultan Khalil, of course," William said with a furrowed brow. "But Prince Xander came to us by his own choice and without entourage. And he told us from the beginning that he had come to Northhelm following rumors of the missing princess. Celeste has been greatly frustrated by her inability to track the girl down, so I know she was happy to consult with him and even suggest locations for him to investigate further. So we can't be surprised that he has left to follow this lead."

"We won't go after him, then?" the senior guard asked.

William shook his head. "We weren't the ones to send him on this tour or on his quest. If he's decided our paths need to diverge, I don't think we can attempt to recall him, and I don't believe his father would blame us for not doing so." He frowned. "I do wish he'd taken the time for a proper farewell, though. It's hard to be entirely at ease without one. Did he think we would try to restrain him?"

Xander sighed. "It makes both me and Kuralan look terrible. I know they were hoping we could talk further about the possibility of a treaty before I left."

I patted his arm as reassuringly as I could. "Once we work out how to free ourselves, you can discuss all the treaties your heart desires."

"None, then?" he grinned at me. "You must be thinking of my older brother."

I laughed. "Very well, you can leave the treaty making to the more responsible members of your family, but at least you can give your own farewells."

His expression grew serious again, and I could see he felt true distress over that part of his disappearance. He didn't like these new friends thinking he had spurned them and run off.

"I suppose that's the famous jewel of the true ruler," Lori said, eyes locked on the glowing blue gem resting against the king's chest.

"The jewel of what?" I asked, only half listening, my attention distracted by William.

The crown prince had subtly slipped the letter into his pocket instead of handing it back to the king. Was he planning to send it to his wife for further analysis? Would she be able to tell it hadn't been written with Xander's hand?

"Didn't you learn about the jewel before we left Trione to join the delegation?" Lori asked. "You seemed to be studying everything about the Four Kingdoms you could get your hands on."

"Learn about what?" I asked, finally refocusing on our conversation.

"I can see you must have been beloved of your tutors," Xander said with an infuriating grin.

"While yours no doubt adored you," I said back, but he merely grinned more broadly, owning it.

"We were talking of the Northhelmian jewel of the true ruler," he said. "Also known as that giant blue stone that King Richard carts around on his chest. I think it's the real reason for this tour. He wants everyone in the kingdom to have a chance to see it and believe in its power."

"What is its power?" I examined it more closely. There was no point denying it had power of some sort. No jewel could glow like that otherwise. "Oh wait! Is that the godmother object that they received because of the princess being secretly adopted?"

"I'm not sure that's the exact reason the godmothers gave for the gift," Xander said, looking suspiciously like he was trying not to laugh at me. "But King Richard did receive it following that business with the rebel fifteen years ago."

The king and prince finished their conversation about contacting the Kuralanis and returned to the tap room, allowing us to finally move away from the walls.

"That's right." I nodded. "I do remember learning about it—I just hadn't thought about it in years. There was some unrest among the nobles after the attempted rebellion, especially given the king and queen had been keeping secrets from them. Since the whole rebellion centered around who had the true birthright to rule, the godmothers gave the king a jewel that would glow in the presence of the true ruler. That way his people could always remain confident in the identity of their king." I beamed, proud of myself for remembering the old lesson.

"So what happens now that he's abdicating?" Lori asked.

"Supposedly it has all been discussed with the godmothers," Xander said, "and the jewel was always intended to be passed down through rulers. The king and prince will withdraw for a private ceremony of some sort—only they know the details—and as long as William emerges with the jewel glowing on his chest, then the handover of power is considered complete and a coronation will be held immediately."

"I wonder if he's nervous." I gazed at the closed tap room door.

"He has no reason to be," Xander said. "William is the oldest child of the current king and has been the undisputed crown prince since his father took the throne. On top of that, the populace like him, and it's hard to imagine a more capable team than him and his wife. I've traveled through half the kingdom with them, and I haven't heard a single suggestion he might not have the necessary qualities of a ruler."

"May we all hope for such glowing tributes to be paid us," Lori said, looking at me with a heavy look that suggested she had long since despaired of hearing such praises directed toward her ward.

I smiled sweetly at her. "I love you too, Lori."

"So it's all a formality for the prince," I mused. "But the king thinks the authority of the jewel will be solidified if all his people have seen it for themselves. Now when the news spreads that the new king has been crowned and that he wears the glowing jewel, there will be utmost confidence in his reign."

"Exactly." Xander was also staring at the tap room door, but he sounded concerned.

"What is it?" I asked.

"I'm hoping it's nothing but a flight of fancy," Xander said. "If you could both laugh at me, I'd be most grateful."

"Uh oh, that sounds ominous," I said. "While I would usually be more than happy to laugh at you, I feel a sinking certainty I won't be able to do so in this instance."

Xander grimaced. "I just keep thinking about what Eulalie

said about having one chance, and it seems awfully coincidental that Northhelm is so close to the coronation of a new ruler."

"You think she means to disrupt the handover of power?" I asked. "Why would she want to do that?"

"As to that…" He hesitated. "I have an idea, but it's far-fetched. Like I told you before, I need to check something before I say anything more."

"Check what?" I asked suspiciously.

"Just give me a day," he pleaded. "I'll tell you everything in the morning, proved or not."

"That's fair," Lori said with a quelling look at me, cutting off my budding protests. "We don't have time to be standing around talking anyway. While we're here jabbering, Eulalie could have waltzed out the front door of the inn and disappeared. We need to split up and keep a watch on all the inn's exits. We just have to make sure we find somewhere hidden to watch from. That should be our priority."

Reluctantly I subsided, unable to dispute her point.

Since Eulalie still didn't know Lori had been caught in her enchantment, Lori volunteered to check she was still in the tap room. And once she'd ascertained her presence, she would be the one to keep watch on the front door of the inn. Since the inn was located in the center of town, watching the front door from a hidden location would be difficult, so Xander and I accepted our assignments at the back and side doors.

We circled the inn together, choosing our hiding places and being sure each of us knew where to find the others in case our target appeared.

But as soon as that initial excitement was over, a long period of boredom set in. Thankfully, I had plenty of experience with boredom. And even the side door of the inn saw more activity in an afternoon than my tower used to see in a full day.

The time passed eventually without Eulalie ever appearing, and we reconvened in the street outside the inn.

"There's no reason for her to sneak away from the inn in the middle of the night," Lori said with a sideways look at me. "We should get some sleep."

I sighed. She was putting mothering me ahead of our quest.

But Xander jumped in to agree, surprisingly eager. "She must have rented a room for the night—she's not invisible like us, just anonymous—and we need to get some sleep."

I looked between them suspiciously, but Lori seemed surprised and pleased at his easy acquiescence, so I couldn't suspect them of a plot against me.

"We should take watches," I said. "That way we can take it in turns to keep an eye on the main street at least while the other two sleep."

Xander again agreed readily, Lori following more reluctantly behind. I ended up assigned the first watch, which suited me perfectly. I didn't trust either of them to wake me up when my turn came otherwise.

I, on the other hand, had no problem waking Xander up after a third of the night had passed. He looked peaceful sleeping next to Lori behind the inn—a position chosen to keep the bedrolls out of casual sight and to offer at least a little coverage of the back exit. I still shook him heartlessly awake, however, and he leaped to his feet with surprising alacrity.

I lay down in his place, but sleep didn't come as quickly as I had expected. I kept thinking of his insistence that he needed to check something before sharing his theory, and his statement that he would share the information in the morning.

I eventually grew suspicious enough to abandon sleep altogether and creep back out of the bedroll. Rounding the inn, I almost collided with him.

Not only was he far from his assigned watch, but he had his hand on the inn's side door.

"Don't even bother trying to deny whatever is going on here," I said dryly.

He glanced back in the direction of the sleeping Lori before smiling slowly.

"I don't mind having company."

I raised an eyebrow. "While doing what, exactly?"

"How would you feel about using our fancy powers to sneak into the king's bedchamber?"

My other eyebrow shot up to join the first. "If you have secret plans to assassinate the Northhelmian king, then I'm going to have to object."

"What if I promise there's no killing involved?"

"What about abducting? General bodily harm? Pulling out hairs for use in some sort of forbidden enchantment?" I examined the shape of his pockets with narrowed eyes. "Be honest—do you have some of that nayera gas concealed on your person right now?"

He snorted. "I already told you—only doctors are allowed to have it. Being a prince doesn't exempt me from that particular rule."

I crossed my arms. "You haven't fallen in love with Queen Louise and devised a dastardly plot to dispose of her husband?"

He laughed. "She seems a lovely lady, but given she has grandchildren nearly my age, I can assure you that is not the case."

I sighed. "I give up. Why are we sneaking into his bedchamber?"

"We? You'll come?" He sounded pleased, and my heart swelled

in response. No one had ever wanted to include me in their adventures before. I had always needed to force my way in.

I glanced around to check there was still no one in sight and pulled open the door. I gestured for Xander to precede me inside.

"Please tell me we're not looking for top secret trade documents," I said as we moved into the building, "because that would be most disappointing. If secrets are involved, I at least want a baby stolen at birth or something equally thrilling."

"I think the Northhelmians have had enough of that sort of thing," Xander said in a choked voice. "But there is magic involved, if that helps."

I brightened. "A godmother object? What does it do?" I stopped in the middle of the stairs. "Wait. We're not going to steal the jewel of the true ruler, are we?"

"Just briefly?"

I stared at him. "The jewel of the—that name is ridiculous and way too long. But we're not actually stealing the king's jewel, right? That's not the sort of royal artifact you can mess around with, even temporarily."

"If I still had the ability to ask the king for information directly, I wouldn't need to resort to temporary theft," Xander said, his manner serious for the first time since the start of our conversation. "But I can't do that anymore, and this is the only way I can think of to confirm if my idea is just far-fetched or totally impossible. I'm hoping totally impossible, but if not... Well, I'm worried I might not be the first person to have put it to the test."

"You think Eulalie has tested the jewel already."

He shrugged. "Maybe. Or maybe she didn't need to test it. Maybe she has some other way to find out the details of how it works."

"Don't you think it's time you told me what this is all about?"

He resumed climbing, overtaking me and forcing me to continue upward in his wake.

"I've been wracking my brains trying to work out how an invisibility enchantment could be used to take over a kingdom," he said as he reached the hallway with the guest rooms. "It didn't make much sense until I put it together with the upcoming coronation, and then I had an outrageous idea."

It was odd to hear him talking at full volume in the quiet of the sleeping inn. But, of course, no one stirred at his words. Instead we moved down the hall unchallenged, stopping in front of one of the doors.

I tried to work out what possibility Xander had imagined. "You think Eulalie intends to enchant King Richard and Prince William during their private ceremony to hand over power?"

He nodded and eased open the door. A guard slept inside, stretched out across the floor. His body should have blocked our access to the room, but he had rolled just enough for us to squeeze inside.

I went through after Xander, closing the door softly behind me and turning to face the unnatural blue glow that lit the room. When I joined Xander at the side of the bed, I saw the source of the light—the king's jewel.

"I have no idea what claim Eulalie thinks she can make on the throne," Xander said. "But when I tried to think what plan would require an invisible king instead of a dead one, *that* was all I could come up with." He pointed at the blue gem.

Startled, I tore my mesmerized gaze from the jewel to stare at Xander instead. "You think she means to wear the jewel herself, even though she's not the true ruler? You're thinking that if she keeps the true ruler with her, invisible to others, it will keep glowing because of his presence?"

Xander shrugged. "If the gem has to actually be worn by the king to glow, then the plan wouldn't work. But surely he takes it off to wash, at the very least. From what I've heard, it wasn't in the form of a necklace when it was first gifted to him. It was just a gem. King Richard had it placed in its current setting so he could carry it with him where it would be visible to others. So my theory is that it's not about wearing the necklace, it's about the jewel itself and the jewel remaining in close proximity to the king."

"And you want to test that by seeing what happens when you take it off him?" I asked, realizing why we were here.

"Exactly." He shuffled closer to the bed. "If the jewel will still glow anywhere in this room, then we'll have our answer."

"And if it stops glowing and the king and guard wake up as a consequence?"

He smiled mischievously. "We shove it back over his head and run? It's not like they can catch us."

I groaned. "Clearly there's no arguing you out of this."

"Do you even want to try?" he asked with a little too much perspicacity.

I stayed silent, not wanting to admit he was right. Now that he'd planted the idea in my head, I was feeling extremely unsettled and wanted the answer myself.

"How are we going to get it off?" I asked instead, eyeing the necklace which had fallen askew during the king's sleep but which was still very much around his neck.

"Very, very carefully." Xander reached for the chain. He looked up at me. "You raise his head?"

I moved into a better position, reaching tentatively for the king's head. "The enchantment might not let me."

"As long as he stays asleep, I think it should," Xander said, falling unnecessarily into a whisper.

Sure enough, my hands successfully touched the king's hair, my touch gentle. I eased my hands underneath his hair and lifted his head the tiniest fraction.

"How is this not waking him up?" I asked in astonishment as Xander worked the chain up and over his head, trying not to let it touch him any more than necessary.

"Remember he can't hear any sound we're making or even

sense our presence. That helps. So it's just the movement itself. And you'd be surprised what most people can sleep through at this point of the night."

I gave him a disapproving look. "Now I know why you volunteered for middle watch."

"Of course." He sighed with relief as the chain eased over the last of the king's hair and up onto my arms instead. "Now you let go."

I forced myself to move slowly as I eased the king's head back down and pulled back. Immediately, I slid the chain down my arms and into Xander's hands, wanting as little contact with the thing as possible. I still wasn't entirely sure it was all right for us to be touching it.

"It's still glowing." Xander sounded disappointed to be right.

He strode toward the farthest corner of the room, while I stared at the gem in his hands. Was it starting to dim? Was that a flicker? Was it about to go out and send the kingdom of Northhelm into some sort of crisis of confidence in its ruler?

"It's still glowing," Xander announced, making me admit the dimming had only been in my imagination. "We were right that it only needs general proximity. I'm not going to test how far it stretches because that's unnecessary for our purposes, and I'd prefer it didn't actually go out."

I nodded fervently, glad he felt some sense of caution.

"We have to put it back on, don't we?" I asked with a groan.

He joined me beside the bed again. "I'm afraid so."

But he didn't move toward the king. Instead he looked down at the jewel in his hand and then apologetically up at me. "There's one more test we have to do, though."

"Another one?"

"We know the jewel won't stop glowing if it's removed from the king's neck, but what about if someone else puts it on?"

I stepped back, raising both hands defensively. "I am not

putting that thing on. What if it decides *I'm* the next ruler of Northhelm?"

I was only half joking. I had no desire to get any more involved with an object that was so intertwined with another kingdom's succession.

Xander grimaced. "I don't want to wear it either. But it's not a proper test unless we try." With an exhale, he whisked the chain over his head and let the gem settle against his chest.

We held our breath and waited. It continued to glow.

"The godmothers could have designed it better," I said disapprovingly. "Why does it glow when it's out of contact with the king?"

"He probably doesn't want to have a stone chained to his skin every second of the day," Xander pointed out. "I'm sure he takes it off to wash among other things. And it wouldn't inspire confidence in his subjects if the light was constantly going out."

I sighed. "Fine. Please just take it off, all right?"

He willingly slipped it back over his head. "Now we need to return it to its proper place and it will be like we were never here."

"I really hope so," I said, "because if they wake up, we're not going to be able to open that door without them noticing."

"We'll just have to open it regardless," Xander said. "They'll be surprised, but they can't stop us leaving."

"It's not that we shouldn't open it, but that we won't be able to. The enchantment doesn't approve of doors opening on their own. If these two wake up, we'll be stuck in here unless they open the door themselves and leave it open."

Xander grimaced. "Let's be extra careful, then."

But as soon as my hands touched the king's head, he stirred. I froze, holding my breath—an instinctive, if futile, gesture. Our previous contact must have brought him out of a deep sleep, leaving him in a much lighter state of sleep for this second attempt. He began to wake.

"Quick!" I screamed, abandoning the pointless silence. "Get it back on!"

Xander shoved the chain over the king's neck one second before his eyes fluttered open. It was just in time because the moment they opened, both Xander and I were forced back out of contact with him by the enchantment.

"That was close," I breathed, staring thankfully at the chain around King Richard's neck. It was tangled and twisted, but that could easily be explained by sleep.

The king sat up, and the guard sleeping by the door instantly woke. He leaped to his feet, gazing around the room.

"Is something wrong, Your Majesty?" he asked.

The king blinked slowly, also looking around the room. "It felt as if someone was touching me."

"Touching you, Your Majesty?" the guard cried, alarmed. "Are you injured?"

"No, no, I don't think so." The king took stock of himself, running his hands over his hair and then letting them fall to the gem on the chain. "It must have been a dream."

"Yes," I whispered encouragingly, although I knew he couldn't hear me. "Think of it as a dream!"

The guard relaxed a little, but he was still tense, his eyes darting into the corners of the room one by one. King Richard sighed and lay back down.

"My apologies for disturbing you. We should both get sleep while we can."

The guard nodded, watching as the king lay back down. But while the king soon settled back into steady breathing, the guard remained sitting upright, his back to the door, clearly reluctant to sleep after the king's alarm.

"Well, that's unfortunate," Xander said in what I felt was too calm a tone.

"Just unfortunate?" I asked. "It's a disaster."

Once again, I had gone chasing adventure and ended up in trouble.

"It's not that bad." Xander took a seat against one of the walls. "They'll leave the room eventually, and then we'll have our chance to escape."

"What about all those important documents I was joking about?" I looked around the room. "Are you sure they just leave the king's room unguarded during the day?"

Xander went still, and I gave him a knowing look.

"I'm right, aren't I? They leave a guard here during the day to watch the king's possessions."

Xander groaned. "I'd forgotten that. We'll just have to be ready to sneak out behind the king."

"It might work," I said. "And it might not. The enchantment pushes us away from people, remember? And we can't stop the door from closing. If they close it quickly enough, the enchantment won't give us a chance."

"An opportunity has to come eventually!"

"I assume so," I agreed. "And in the meantime, Eulalie may well leave the inn and the village altogether."

Xander gave me a guilty look, and I continued on unrelentingly. "But that would still not be the worst outcome. What do you think Lori will do when she wakes up for her turn at watch and we've both disappeared?"

"Not quietly complete her shift, I'm guessing."

I rolled my eyes. "I see you've met her. She'll tear the inn and village apart looking for me, regardless of whether or not that brings her to Eulalie's attention. We might all end up exposed from this."

Xander rubbed the back of his head. "It's possible I may not have entirely thought this through. In my defense, I'm still new to these powers of ours."

"They're not powers!" I said. "It's an enchantment—a bad one that we want to be free from. Please don't forget that."

"Yes, Your Highness," he said, making me frown even more deeply.

"We need a plan," I announced.

"Then it's a good thing we have the queen of plans with us." He looked at me hopefully. "You've concocted a plan for this sort of situation, right?"

"Might I remind you that I've been captive in a one-room tower with only a window as entry and exit? I didn't put a lot of thought into how to get through doors."

"Well, there's no time like the present!"

"Actually," I said slowly, struck by my own words, "maybe I am the expert on this situation."

He followed the direction of my gaze toward the window, his brows rising. "You do remember we had to climb stairs to get here?"

I turned to him, giving my words a slight mocking air. "Why, are you scared?"

He laughed. "If you knew me from Kuralan, you wouldn't be worried about that." He winked. "You wouldn't think you needed to resort to daring me either. I've done far more foolish things from just a polite request. In fact, it doesn't even have to be that polite."

"I wish you and your siblings were Trionian," I said wistfully. "I love Teddy and Millie, of course, but it sounds like you were all much more fun as children."

"I, on the other hand, am very grateful not to be your brother." There was a light in Xander's eyes that made me squirm and look away.

I considered pretending to be offended and decided it was safer to ignore the whole thing. Standing, I hurried toward the window, his chuckle chasing my cowardly retreat.

When I reached the window, I peered down at the ground below. The only reason we even had a chance was thanks to the warm spring nights. Given the lovely outside temperature, the king had decided to leave his window open for some fresh air, meaning there was no solid barrier blocking our way.

The guard was sitting staring fixedly at the window, so we wouldn't have been able to open it. But given it was already open, he could stare at it forever and he wasn't going to see our escape.

I looked back at Xander. "I think we can do it. We might break a bone or two, but we'll be free. What do you say?"

He reached my side and peered over the windowsill. When he looked back at me, he was smiling.

"Who could say no to a proposition like that?"

CHAPTER 15

I glanced back at the guard and shivered at the unnerving sight of him staring straight at us with blank, unrecognizing eyes.

Xander followed my gaze. "He's awake, so we won't be able to use anything from the room. No ropes made of blankets this time."

I looked dubiously at the distance to the ground and then around at the inn's dark surroundings.

"Can you see Lori?" Xander leaned out the window to get a better look, and I instinctively grabbed him before he toppled out.

He looked back at me. "Don't worry, I have excellent balance."

I quickly let go, shaking my head.

"We could try calling to wake Lori up," Xander suggested. "Maybe she has a handy pile of branches she can pull over."

I snorted. "Good to know you're taking the situation with utmost seriousness."

"Naturally," he said. "I'm always serious. It's my most defining feature, constantly bemoaned by my siblings since childhood."

I ignored him, still peering at the drop. "If only my hair had grown a bit faster. We really could have plaited it and used it as a rope."

I sighed, realizing that standing around talking about it was only delaying the inevitable. "As long as we land on our feet and absorb the fall well, I think we can manage it without too much injury. I'll go first."

I didn't mention how many times I'd calculated the best way to survive a fall from my tower.

"Absolutely not," Xander said immediately. "I'll go first and then catch you."

"I'll squish you!" I protested.

He grabbed the windowsill, pushing me sideways with his shoulder so he occupied the space alone. Pausing, he looked at me with a pleading expression. "I came all this way to rescue you, and I've been no use at all. Can't you at least give me this?"

He didn't wait for an answer, putting his boot on the windowsill between his hands and vaulting through.

I gasped, rushing forward. For a second I saw his fingers wrapped around the sill, his body presumably dangling down the side of the building. But by the time I reached the window, he had dropped.

I just caught his landing. He hit the ground feet first, moving immediately into a fluid drop. I watched admiringly as he allowed his momentum to carry him forward in a flip over his shoulders, the other side of his body slamming into the ground to dissipate the last of the landing force.

He sprang immediately back to his feet, turning to smile cheerfully up at me.

"Are you all right?" I called, although I could already see he was.

He spread his arms wide. "As you see. Now you just need to jump, and I'll catch you." He held his arms out encouragingly, but I eyed the distance between us uncertainly.

"Lower yourself out the window first," he said. "If you dangle down at full length, you'll take a lot of height off the drop. Add in how tall I am, and I won't have any trouble catching you."

I bit my lip, considering my options. I could insist on landing on my own, which would ensure I didn't injure anyone but myself. But from his landing, Xander clearly knew what he was doing when it came to falls, and if I was honest, I had nothing but endless fantasizing to draw on.

He had already proved his confidence in his own landing. I should trust that he knew what he was doing when he said he could safely catch me. If I tried to jump on my own and broke a leg, we'd never be able to track Eulalie.

"Fine!" I called down, making his eyes light up. "Don't drop me!"

"Never," he assured me, unusually serious.

I pulled back for a moment, waiting for the flush on my cheeks to die down. Even as a child, I had always wanted to go on adventures myself rather than be rescued, and from the very beginning I had made plans to save myself from the tower. But I couldn't deny the warm feeling that filled me at Xander's words. Apparently part of me did want to be rescued after all.

And what's so wrong with that? I asked myself. I had always envied the way my twin siblings always had each other. We all needed other people sometimes. *And if they happen to have strong arms that are good at catching, there's nothing wrong with that.*

"Daisy?" Xander called up. "Are you coming? You can trust me!"

I grabbed the window and swung my legs over the sill. Sitting perched there, I smiled down at him. "I know."

I pushed myself off, letting my body drop down as I twisted and gripped the sill with both hands. Once I was dangling down against the wall, I held position for a second, my arms straining.

"Ready?" I called.

"Ready," came Xander's reassuring voice.

I took a breath, pushed slightly off the wall with my feet, and let myself drop.

"Oof!" The breath rushed out of me as I landed in strong arms, my momentum carrying us both downward.

Xander kept his feet, however, stopping my downward force before I reached the ground and straightening so that he stood, cradling me in his arms. I looked up at him and immediately realized how close our faces were.

"Good job," he said softly. "A beautiful fall."

He hesitated, as if he wanted to say something else, but stayed silent. Instead of speaking, his eyes traveled over my face, catching briefly on my lips before returning to my eyes.

I remained in place, too frozen to move or respond. The night air grew warmer, tension stretching between us in the silence.

Just as it was about to snap, a third voice shocked us out of the moment.

"What in the kingdoms is going on here?" Lori exclaimed.

Xander released the arm beneath my knees, letting my legs drop to the ground. I stumbled slightly finding my balance, and he left his other arm curled around my shoulders. But as soon as I was steady, he stepped back, clearing his throat and adopting an expression that somehow perfectly combined respectability and innocence.

"We had to jump out the window," I said quickly. "Xander jumped first and then caught me. I'm very grateful."

Lori looked slowly up at the open window and then back at me, eyes narrowed. "You had to jump out the window," she said in measured tones that only made me more nervous. "And what exactly were you doing inside the inn?"

"I needed to test something," Xander said, his expression becoming deadly serious. "And unfortunately my guesses were proved correct. We may have a big problem on our hands."

Lori's eyebrows rose. "It's not quite morning yet, but I suppose you're sharing your theory now." She glanced at me. "I can't imagine any of us will be getting back to sleep until we've talked this out."

I slipped my arms around her and squeezed. Lori knew me well.

She sighed, but her eyes were smiling. "Let's at least go to the front of the inn so we can keep watch while we talk. You had better hope Eulalie didn't slip away while the two of you were playing detectives, or whatever you were doing in there."

"You don't suspect us of playing assassins?" I asked as we walked around the side of the inn.

"Of all the ridiculous things to say!" Lori exclaimed, incensed.

We found an out-of-sight place to sit that still had a view of the inn's front door—an easier feat to achieve in the shadows of nighttime. Lori turned to Xander with an expectant expression.

"We went into the king's bedchamber to test his jewel of the true ruler. We ascertained that the king doesn't need to actually wear it, he just needs to be near it."

Lori raised an eyebrow. "That sounds like it could become confusing. What if the true ruler is actually someone near the king?"

"I see you've reached straight for the heart of the issue," Xander said. "Normally it wouldn't be a problem since no one individual is always in the king's vicinity. His guards take shifts, and none of his family and advisors are at his side all day and night without fail. If someone did shadow the king like that, then I imagine some questions would be asked."

"Unless," I said glumly, "one of the two of them was invisible —unable to be seen or heard by anyone else."

Lori's eyes widened. "You think Eulalie means to put her blinding enchantment on the king in order to do that? Who does she want to make ruler in his place?"

"Herself," I said without hesitation. "She mentioned once that her family are all dead, and she never talks about anyone else. She definitely wants Northhelm for herself. From the way she talks, she thinks she has some right to the kingdom, although I can't imagine…"

My voice trailed off as a thought occurred to me, but the others kept talking.

"Could she really manage it?" Lori sounded doubtful. "How would she keep the king restrained at her side at all times? He's larger and stronger than her, and you'd think he would eventually escape or attack her."

"She's been preparing for this for five years," Xander said, "all the while testing to see that the enchantment would hold up for the long term. She may well have found a way."

"Perhaps she has another gas or drug that will keep him docile?" Lori mused. She looked at me. "It's a good thing you always played along with being so submissive or she might have used it on you."

"Mmmm," I said, still distracted by my thoughts.

Xander gave me an odd look but was distracted by Lori's continued speech.

"But why has she waited so long?" she asked. "Is she really waiting to see what happens when Daisy reaches eighteen? Is she worried that the kingdom's children might be able to see the true king at her side?"

"I suspect she means to trap both the king and the prince," Xander said. "The king is abdicating soon, and a new coronation is being planned. It's the ideal time for her to step in if she wants her takeover to go as smoothly as possible."

Lori shook her head. "I understand why you're concerned at the possibility, but I still can't see how it would work. Let's say Eulalie manages to infiltrate the location where the king and prince are conducting their private ceremony to transfer the authority of the jewel. And let's say she manages to enchant them both so that she's the one to walk back out with the glowing gem around her neck. What claim can she make on the throne? Does she think everyone will just accept a completely unknown commoner claiming to be their new queen?" She looked between us. "Do the Northhelmians trust the jewel that much?"

"I'm not sure," Xander admitted. "They've all been very impressed by it from what I've seen of the tour, but it does seem like a far-fetched claim."

"How about this for another far-fetched claim?" I said. "Do you remember yesterday when you were talking about that rebel from fifteen years ago and we were guessing that maybe Eulalie had found his stash of godmother objects?"

"The man with the leathery skin like hers?" Xander clarified, and I nodded.

"This conversation reminded me of something Eulalie told me when we first met. She claimed she got her godmother objects from her brother. A brother who is now dead."

"We must have been wrong about the rebel, then," Lori said, clearly unsure why this was significant.

"Maybe," I replied. "Or maybe we weren't wrong at all and the rebel from fifteen years ago was her brother."

Xander rocked back, amazement on his face. "The rebel was trying to take the throne because he believed he was the one with the true birthright to rule. He said the throne had been stolen by his younger brother generations before. If Eulalie truly is part of that family, then she's of royal Northhelmian blood herself. She could say she's the long-lost heir returned, and that the jewel recognizes her claim."

"She'll still be a stranger to everyone in the capital," Lori objected. "They're not going to like it."

"No, I'm sure they won't," Xander said. "But will they dare go against the object provided by the godmothers for exactly this purpose? Everyone knows the Four Kingdoms have been prospering in recent years due to the High King's blessing. They won't want to defy his godmothers."

"So she has a claim to the throne—however shaky—and a plan on how to get it that has a chance at working," I said. "But we know she's missing something she needs to make the whole thing work."

"What is it that she still needs?" Xander asked, thoughtfully.

"A way to keep the king and the prince compliant?" Lori suggested. "That seems the biggest flaw in her plan to me."

"If she can find that, it will become difficult for anyone to stop her." Xander sounded alarmed.

"Difficult for anyone else, maybe," I said decisively, "but we can do it. We can see her true face and recognize her through her disguise enchantment. We know what she's planning. We can stop her."

Lori looked at me with concern. "What are you suggesting? That the three of us should storm the inn and attack her?"

I shook my head. "I don't think that's a good idea. We still have the same problems we always had. If it's necessary to sacrifice ourselves in order to stop her taking over an entire kingdom, I'm willing to give up my life. But only as a last resort. We still have time before the king steps down, and I still have hope we'll find a way to both free ourselves and stop Eulalie."

Xander nodded fervently. "I vote we follow and watch her for now. We need to find out what she's looking for and stop her getting it."

Lori relaxed, clearly relieved I wasn't suggesting we go charging in immediately.

"Eulalie doesn't know what I look like or that I'm under her enchantment," she said, "but she'll recognize either of you. Which means you both need to stay out of sight." She gave us both a stern look. "If we're going to be traipsing around the kingdom after Eulalie during the day, you'd both better get some sleep." Her eyes narrowed. "I'm sending you back to the bedrolls to sleep so don't let me find you sneaking off for any more of your so-called adventures."

"Yes, Lori," I said so meekly that she added, "I'll be coming past every few minutes to check you haven't done something reckless."

I laughed. "That really isn't necessary."

"I'll be the judge of that," she muttered, and my smile slipped away, replaced by guilt. Apparently doing reckless things really was in my nature, and even five years in a tower couldn't beat it out of me.

CHAPTER 16

We did sleep, in my case because exhaustion overtook me despite my churning thoughts. The sun and noise of the village woke me early, though, and the three of us were soon huddled in the main street again.

We were just discussing positions for the day's watch when the inn door opened and Eulalie walked out, a bag over her shoulder. Lori instantly thrust us both behind her, her presence enough to shield us given our secluded corner.

As Eulalie's eyes swept over the street, I held my breath. Did she have some way to tell that someone was linked to her enchantment—some hidden sign we didn't know anything about?

Her gaze didn't pause, however, passing over Lori as it did the other villagers in view. I let out a sigh.

"She doesn't recognize you," I whispered to Lori. "We can be grateful for that, at least."

"Personally I'm just grateful I don't have to sit on this street all day watching a door," Lori said, making me swallow a laugh.

"If the people my parents assigned to watch over Xavier and me had been more like you, Lori, I might not have been such a rebellious child," Xander murmured from where he was crouched behind Lori, trying to remain unseen.

She snorted. "Pretty thoughts make pretty tales. But I wasn't born yesterday nor the day before neither."

Eulalie turned onto the street, moving southward. She was heading toward the rest of Northhelm, not my tower. I released another anxious breath.

"How long should we wait before following her?" I asked, unsure how to trail her without being seen.

No one replied, so I looked away from Eulalie's retreating back to discover Xander was no longer beside me.

"Where's Xander?" I asked sharply.

"Right here." He appeared at Lori's side with a smile.

When he handed me my bag, I noticed he had another one slung over his own shoulder, this one with all three bedrolls attached.

"That was fast," I said while Lori gave an approving grunt.

"We should move quickly," he said. "We'll want to stick fairly close to her in the village. It'll be easy enough to do since there are so many more people moving around than usual thanks to the tour group, plus we have buildings and objects to conceal ourselves behind. But once she moves out of the village, we'll have to fall back and follow out of sight, trusting that she'll keep to the road."

I grimaced, and he shrugged in response. "There's no way she won't notice us if we follow within her sight line."

Begrudgingly I was forced to admit that was true. Hopefully she wasn't planning any side trips into the forest.

But as we finally moved into the street to follow Eulalie through the village, I squinted at Xander's back. "You seem to know a lot about trailing someone."

"I may have done it once or twice before," he admitted, grinning back at me.

"Why am I not surprised?" I rolled my eyes but finished on a sigh. "I really wish I had a twin."

"Whereas I've always been glad there's only one of you," Lori muttered, making Xander laugh.

He'd barely fallen silent when he took my arm and whisked me behind a stationary cart.

"Wha—?" I managed to start before realizing Eulalie had stopped. I peeked around the edge as she started moving again. "I see why we can't do this on the forest road," I acknowledged.

My eyes dropped to where Xander's hand still lightly gripped my elbow. He let go quickly in response, and I wanted to tell him the contact hadn't been unpleasant. But Lori had already returned to the road, and we had to hurry to catch up.

Twice more we had to duck out of the way, the final time sending us huddling behind the last house in the village.

"We'll have to give it longer this time," Xander said, "to let her get properly ahead of us."

"How will we stop ourselves running into her when she stops for the night or even just stops for a rest or to prepare a meal?"

"If she makes a fire, we'll hopefully smell it before we reach her," Xander said. "And it's likely that she'll camp just off the road, rather than in view of it. She's a lone traveler, so she won't want to attract attention. Even though she has enchantments to protect her, it's still simpler to avoid trouble if she can."

"So we might walk right past her?" I asked, alarmed.

"We'll keep our eyes out." Lori didn't sound in the least concerned. "I'm sure between the three of us we'll see signs of her." She hesitated for a moment. "I've followed her before—for a day or two at least—so I have a sense of her pace. We'll naturally move at a similar speed, I expect, so it shouldn't be too hard to guess where and when she'll stop."

"You've followed her before?" I stared at Lori, my mouth gaping open. "When?"

"At various times," she said evasively. "How did you think I was so certain she was leaving the region entirely?"

"Why didn't you tell me?" I asked, still shocked to think I'd been so unaware of Lori's movements. I knew we often went days without seeing each other, but I had thought it was because she was busy tending her garden, catching game, and sourcing our supplies.

Lori didn't reply, and my frown deepened.

"I think she felt bad," Xander said in a surprisingly gentle voice. "She didn't want to tell you she was going so far when you were trapped in the tower."

Lori sighed. "Aye, that's it. You're a perceptive one, young master."

"I understand because I've never liked having to leave anyone behind," he said in a murmur, and I believed him.

From the moment I'd met him, he'd been easy-going and inclusive. I'd thought my insistence on including Lori on our trip would throw him off, but he'd responded with warm welcome. And even when I'd discovered him about to sneak into the king's chamber, he'd been quick to invite me to join him.

Being around Xander was nothing like being around the princes of my childhood—especially my own brother who had been the most enthusiastic at excluding me from anything that could possibly be considered dangerous.

It was incredibly endearing that Xander didn't feel any need to cosset me. I might be about to turn eighteen, but I had missed five years of normal life experience, and he could easily have used my imprisonment as an excuse to treat me as weak and helpless.

I couldn't entirely trust that instinct, though. I was far too aware of the way I responded to his presence. I had watched various courtships from my window, but I had been barred from participating in any, and there was no denying Xander was extremely handsome.

Was I seeing what I wanted to see in him? He had exactly the sort of lighthearted, adventurous charm that had appealed to me from childhood. But I couldn't let myself forget that he had left all his family and friends and gone off in search of the missing princess. I might be attracted to Xander, but I didn't need a prince who thought the role of a princess was to sit around meekly and wait for a prince to rescue her.

He might be entertained by me now—the charm of the unexpected—but how long before he got bored of my real personality and decided it was time for me to step aside, be quiet, and let him be the one to shine? I refused to marry anyone unless we would have an equal partnership. A third prince and second princess from allied kingdoms might appear to be a perfect pairing, but I had finally escaped my tower, and I would rather marry a commoner than find myself in a larger, fancier cage.

Gabe's charm had been paired with a good heart, but what did I really know about Xander? I had spent my whole life watching the world from the sidelines—both in my childhood and from the tower. I had no personal experience with charming scoundrels. Could I trust myself to recognize one if he appeared?

"I think it's safe to go now," Xander said, startling me out of my thoughts.

How long had I been standing there, staring at a wall? I flushed, but neither of the other two noticed. Their full attention was on the main road, which extended beyond the village, cutting through the forest to connect this remote northeastern corner with the rest of the kingdom.

"The tour came on horseback or in carriages," I said, struck by a sudden thought. "Won't they overtake us when they return this way? How is Eulalie expecting to stay ahead of them?"

"They're not heading back by this route," Xander said. "They're continuing out of the forest into the foothills of the mountain range that separates Northhelm from Rangmere. They'll then skirt the southern edge of the forest on their way back to the capital."

I recalled the maps of the Four Kingdoms that I used to study. "That makes sense. I know there are mining communities in the mountains since they trade with the villagers. That must be the last leg of the tour, though. The day of the transfer of power is getting close."

Xander nodded, stepping confidently onto the road and leaving me to trail behind with Lori. It didn't take long for him to drop back to walk next to me, though, and he was soon regaling both me and Lori with tales of his distant home kingdom.

"Kuralan sounds fascinating," I said, "and I'd love to know more about it. But I'm desperate to find out what happened to my old friends. I heard that someone from my own lands made it across the desert and discovered two new kingdoms, so when I heard the adventurer was called Cassandra, of course I guessed it was Cassie. But it all happened so far from here, and you're the first person from either of the new kingdoms to make it this far north, so I've barely heard any details."

"You must have been worried about them," Xander said with quick sympathy. "It's been hard for them not knowing what happened to you, but at least they had the godmothers' reassurances."

I frowned at his words, but I didn't feel the outrage I'd felt at his first mention of the godmothers' involvement. I had thought then that the godmothers had glibly assured the others while abandoning me entirely. Now I wasn't so sure.

"Can you tell me exactly what happened to them all?" I asked.

"I'm afraid I don't know much about Princess Daria," he said apologetically. "I never met her because she returned to Talinos before I first crossed the desert, and I haven't made it across the sea myself yet."

"She returned to Talinos?" I asked, confused. "But Daria is from Eliam."

"You mentioned she's a princess now?" Lori said to Xander. "I suppose she married Prince Percival of Talinos."

"Percy?" I gasped and then fell into laughter. "I should have realized that for myself. I thought he was supposed to marry Giselle, though. I hope the Eldonians aren't too disappointed to have missed out on the opportunity for an alliance with Talinos."

"I admit I know nothing about the inter-kingdom politics of your group of kingdoms," Xander said cheerfully. "But everyone I've spoken to seems perfectly content with how matters worked out."

"So Daria ended up with Percy," I said when my amusement subsided. "She was never rolling around the Four Kingdoms with the traveling merchants, then."

It was surprisingly hard to let go of the stories that had kept me company during my years of captivity. The Daria of my dreams felt as much like a real person as the actual Daria in my memories. For a few minutes, I had thought maybe...

"How did you know that?" Xander sounded startled. "Daria spent two years hidden among the traveling merchants before Percy found her."

I gasped. "Are you sure? She was definitely among the merchants—living in a wagon and everything?"

He nodded, bemused. "Yes, I'm quite certain. But how did you know?"

"And what about Giselle?" I asked eagerly, carried away by my wild suspicions. "Surely she wasn't really herding geese?"

Xander's confused expression deepened. "I thought you said you didn't know what happened to them? I suppose someone in the village has heard the stories and the children—"

"No." I shook my head. "No one has told me stories about them at all. It's so remote here that I sometimes think the villagers forget the rest of the kingdoms exist. But are you saying I'm right? She really does herd geese?"

He smiled despite his obvious confusion. "I don't think she does so any more, to be fair. But there was a...mix-up for a while."

"A mix-up?" I waved my hand. "No, never mind that. Giselle really was with the geese, Daria was with the traveling merchants, and Cassie was exploring the deserted tunnels of an abandoned city. I can't believe they were all real!" I jumped up and down, clapping my hands. "They're all real, Lori!"

"I'll admit I didn't think the geese sounded very likely," she said. "But I hope I'm able to admit to my errors."

"I thought the godmothers abandoned me, but they were sending me reassurances, after all," I said, inordinately pleased by my discovery.

"Hold on!" I cried, struck by a new thought. "You've talked about your siblings, Xander, but who are they exactly?"

I fixed him with an intent look, and he stared back at me, apparently disconcerted by the abrupt change of topic. "My siblings?"

I nodded and continued to look at him expectantly, so he shrugged.

"The oldest of us is Tarek—Rek we call him. Then it's my sister, Adara, and Xavier and I are the babies of the family. All of my siblings are married, though, so I also have—"

"Zaria and Kali!" I cried in tones of triumph. "They're real!"

Xander stopped in the middle of the road, looking helplessly at Lori. "What is happening right now?"

"I've dreamed about them all!" I told him in breathless excitement. "I thought my subconscious was making up pleasant stories about my missing friends as well as making up extra friends. But the dreams were all real! I feel like I already know Zaria and Kali, although they won't know me, of course."

My spirits briefly dropped at that thought, but they quickly recovered. The imaginary friends who had kept me company hadn't been imaginary at all. I would get the chance to meet them in person one day.

At least, I would if we managed to break our enchantment.

But in the meantime, I had already met one of them. He was standing right beside me.

"You seemed familiar the first time I saw you in the clearing," I told Xander as I pulled him back into motion. "I thought it was because you reminded me of someone from my childhood, but I've just realized it was actually from my dreams about Zaria and Kali. You were in some of them, briefly."

"I was in your dreams?" He sounded slightly awed, and I suddenly wished I'd stayed quiet.

If he had ideas of us being some sort of destined couple because he'd been the one to find me, then the last thing I wanted to do was feed his fantasy. I didn't want someone to imagine themselves in love with me just because I was the girl in the tower.

"Was there really a treasure cave?" I asked quickly, changing the subject.

"Two actually," he said after only the slightest hesitation at my abrupt change of topic.

"Oh yes, of course! Cassie found one too, didn't she?" I sighed in delight at the idea of a magic cave full of untold riches. "How come she got a treasure cave and I only got a tower?"

"Maybe she didn't go plunging headlong into danger at every opportunity," Lori grumbled, and I winced.

"I really thought I'd learned my lesson after all those years in the tower," I said sadly. "But apparently I can't help wanting to rush into situations."

Xander smiled down at me so warmly that I quickly looked away, trying to remember my earlier concerns about him.

"I've always preferred action myself," he said. "So I hope you never change."

"Lori might not agree with you." I fervently hoped my cheeks weren't as red as they felt.

"I'm not saying it wouldn't make my life easier," Lori said in a calm voice. "But that's hardly a reason to change who you are."

I blinked at her, taken off guard by her words.

She continued on in the same matter-of-fact way. "I'm not saying a little extra maturity wouldn't be helpful, mind you. There's nothing wrong with having a desire for action, though— just as long as you're not leaping into that action without thought. As a child and a royal princess, you had layers of protection to shield you from the consequences of youthful rash behavior. And for the last five years, the tower has kept you from almost any action at all. I just hope you realize that there's no one to help us now but the three of us ourselves. Getting trapped in royal bedchambers might be the least of your worries." She gave me a warning look.

I hugged her, trying to hide the tears in my eyes. "I promise not to sneak into the bedchambers of any more sleeping royals."

"Somehow I'm not sure you grasped the point of that speech," she muttered, but as always I could hear the overtones of her affection.

Despite my words, however, I did understand, and I felt simultaneously both more free and more burdened than before. I could stop feeling guilty about the return of my old nature. I could be myself. But I had to ensure the delight in my new freedom didn't make me forget the lessons of the tower. I could feel joy at the adventures in front of me, but I had to make sure I didn't rush foolishly and unnecessarily into danger.

CHAPTER 17

My thoughts on the matter kept me subdued most of the morning, so I was caught off guard when Xander put up his arm, blocking my forward progress. I was about to indignantly question him when I absorbed his posture and expression. I stayed silent instead.

"Back up," he whispered, and I instantly obeyed, returning around the sweeping bend we had just followed, Lori ahead of me.

Once we'd made it some way back, he relaxed. "I don't think she saw us."

"Was Eulalie stopped? Did we catch up to her?" I asked in a whisper.

"She's either moving a little slower than I expected or has taken a longer break for her midday meal," he said. "Either way, we should eat now too."

"Oh thank goodness." I flopped onto a soft-looking patch of grass beside the dirt road and lay with my arms spread wide. "I'm exhausted and everything hurts," I groaned. "Including my pride. I may have been confined to the top of a tower, but I can climb up and down its side with relative ease, and I spent a lot of time developing and carrying out complex exercise routines. I thought walking would be a breeze."

I expected Xander to tease me, but he looked sympathetic. "I'll confess my feet are hurting as well. I've done all my travel mounted since before I arrived in Northhelm, so my feet aren't used to it."

"We'll all have aching muscles," Lori said. "Regardless of our usual level of activity, we aren't accustomed to using these specific muscles so repetitively for such a prolonged time. Eulalie has the advantage on us there. I wonder why she doesn't ride herself."

"Maybe because she couldn't as easily remain anonymous then?" I asked. "Her second enchantment hides her identity and makes people forget it as soon as she's out of their sight, but it probably wouldn't work on her horse. If people could describe her as the woman on the chestnut mare with the white stripe, she would lose her anonymity."

"I don't care why she doesn't have a horse," Xander groaned, "I just wish *we* could have them." He sat down on the grass beside me. "What if we did find horses? Would they be invisible while we rode them?"

"They might be." Lori pulled out packed food from her bag. "But they wouldn't be when we weren't riding them, so camping inconspicuously would become a problem."

"I suppose so." Xander sighed and accepted some food. "Still, a man can dream."

Getting back up to continue walking proved more difficult than I'd expected, as if the break had convinced my body that it never wanted to engage in that particular activity again.

At least I had Xander's stories to distract me from the discomfort. He described each of his siblings for me, his descriptions matching the pieces of their lives that the godmothers had shown me. He had far more stories than the ones I'd seen in my dreams, though, including a whole childhood full of outrageous escapades in the company of his twin.

"You must miss him," I said as the light started to fade.

"Every day." He hesitated. "I would never want to live away from him permanently."

I glanced sideways at him, wondering if I'd misheard the extra note of meaning in his second sentence. Was he trying to tell me that while he might happily travel the Four Kingdoms alone, his eventual home would be with his family?

Did I feel the same way? I could almost feel the unspoken question in the air, but I wasn't ready to answer it—either aloud, given what the words might imply, or even to myself. I didn't know the answer.

I considered the question, though, thinking it through from every angle. I knew that Giselle had been sent to the Four Kingdoms in the hope of a marriage alliance, but since I had been thirteen at the time of the delegation, it hadn't been in my thoughts for myself. Of course I had always known the likelihood of princesses —especially younger ones—being used in marriage alliances. But there had been no obvious candidates among the royal circles from my home kingdoms or even among the Four Kingdoms.

As a child I had dreamed of going on grand adventures, but I had always pictured myself returning home afterward, and home had always meant Trione. I certainly longed to see it again, and my family especially. If I did ever get my home back, could I bring myself to leave it again?

I didn't have to consider the question long. I had only been out of the tower for two days and I was already caught up in the thrill of adventure once more. I might have spent time dreaming of a calm life at home, but it wouldn't hold my interest for long. I was determined to return to Trione, but I wouldn't stay there forever.

A deeper realization hit me, shaking me. Trione represented

my childhood and family, and it would always be in my heart, but I hadn't set foot there in five years. It hadn't been my choice to leave, but it wasn't my home anymore.

"The tower isn't my home!" I said fiercely, causing both Xander and Lori to give me odd looks. "Sorry," I muttered, "just talking to myself."

"The tower was your prison," Xander said. "That's not the same thing as a home." He paused. "But it's only natural that it would have gained the familiarity of a home. It was your world for years. It's equally natural that it might feel strange to leave it and know you're never going back. There's no reason to feel bad about that."

"Most of the time, I just wanted to be free of it," I said quietly. "But sometimes, when Eulalie was far away, and the wind was howling, I would close the shutters and feel…safe."

Xander stopped in the middle of the road and swept his arms around me, pulling me into a hug and holding me tight against his chest. I gave a small squeak but made no effort to pull away.

"What are you doing?" Lori cried in scandalized tones, but Xander ignored her.

"You're a remarkable girl, Daisy," he murmured against my hair. "In case no one's said it to you before, you've done incredibly. While I was searching for you, I used to worry about what state you might be in after all this time. And when I heard there was a girl who'd been alone in a tower for five years…" He shook his head, still holding me tight against him.

"I didn't dare hope you would be, well—you. You went into the tower a child, but you've come out an adult. Your old place won't fit you anymore, but that doesn't mean the tower is where you belong." He leaned back to look down into my face. "It just means you need to find the place where the adult you belongs."

I stared at him, willing my bottom lip not to tremble. I lost the battle, the tears spilling out of my eyes. I pushed my face back into his chest and let them fall, my shoulders shaking with silent sobs.

Lori was making distressed clucking sounds in the background, but it was the anchor of Xander's firm hold that made the tears slowly fade. When they finally stopped completely, I pulled away from him.

I knew I should be embarrassed, but I couldn't muster the feeling.

"I don't want to be lost in anger," I said. "I don't want to lose even more years of my life that way. But sometimes I feel *furious* at what Eulalie took from me."

I looked up into Xander's face and felt a ripple of shock at the anger in his eyes that mirrored my own.

"I can assure you that her days of freedom are about to end," he said in such a menacing voice that I fell back a step.

"I'm sorry." I wiped my eyes on my sleeves, taking the opportunity to break eye contact. "I've made a mess of us both."

"I can smell smoke," Lori said suddenly, her nose raised toward the road in front of us.

"Eulalie?" I asked, struggling to adjust my thoughts to the change of topic and tone. "Has she stopped for the night?"

"It looks like it," Xander said. "I'll just go and check—"

"I will go," Lori said firmly. "She knows what you look like, remember?"

When Xander appeared rebellious, she continued. "For all your adventures, lad, I'll warrant I've more experience creeping through forests after Eulalie than you."

His lips twitched. "I certainly can't fight that claim. Consider me put in my place."

She shook her head as she hurried off with a final warning to us not to move an inch in her absence. As soon as she was gone, however, Xander started scouting the forest on either side of the road for a good spot to set ourselves up for the night.

By the time Lori came back to confirm that Eulalie was

settled for the evening with a campfire and cooking food, Xander had already chosen a location for our own camp and I'd started gathering firewood.

"Won't Eulalie smell our smoke like we smelled hers?" I asked warily, but he brushed the concerns aside.

"Her nose will already be full of her own smoke. And if she does realize there's a second fire somewhere, she'll assume it's other travelers. This isn't a highly frequented part of the road, but there's the occasional traffic in both directions."

I didn't fight any harder, already looking forward to the warmth of the fire overnight and the lure of hot food. Sitting down was even more luxurious, although I wasn't sure I'd manage to fall asleep when every part of my body was hurting.

"How can every single one of my muscles hurt?" I groaned when we were finally eating the meal Lori prepared.

"It only feels like it's all of them," Lori said heartlessly. "There are plenty more that could be hurting still."

"Shouldn't you be saying something encouraging?" I gave her a mock glare.

She looked back at me blankly. "I did."

I groaned again. "I'm not going to make it. You should abandon me now and save yourselves."

Xander laughed. "I can't promise it won't get worse first, but it will eventually get better. And that comes from personal experience. I felt even more dreadful than this after my first full day on horseback."

When I lay down to sleep with nothing but a bedroll beneath me, I wasn't convinced by his words. I had no idea how I was going to sleep with so little padding for all my poor, abused muscles. Thankfully my exhaustion was a fraction greater than my discomfort, and I fell asleep after all, sleeping undisturbed until the sun rose.

Unfortunately, Xander's words were proved correct, and dragging myself along the forest road all day for a second time was worse than it had been on the first day. The only thing that saved me was Xander's insistence on hearing stories about my own home and childhood. Immersing myself in the memories made me temporarily forget my aching body, one foot somehow plodding along in front of the other.

By the third day, we had settled into Eulalie's rhythm and no longer stumbled over her by accident. Xander and Lori took turns creeping forward at opportune moments to check she was still keeping to the expected path, but I didn't see her at all for four days.

On the fifth day, we reached a town of significantly greater size than Charli's village. The worst of my aches had finally subsided, but several spots on my feet were still raw, and I greeted the prospect of a hay bed in the rafters of a stable with joy.

We increased our pace enough to watch Eulalie disappear among the houses, confirming her intention to enter the town and allowing us to hurry after her. Her steady pace so far had made it clear her search lay in front of her, and we guessed she would continue to move on quickly from this town. Xander suggested she was heading for the capital, making me propose the ocean, merely to be contrary. But we still needed to watch her movements in the town, just in case we were wrong.

But it was hard to stay focused on Eulalie once we reached the center of the town and discovered it was market day. It had been years since I attended a market, and I had usually gone to the large ones in Trione's capital. But something about the sight of the stalls and the familiar sounds and smells took me straight back to those days.

"It's a market!" I clapped my hands, my eyes growing round. "I wish we were able to buy something!"

"I have plenty of coins," Xander said. "If there's something you want, we can try. You had a method worked out, didn't you, Lori?

Something about taking it when they weren't looking and leaving coin behind."

"We should save our coins for things we really need," she said repressively. "I wouldn't mind buying some more travel bread. My snares have been doing well enough during the nights, but we've run out of any sort of bread to go with the meat."

"Over there!" I pointed toward a distant stall. "The baker has a stall over there."

She peered in the direction I was indicating, searching until her eyes found the stall. "You'd better come with me," she said to Xander. "I can take the bread, and you can leave the coin."

She turned to give me a repressive look. "You can find a place to hide. The last thing we need is for Eulalie to spot you in this crowd."

I considered arguing, but I knew she was right. Reluctantly I withdrew to the edge of the market, only stopping when I noticed a spot between two stalls. If I sat down and tucked up my knees, I would be out of the way as well as mostly out of sight, but I would still be able to see something of the market's activity.

Hurrying to my hiding place, I scooted myself inside and wrapped my arms around my knees. I would have preferred to be immersed in the middle of the market, but just being present was overwhelming after so long in the isolation of my clearing. Even when multiple people visited the clearing at once, it had never had the bustle and buzz of a market.

Xander came strolling back into sight, Lori no longer beside him. From his relaxed air, I guessed she must have stopped to collect something else, and he was waiting for her to catch up. He glanced around, clearly not seeing me, and I gave myself a mental clap on my excellent hiding place.

Stepping up to one of the stalls, Xander ignored the customer already there and examined the wares laid out for perusal. My heart beat a little faster as I noticed what this particular stall sold.

Xander could have no use for silk scarves and purses or jeweled hair clips. Was he thinking of me while he looked at them?

I had barely formulated the thought when a flash of something familiar caught my attention from the corner of my eye. I turned my head to look straight at the unsettling leathery face of Eulalie.

She was standing several yards away from me, her eyes trained in Xander's direction.

My own gaze darted back to him in time to see him stiffen slightly. It was a subtle gesture, and I wasn't sure what it meant. Had he also seen Eulalie out of the corner of his eye? What could he do to escape her when she was already so close?

My heart was racing even faster, my breath coming in fits and spurts as I tried to decide what to do. Should I leap up to help him? Or was it still possible he could get away unnoticed? Had Eulalie definitely recognized him?

While I was still trying to decide whether or not she knew it was him, Xander straightened, turned his head, and looked directly at her.

CHAPTER 18

I gasped. Was he challenging her? She had fled my clearing in fear of him, but she'd had time to recover since then.

Eulalie had been the focus of all my dread for so long that every one of my nerves was screaming at me. I wanted to leap to my feet and shout for Xander to run.

But something strange was happening. Xander had looked straight at Eulalie, but it was like he didn't see her. His gaze passed over her as if she was just another member of the crowd. As if he himself was an ordinary person who saw her as a forgettable woman like any other. As if he wasn't under the enchantment.

I saw the moment the same thought hit Eulalie, saw the shock ripple through her. If Xander couldn't see her as herself, then he was no longer inside the bubble of her enchantment.

When she looked down at her ring, her eyes wide, it confirmed her thoughts. Xander had fooled her. But when she looked back up, a determined light had entered her eyes. She trusted the ring more than him.

She started toward him, and I maneuvered onto my knees—

still lurking in the shadows but ready to leap up and dive into the fray if needed.

But before Eulalie reached the stall where Xander was standing, the stall keeper spoke in a conversational tone.

"You won't find finer silk anywhere this side of the ocean!"

Xander looked at him and smiled. "It's very impressive."

"It's spun here in our own town." The man's chest swelled, as if filled with pride in the local people. "I'm sure you've traveled all over, but you won't have seen finer wares than this. Not in the capital itself!"

Eulalie froze mid-step, clearly thrown off balance by this evidence of Xander's freedom.

The stall keeper picked up one of the silk purses and held it out, angled to show to best advantage. Xander dutifully leaned forward to touch it, running his hand down the length of it and making an admiring noise.

Thanks to my odd angle, I could see that he never actually made contact with the purse, keeping his hand an inch or so above it. Since he never tried to get closer, the enchantment did nothing to repel him.

"Clever," I murmured to myself as Xander spoke again to the stall keeper.

"Very nice, indeed," he said. "But I'm afraid I'm not in the market for a purse today."

"A hair pin, then?" the stall keeper suggested, and I blinked, almost starting to believe they were having a real conversation.

"I'm afraid not today," Xander said with an apologetic smile. "But perhaps—" He moved aside slightly, gesturing to the man beside him, and the true customer stepped slightly sideways, putting himself into a better position to see the pin the stall keeper was now holding out.

"Another day," Xander called to the stall keeper with a wave of farewell and strode off into the crowd.

Eulalie did nothing to follow him. She was trembling slightly, clearly unnerved and unsure what to do.

But eventually she pulled herself together, looking down at the ring and stroking it reassuringly.

"Why not?" she murmured so that I only just caught the words over the sounds of the market. "He added himself to the enchantment somehow, so mayhap he knows a way out. But he can't have broken it over Daisy. The ring would have responded to that."

She still hesitated, though, glancing back in the direction of the village. Was she considering rushing back to the tower to check on me? If she did, it would cause all sorts of problems. We still didn't know what she was searching for or where it might be, and I had no interest in trekking back across the ground we'd already covered.

But after a moment of gazing behind her, she shook herself and pushed forward into the market again, moving in the opposite direction.

I slowly relaxed, giving myself a moment to clear my head and settle my breathing. Eulalie had obviously decided that if the prince could no longer recognize her then he wasn't a threat, and that could only be to our advantage.

"How did I do?" a voice asked from behind me, and I leaped to my feet, only just swallowing the scream that rose in my throat.

I whacked Xander lightly on the arm while he pretended to look apologetic.

"Do you want me to scream the town down?" I asked. "Don't terrify me like that."

"I did well, though, didn't I?" He was looking smug, but I couldn't deny his claim.

"Very well! I have no idea how you managed it. It must have looked utterly convincing to Eulalie. I was half convinced myself." I laughed, but it was an uneasy sound.

I knew I should wish for the appearance to be reality. If

Xander was free of the enchantment, he could go to the king and explain the danger directly. But after only a few days, I already couldn't bear the idea of being trapped without him.

"I only managed it because the other customer at the stall was so surly," he said. "He was the one the stall keeper was actually addressing, of course, but his grunts and half-replies were so quiet, you could barely hear them. As soon as I could see which way each reply was going, I said something more elaborate at a much louder volume. Neither the stall keeper nor customer noticed, but my words drowned the other man out for you and Eulalie."

"I was afraid she was going to go running back to the tower to check on me."

He leaned over to examine the other side of the marketplace, checking for Eulalie's retreating figure. Whatever he saw reassured him, because he pulled me out of the uncomfortably tight quarters between the two stalls.

"I think her reaction was quite revealing. It confirms that she's feeling time pressure leading up to the handover of power. If she turned back now, she'd lose ten days, and she wouldn't make it to the capital in time."

"You're still sure that's where she's going? What if she needs to go somewhere else first to find the object she's searching for?"

"Even if she does, the important thing is that she'll end in the capital, and she'll get there before the ceremony. Not even my appearance is going to derail her from that goal."

"I step away for one minute and you let her see you," Lori said in a despairing voice, her arms full of parcels.

Xander took them from her with his most charming grin, somehow managing to fit them all into his own bag.

"I think I've managed to turn my carelessness to our advantage. She's rattled, and the more rattled she is, the better for us. She'll make mistakes that way."

When Lori heard the whole story of exactly what had

happened, I could tell she was impressed. But she still insisted that Xander and I follow her to the stable loft she had found and remain there while she tailed Eulalie around the town for the day.

I made only the vaguest attempt to protest and was soon collapsing into the hay with relief.

"I know I should feel guilty," I said to Xander, "but I can't manage it. I'm just so relieved to be off my feet and lying on something soft. When I look back on my childhood now, I see only a sea of foolishness. I really had no idea adventures would be so unpleasant."

Xander lay in the hay with his arms under his head. "Do you think Lori will believe me if I tell her I didn't expose myself to Eulalie on purpose so I could laze around for the rest of the day?"

"The real challenge will be not falling asleep. I just know if I nap now that I'll be lying awake half the night."

Xander rolled over, propping himself up on one hand. "In that case, you should tell me more about your siblings becoming merfolk. I'm still not sure I understand that one."

I also rolled onto my side to face him. "That's reasonable considering it's a long and complicated story."

I went back over the story from the beginning with frequent interjections from Xander, most of which left me curled up from laughter. By the time Lori returned with hot food, I couldn't believe it was already getting dark. Spending time with Xander was dangerously easy.

"Eulalie has booked one night at the inn here and is clearly planning to move on in the morning," Lori told us. "So I've decided we can all sleep here for the night. As long as we're up early enough, we should have no problem locating and following her."

"Ha!" I cried. "I see I'm not the only one looking forward to a softer bed for the night."

Lori apparently felt that comment didn't need to be dignified with an answer because she merely handed out the food.

I woke the next morning feeling more refreshed than seemed possible. A half day of rest and a soft bed had worked wonders, despite the early hour of our wake-up.

Lori was right to get us going, however, since Eulalie was the first traveler to emerge from the inn and take the road straight out of town.

"It would have been nice to stay another day or two," I said wistfully, looking at the disappearing town over my shoulder.

"Eulalie is clearly still perturbed from seeing Xander in the market yesterday, and she's moving faster than before." Lori seemed pleased with this development.

"From here she'll surely stay on the road at least as far as Greenwood," Xander said. "That's only a small village, like the one near the tower, except instead of being remote, it's the closest forest town to the capital. It will take us another four or five days to get to Greenwood, but it won't take us long to get from there to the capital."

We easily fell back into our previous rhythm of travel, with the great advantage that my feet and muscles had grown much more accustomed to the activity.

On our second day back in the forest, however, I woke up to an unfamiliar view. The scent was the first thing to call me from my dreams, but when I opened my eyes, all I could see was a riot of color.

I sat up, blinking to clear my vision, and discovered I was lying in a bed of flowers. While I slept, someone had collected countless wildflowers in every color imaginable and piled them all around my bedroll.

"Happy Birthday!" Xander stepped back into our makeshift camp, a full pot of water dangling from his hand. "I meant to be here when you woke up. Do you like it?"

"It's...incredible." The smile on my face grew broader as I

realized Xander must have been the one to arrange the surprise. "I didn't know you even knew it was today."

He laughed. "You did mention it three times yesterday."

"Did I?" I asked guiltily. "I didn't even realize. I've just always loved birthdays."

"I could tell." His voice went soft. "We can't do much for you here on the road, but it's not just your first birthday free of the tower, it's also your eighteenth. We couldn't let it pass unmarked."

"Here." Lori pushed a small package into my hands. "The prince says this is from both of us, but we all know only one of us has the coin to be buying presents."

"But you were the one to manage the actual purchase," Xander said quickly, "which is not a small feat given our current state."

"Did you go back to the market while we were in the stable loft?" I unwrapped the package, my mouth dropping open when I saw the contents. "They're beautiful!"

It was a matching pair of hairpins, each decorated with amethysts arranged in the shape of a flower.

"This decides it." I looked from Xander to Lori. "Please tell me one of you brought scissors. Because if you didn't we're using a knife."

"To cut what exactly?" Xander asked in the voice of one who already knew the answer.

"It's about time," Lori said briskly. "I wasn't going to rush you, but your hair is a most impractical length. Do you want me to cut it all off like you always said?"

"Yes," I said, but the word came out much more hesitantly than I had intended. Looking at the new hairpins clutched in my hand, I ran my fingers over the length of my hair.

I had spent so long in the tower dreaming of chopping it all off and becoming a new person. But now that the moment had come and I was free to do whatever I wanted with it, I was uncertain. Did I actually want to become a new person? I had always had long hair, and it was suddenly a link with my past I wanted to preserve.

Since leaving the tower, I'd realized that my years of captivity hadn't transformed me as thoroughly as I'd thought. The old me was still there, just grown and changed—as I always would have between thirteen and eighteen. I was standing on the cusp of adulthood, but I couldn't bring myself to cut the last tie to my old self. I didn't want to abandon my childhood self because she had led me to the tower. The way to win was not to let Eulalie completely strip her away.

"Actually, I don't want it short. I want it how it was before. About here." I indicated a spot three-quarters of the way down my back.

"Perfect." Lori's smile told me she approved of my decision.

Within minutes she had produced scissors and deposited me on a fallen tree. I sighed with relief as the weight of the extra length fell off, and when she declared herself finished, I shook my head from side to side in delight.

"It feels so light! Look how I can swish it around."

"If you hold still for a minute, I'll do some braiding," Lori said, making me go motionless beneath her hands.

Within a short time, she had a braid running across the top of my head, like a makeshift crown, although she let the rest of it hang loosely down my back.

"Now you just need these." Xander stepped in front of me, his eyes on my head as he carefully placed the pins in the braid.

I held my breath at the feeling of his fingers in my hair, only breathing again when he stood back and gave me a critical exam-ination.

"Perfect," he pronounced, with a wide smile.

"Thank you," I said first to him and then to Lori. "Thank you for remembering and for making it special."

"It's not the eighteenth birthday you must have dreamed of back home in your palace," Xander said regretfully.

But I beamed at him, refusing to be pulled down by thoughts of the distant past.

"Perhaps not, but it's a great deal better than the birthday I expected alone in the tower, waiting for Eulalie's visit."

That made both of them smile before Lori pointed out that if we dallied too long, we'd fall far behind Eulalie.

I spent a large part of my birthday walking, but I was waited on hand and foot at each stop, and at the evening meal, Lori produced a cake from her capacious bag.

"Cake!" I pounced on it in delight. "How did you smuggle that here?"

"It's a little squished," Lori said with a critical examination. "But we left the town recently enough that it should still be edible."

I stayed up later than usual, my eyes on the small flames of our campfire as I enjoyed the warmth of it washing over me. I didn't want to go to sleep and miss one moment of my birthday.

Lori gave up first, falling asleep the moment she crawled into her sleep sack, and I knew I should follow, but I couldn't resist a few more minutes. I pulled my knees up and wrapped my arms around them, resting my chin against my knees.

Eighteen. How many years I had longed for it—first for one reason and then for another. I had always thought Eulalie would appear on my birthday, and it would be my chance to make a bid for my freedom. But I now knew the timing of the coronation meant she had to be in the capital too soon after my birthday for her to have ever been at the tower on that date.

If Xander hadn't appeared, how crushingly disappointed I would have been when the day came and went with no confrontation with Eulalie. Would I have stayed there, still waiting, until she tried to enchant the king and blew the whole thing up in our faces?

My eyelids began drooping shut as I thought of Xander and

all the changes in my life since he'd appeared. When I felt his arms around me, lifting me up, I struggled to open my eyes.

"I'm so glad you came," I said, my words slurred with sleep. "You saved me."

"No," said the deep rumble of his voice as he cradled me against his chest. "You saved yourself." He placed me gently on my bedroll. "Happy birthday, Daisy." But he didn't immediately pull back, instead hovering there beside me.

I fought one of my eyes open and gazed up at him. "What is it? Do you have something else for me?" I smiled in sleepy contentment.

He sucked in a breath, his eyes on my lips. "Don't tempt me," he whispered. "I promised no more surprises."

My eyes drifted rebelliously shut again as a frown curved my lips downward. "But I like surprises, especially birthday ones."

"You're making it very hard for me to keep my promise." His voice trembled slightly. "But this isn't the right moment."

I pouted, but my body was slowly sliding down to lie flat. I must have already been in the grip of sleep because I was fairly sure I dreamed his quiet voice saying, "Well, perhaps just this doesn't count." And I definitely must have dreamed the feel of his lips pressed briefly against my palm before he tucked my hand down beside me and murmured a final goodnight.

CHAPTER 19

My dreams that night were full of Xander, and I would have avoided him in the morning out of embarrassment for my rogue mind if it wasn't impossible to do so. With only the three of us, it would have been painfully obvious if I'd suddenly changed my behavior.

Thankfully, the routine of the walking soon calmed my nerves, and by the time we were eating the midday meal, I was comfortable around him again. We didn't stop for long due to Eulalie's increased pace and were soon back walking again.

"It's one thing to see a forest on a map, and another altogether to walk through it day after day," I said. "I hadn't realized how enormous this one is."

"We have a forest outside our capital," Xander said. "But it isn't nearly as big as the ones you have here. There's an enormous jungle in Lanover and an even vaster forest that crosses the border of Arcadia and Rangmere. I've visited at least the edges of both and been almost as awed as I was by the ocean. We have the Sea of Sand, but this is like a sea of trees."

"I hope I get to see the Great Desert one day," I said.

"I would love to hear your thoughts when you do," Xander said. "I always used to—" he broke off, his brows pulling together.

We all stopped walking and peered into the trees north of the road.

"Is that someone shouting?" I asked, just as a clearer call came.

"Liam!!" a woman's voice screamed. "Liam! Where are you?"

"It sounds like someone's missing," Xander said at the same moment as Lori said, "Who could it be?"

He sounded concerned, she sounded suspicious.

"The tour traveled through the forest," Xander said, "and William gave me information about the environment and the locals. Most of the forest dwellers live in towns or villages, but there is the occasional individual or family who has chosen a more remote home."

Lori looked skeptical. "I've been one such individual since I was enchanted, but I've never met another."

"There aren't many in the northeastern tip of the forest near you," Xander said, "because it's too remote, even for those who prefer the solitude and privacy. They tend to be located within a day or two's travel from a larger town. They're not hermits—they still come into the towns for trade, shopping, and medical care. They generally balance the isolation of their home by locating themselves near a larger town."

"LIAM!" The distraught woman sounded closer.

I swayed back and forth, trying to see through the trees, but I still couldn't locate her. We would need to leave the road and follow her voice to find out what was going on. I was about to say as much to the others when Xander spoke.

"They might be searching for a child. We need to go and help."

I beamed at him, but Lori frowned.

"Eulalie has been moving more quickly, remember, and we have no idea of the details of this situation. We might end up delayed for a significant length of time, and we could lose her completely."

"We won't lose her," Xander said confidently, "because we know she's heading for Greenwood, and that's still several days away. We'll just have to move at faster speed ourselves to catch up."

"We *think* she's going to Greenwood," Lori said.

"Can't you hear the desperation in her voice?" I asked softly. "She and her family must live alone out here, and we rarely pass other travelers on this road."

"If we don't help, who will?" Xander added, and Lori finally capitulated.

"Fine, if you both insist." She shook her head, but Xander caught her up in an enthusiastic embrace.

"You're a good woman under all that practicality," he said as he released her.

"Someone has to keep their head on their shoulders with you two around," she replied, but she looked a little pink.

I plunged into the trees beside the road, Xander a step ahead of me. Lori sighed and followed us, and I turned my attention on the continued cries.

"We won't be able to offer help," Xander said, "so we'll just have to hope we can work out the situation."

We reached the woman easily. Her twisted, tear-streaked face made my own heart twist, and I desperately wished she could see and hear us.

"We're here to help," I said uselessly. "What's wrong?"

"We found him!" a male voice called through the trees, and the woman's face lit up.

I relaxed, glad the crisis was so easily solved, but I tensed again when the man came into view and I caught sight of his expression. He didn't look like someone released from tension. Surely the boy hadn't been—

"Is he alive?" the mother gasped, clearly caught by the same fear.

The man nodded quickly, and we both relaxed.

"He doesn't seem injured, but…" The man's voice trailed off, leaving me concerned about what was so bad he didn't want to say it.

The mother grasped his arm, her voice urgent. "Tell me! What is it?"

"It will be easier to show you." The man towed her along, and I didn't even look to the others for confirmation before following. I couldn't walk away until I was sure the situation was resolved.

"He's climbed up beside the falls," the man said. "You know how fascinated he always is by them."

The woman gasped and began shaking, while I registered a dull roaring sound I hadn't noticed before. Now that I was hearing it, it was clearly the waterfall in question.

"The problem is his mood," the man said, and the woman gave a small wail as if she knew exactly what he was talking about and was terrified by it. "You know how he was when he ran off. When he gets like that, he won't let anyone near him."

I exchanged a concerned look with Xander, who was keeping pace beside me. What sort of child was this?

I willed the mother to ask some more clarifying questions, but before she could do so, the trees abruptly ended and were replaced with a small pool. The irregular circle of water had trees growing right up to it on this side, but on the other, there was a stretch of clear ground.

A stream ran out of the pool, running toward the east on a parallel path with the road. Opposite it, a waterfall thundered into the pond, agitating the water on that side. It wasn't a particularly high waterfall, but the rocks around it were sharp and jagged, slippery with spray.

The man and woman froze instantly, both of their attention on a rock on the other side of the water. A small child who looked about two years old stood on the rock, staring back at the adults with an expression of defiance on his face.

"Oh, he's a toddler," I said, understanding the situation at last.

Although I had been the youngest in my own family, the palace and its surrounds had housed enough families that I had grown up around younger children. Since I had always defied royal protocol by befriending the servants, I had known many of them through pregnancy and early motherhood when they would sometimes bring their little ones along while they completed their tasks.

And even in my tower, I had encountered children of this age since older siblings would start bringing them along on their adventures as soon as they were established walkers. Two could be a difficult age, and when the more defiant children became enraged, they responded badly to any attempts to interfere with them.

"Liam," the mother called, in what was clearly an attempt at a calm voice. "Won't you come down from there and come to mama? We can go back home and have a piece of cake."

The toddler hesitated at the word cake, and I held my breath, hoping he would capitulate. He had obviously climbed onto the rock from the stretch of open ground, its rough surface providing easy climbing holds. In that direction, the layer of undergrowth at its base created a soft surface. Even if he tumbled on his way back down, he would be fine.

Behind him, however, the rock backed onto the edge of the waterfall. If he slipped in that direction, he would crash against jagged rocks before being thrown into the depths of the churn at the base of the fall.

"Cake?" The toddler took a single step forward, and I was about to cheer when the man responded by jumping over the stream, clearly preparing himself to extract the boy.

The child immediately stiffened at this sign of approach and took a step backward, his face screwing up. "No!" he screamed. "Don't want cake! No cake!"

The man, who I assumed to be the father, froze, but the

damage had already been done. The mother glared at him before speaking to the toddler in soothing tones that sounded forced.

"All right, then. No cake. We can have whatever food you want. Just climb down, and you can—"

"NO!" screamed the boy again. "Not wot-ever I want!"

The mother threw a despairing look at the father. In less serious circumstances I would have laughed. It was hard to be small with limited language and little control over your world.

One of the assistant cooks in our palace had a daughter who had gone through this stage. The head cook had always taken any outbursts in her kitchen in stride, explaining to me that it was part of growing up.

"When small children reach that point, there's no reasoning with them," she had said. "Specially not the fiery ones. All you can do is offer them hugs and sit with them until they calm down enough to start thinking again. If you yell at a new apprentice when they make mistakes or burn the pastries, they might eventually become competent enough, but they'll never turn into master chefs. They need freedom to learn. It's the same with children—it's just that they're learning how to manage their emotions, instead of pastries."

She had laughed then, the deep belly laugh that I had always loved, before leaning over and whispering conspiratorially, "Pastries might not be like emotions, but they can sure have a positive effect on them." She had accompanied the pronouncement with a wink and a sneakily delivered pastry into my lap.

The whole situation brought back such clear memories of those days that my chest hurt. But the memories also told me that we needed to take drastic action, and we needed to do it straight away.

"It's clear from the parents' reactions that they know how long Liam can hold onto his emotions," I said. "In a normal situation, that wouldn't matter. But if he takes one more step backward on that stone, he might slip into the waterfall. He's clearly an adventurous boy to have climbed up there in the first place, but he's too young to understand the danger. His parents can't approach him because that will drive him backward. We can't openly approach him either, but for now, he doesn't know we're here. We have to intervene."

"Are we sure he's even able to see us?" Lori asked. "If he's not, it would make approaching him easier."

I stared at her, and she shrugged. "It was your birthday yesterday, remember?"

My mouth dropped open. I was eighteen now, which meant it was possible children could no longer see or hear me. How could I have forgotten the fear that used to keep me awake at night?

But after a moment's consideration, I shook my head. "It doesn't matter for now. We can't risk testing it because we don't know what he'll do if he can see us. We have to assume he can and proceed carefully."

"But how?" Xander asked, clearly worried.

"We have to approach him from behind. We can try to grab him, but even if we can't do that, we just have to get him to fall forward. The ferns there will give him a soft landing."

"Do I need to point out that the back of that rock is a waterfall?" Lori asked.

I darted forward and picked up a coil of rope that had been discarded on the ground, turning triumphantly to the other two.

"We can use this!"

The father had been carrying it over his shoulder, obviously having brought it in case it was needed in a rescue effort. When he found the child on the rock, he must have dropped it, and the enchantment had let me pick it up because neither of the parents was noticing anything other than the child and their attempts to coax him down.

"Neither of you are strong enough to lower me down," Xander said doubtfully. "But if we can find a tree to tie it to, it should work."

"There's no time for that," I said. "I might not be able to anchor you, but you and Lori could easily anchor me."

Xander frowned, clearly wanting to protest, but I kept talking.

"Besides, I'm the most experienced of us here when it comes to climbing up and down stone walls!"

With that triumphant pronouncement, I darted away through the trees. I headed uphill, half running, half clambering over the rocky ground beside the waterfall. When I reached the top, I saw the other end of the stream—the one that fed the waterfall.

Thankfully it was narrow enough for me to leap across it, while in the background Liam wailed strident denials to the suggestion that he come down from the rock and equally strident denials to the exasperated statement that he should just stay there then.

When I finally reached the spot directly above the boy's stone, I leaned out to peer down at him. A hand caught my elbow, steadying me.

I smiled back at Xander, realizing I had never doubted for a second that he would be right behind me.

"How are you at tying knots?" I asked, as I took one end of the rope and let the rest drop loose.

"Once again, I suspect you're the expert," he said, retrieving the loose end of the rope.

My fingers were already working to tie a loop in the rope that I could slip around me. The rope responded to my movements with delightful ease compared to the dresses and blankets I was used to knotting.

Within seconds, I had the loop under my arms and secured. Lori appeared, and she and Xander conferred quietly, arranging themselves so they both had a secure hold on the rope and pulling it until it became taut.

"I'll go down the same way I used to with the tower," I said, taking the length of the rope in my hands. "Just let it out slowly as I go down."

"We're ready," Xander said in a solid voice, and I once again felt the certainty of knowing I could depend on him.

With a nod, I stepped backward over the side of the waterfall.

Xander grunted, but the rope held firm, letting out gradually as I walked my feet from rock to rock, my back toward the pool, and my hands gripping tightly to the rope above me.

I peered over my shoulder and moved to my right, slightly further away from the waterfall itself. I needed to maneuver myself into the perfect position so that I came down behind the child, out of his sight.

"We're nearly there!" I called up to the others. "Just another yard or two."

I had expected the roar of the waterfall to keep the boy from noticing my words, but he jerked around in response to them. For one heart-stopping moment, we stared at each other, the awareness in his eyes proving that my birthday had changed nothing.

"Let me down!" I screamed, but I was already dropping with a stomach-lurching sensation.

The boy screamed defiance, jerking himself away. And as predicted, his foot slipped, and he began to topple toward the waterfall accompanied by his mother's scream.

I pushed off with one foot, angling myself directly toward him. My swinging bulk collided with him, driving him in the opposite direction. Seesawing wildly, he tried to get his feet under him, only to fail and topple forward off the rock.

His father was already in motion, making a wild leap toward him, and he arrived just in time to catch the toddler in his arms.

I swung at the end of the rope, bumping against the rock as I tried to steady myself. My wild movement prevented me from gaining a clear view of what was happening, but I caught flashes of the mother's arrival and the boy sobbing and reaching for her. Now that shock had overtaken his defiance, he was desperate for his mother's arms.

At no point did the adults give any indication they could see me dangling beside the waterfall on a rope—yet further proof that my birthday had changed nothing. My age might have caused the unexpected hiccup in the enchantment, but it was obviously a permanent hiccup.

A grunt sounded above me, and I began slowly inching upward. I fought to get my feet against the rock again to steady my movement, eventually managing to scramble the last few feet over the top of the rocks.

As soon as I lay sprawled across them, Xander rushed forward to kneel beside me.

"Are you all right?" he asked.

I beamed up at him. "Yes. Thanks to you. And the boy is all right too. Come on, let's go check on him."

"Untie yourself first," Lori said. "We should return the rope."

The knot was just as wet as I was from the spray of the water-fall, and my fingers kept slipping. I eventually gave up and let Lori untangle it before coiling the rope back into its original loops.

We all climbed carefully down the way we had come, keeping as far from the waterfall's spray as possible. Xander kept stopping to offer me a steadying hand, so Lori soon passed us, making her way back to where I had picked up the rope.

When we reached the spot, we all paused to look across at the family. The child was smiling again, babbling happily about cake, both chubby arms wrapped around his mother's neck. The faces of the parents told me they wouldn't so easily forget the stressful moment, however, and I wondered if it might prompt them to move into a town. At least there they would have a community to help keep an eye on the child. No mother, however vigilant, could survive life out here in the forest without ever taking her eyes off an adventurous child.

"I wonder if I was like that as a youngster?" I said. "Some of the palace children were so calm and quiet they would sit at their mother's side for hours, occupied with whatever small toys she gave them."

"I definitely can't imagine you as a compliant child like that," Xander said with a grin. "And even if this family doesn't know it, they can be thankful you're the daring person you are. If you'd been even a few seconds later in getting down there..."

We both shuddered at what would have happened.

"The world needs loud, active people as well as quiet, thoughtful ones," he concluded.

"You were amazing as well," I said. "I couldn't have done it on my own."

I remembered my certainty in his assistance and the way he had been the first to insist we leave the road to help the family. My earlier fears about him were becoming paler and paler. There was no glory in this situation. Even the family involved didn't know we'd helped them. And Xander himself hadn't played the starring role as rescuer. And yet, he had been unswerving in his determination not to abandon someone clearly in distress.

It was becoming more and more obvious that Xander had responded so strongly to the story of my disappearance not because he liked the idea of himself in the role of dashing hero, but because he had a genuine horror of anyone being alone, helpless, and in trouble.

"I think it was fortunate we were enchanted," he said cheerfully, oblivious of the revelation happening in my mind.

I blinked, trying to follow his thoughts as we stepped back onto the road.

"There was no time to explain ourselves to the parents," he added given my look of confusion, "and if they'd reacted to your appearance over the waterfall, Liam might have slipped before you were in position to help him."

"You're right!" I said, struck by his words. "I never thought some good could come out of this situation. But I'm relieved we were able to help. If we hadn't been passing by..."

I shivered, but my mind was preoccupied with remembering previous words of Xander's. I had been bemoaning being overlooked as the youngest, but Xander had pointed out the burdens that came with being heir and always being seen. I had been struck by his words then, and I was struck by them again.

Xander was obviously the sort of person to look for the positives in any situation, and he saw things I should have seen for myself. When I first came out of the tower, I had berated myself because I still leaped into action at the first opportunity. But Lori had told me that was just part of who I was.

She was right, but that wasn't the whole truth. There hadn't been anything wrong with my desire for activity and inclusion as a child, but I had been at fault when I failed to balance that with acknowledgment and gratitude for my situation.

I would have spent those years in a lot greater happiness if I had been grateful for the advantages that came with my place as the youngest princess instead of focused only on the negatives. If I'd spent more time looking for the positives, I would have soon found a whole host of them. And it might even have helped me think a little more carefully before I rushed into danger.

The lesson I needed to take from the tower wasn't that I should change who I was, but that I should remember to be grateful for what I did have instead of focusing on what I thought I lacked.

"Thank you," I said to Xander with so much earnestness that he stared at me in surprise.

"What for?"

"For everything." I beamed at him. "For being you."

"You're welcome," he said with a bemused return smile that slowly grew warmer. "Very welcome."

PART III
THE CAPITAL

Since the detour to help the forest family had proved to be short, we easily resumed our place a safe distance behind Eulalie. When she didn't even stop in Greenwood but continued straight ahead on the road for the capital, I had to concede that Xander was right.

"She's definitely heading for Northgate," I said.

And when the road finally took us beyond the edge of the forest, I was delighted. I had spent five years in that forest, and I was ready to leave it behind, preferably forever.

Other traffic on the road had gradually increased, and it increased even further on the road between Greenwood and the capital.

We closed the distance between us and Eulalie, hanging close behind other groups of travelers to keep ourselves hidden.

"I don't understand why she came to the tower that last time at all," I said. "If what she's looking for is in the capital, why go so far away?"

"I don't think she was there for you," Xander said. "Remember she only came to the tower because the ring cracked. I think she was following the tour. She either thought the king had what she needed with him, or he had information about it that she needed."

"Do you think she might already have everything she needs, then?" I asked, alarmed.

"I think she got some information that told her where to find it," Xander said. "She's been moving too quickly and with too much purpose to already have it. In that case, she could have stayed with the tour all the way back."

I relaxed a little before another thought occurred to me. "If the king was the one with the information she needed, does that mean whatever she's looking for is in the palace?"

"Obviously I can't know for sure," Xander said. "But I suspect so."

"That would explain why she's been searching for it for so long without success," Lori said. "It will be well guarded."

"Should I be concerned that the king might have an object that forces people to docilely follow his commands?" I muttered.

"If he was using it, I hope everyone would be concerned," Xander said. "But I've seen no indication of anything like that. King Richard's advisors are formal in manner, but they're not afraid to speak their minds, even if they disagree with him. And he always listens and takes their perspectives into account. I didn't see any sign that anyone was blindly following him. And Prince William is even more beloved. He won't have any need for such an object."

"I still don't like the idea of one existing," I said stubbornly, and Lori nodded fervently.

We had to fall silent after that, focusing on the approaching gates and on keeping Eulalie in sight. On the road near the capital, the extra traffic had been a help, allowing us to stay hidden, but inside the actual city, it became a hindrance.

Passing through the gates was as easy for us as it was for the magically shielded and innocuous-looking Eulalie, but inside we were in danger of losing her in the crowd.

"It doesn't matter that we know her general destination," Xander said. "We need to be there to see what she does when she actually gets to the palace."

I would have replied, but I was too busy trying to peer around a carriage in order to keep my eyes on Eulalie. It had been a long time since I was in a city as large as Northgate, but there was no time to stop and enjoy the atmosphere and buzz.

I couldn't help enjoying its quaint appearance, however. The neat cobblestoned streets were lined by long unbroken rows of connected houses, all lined with flowering window boxes. I could only imagine it looked even more charming when the street lanterns on their black metal poles were lit.

Given the appearance of the city, I wasn't surprised when the palace came into full view. The tall, elegant building of white stone looked just how I had imagined it, right down to the towers.

A sharp stab of longing for the palace of my childhood made me falter. Lori pulled on my arm, maneuvering me around an oversized cart and donkey, and I tried to pull my thoughts back to the present. It wasn't fair to compare other palaces to the beauty of my home. Nothing could compare to Trione's palace with the sand at its feet and its heights crowned with gold and glass that glittered just as brightly in the sun.

The main palace gates stood open, allowing through a steady stream of traffic.

"They'll be busy preparing for the coming coronation," Lori said, answering my question before I could ask it. "I'm sure they have all sorts of celebrations planned."

We slipped inside behind Eulalie, who attached herself unnoticed to a group delivering boxes. She wasn't even carrying a box, but the guards barely noticed her and clearly didn't perceive her as a possible threat.

"If only they knew the truth," I muttered.

Inside the courtyard, she didn't hesitate, heading for a side door.

The door turned out to be the entry to the kitchen. I paused on the threshold, hit by another wave of nostalgia and longing. I had spent many happy hours of my childhood in the kitchen of my home palace.

But I couldn't linger in a doorway. I barely managed to dodge out of the way in time to stop the enchantment bringing disaster to a young apprentice who was approaching the door with a precariously stacked tray of sandwiches.

The three of us dodged through the kitchen, not wanting to disrupt the hive of industry inside, and reached the internal door to the rest of the palace. Eulalie had already disappeared through it, but Lori got her head around in time to see which way she turned, and we were soon slipping through a maze of white marble corridors.

When Lori peered around yet another corner, however, she held up her hand to stop us instead of gesturing us onward.

"She's finally stopped?" Xander whispered, and Lori nodded.

She remained in place, watching something we couldn't see.

"She's stopped in front of an impressive looking set of double doors," Lori whispered. "They look thick, and they're well-barred. Plus a set of four guards is stationed outside them."

"Be off with you!" a male voice said loudly from around the corner.

"That was one of the guards talking to her," Lori said. "She looks surprised at being addressed, but her reply is too quiet for me to hear."

She paused, and I waited in suspense until she pulled back around the corner and looked at us.

"She's hurried off. She's obviously gotten used to not being noticed, but it doesn't matter how innocent and unremarkable she looks, the guards at the royal vault aren't going to allow anyone to stand around near the doors without purpose."

"Is that the royal vault?" I risked sticking my own head around the corner to stare at the four stiff guards. "How do you know?"

Lori shrugged as Xander rounded the corner and stood there surveying the scene. "Mayhap I'm wrong. But it has that look."

"I agree," Xander said.

"Have we lost Eulalie?" I asked suddenly. "Shouldn't we be continuing on?"

"I don't think we need to tail her so closely anymore," Xander said slowly. "We've found her destination. The object she needs is in the royal vault. It doesn't matter where she goes now because we know she'll be coming back here. It's the vault itself we need to watch from this point on."

"That will be easier than sneaking through the palace." I stepped around the corner to join him. "Since the guards can't see us, we can move around freely—at least until Eulalie returns. Shall we go closer and have a look?"

The three of us strode along the corridor, and as expected, the guards gave no sign of noticing our approach.

One was positioned on each side of the door, and another two stood directly in front of them. So even invisible, we couldn't get close enough to try lifting the large beam that secured the doors.

"It looks extremely secure to me," I said. "Maybe we've been worrying for nothing. I don't think she's going to get in there."

"I wouldn't be so sure," Lori said darkly. "We don't know what that woman has up her sleeve. If she really does have all the objects that used to be owned by that rebel person, she may have something of assistance in a situation like this."

"That's an unnerving thought," I said.

"How come you never let us *loiter* near the vault, but you're ignoring them?" asked a young and indignant voice.

All three of us turned to stare at the speaker. Instead of one child, we found ourselves facing a striking trio.

Two of them—a boy and girl—looked so alike that they had to

be twins. They both had golden skin and black hair that were similar to Xander's, but their eyes were a startling shade of blue. The second boy had a similar appearance, but his brown eyes changed the whole effect. I could easily believe they were all related, however.

But even though we were all staring at them, the trio showed no interest in us. Their reproachful attention was focused on the guards by the vault doors. Two of the guards gave quiet sighs, but only one of those at the front moved in response to the boy's words.

"I don't know what game you're playing now, but our orders are clear. No one—including you—is permitted to linger near the vault."

"*Especially* you," one of the guards muttered under his breath, and despite everything I couldn't help snorting in amusement. It was so exactly the sort of interaction I could imagine having had with our own guards at home.

The three children turned to glare at me in response to the noise, but the second boy quickly turned back to the guards.

"We know those are your orders, so I'm asking why you're letting *them* just stand there." He pointed at us. "Do you even know who they are?"

"That's enough of your games," the front guard said in a long-suffering tone. "If you don't leave the area immediately, we'll be forced to call for reinforcements."

The boy swelled with outrage and looked about to explode, but the girl spoke first.

"Can you really not see them?" She sounded merely curious rather than incensed. "You can't see anyone standing in this corridor except us?"

"Naturally we can't see anyone but the three of you," the guard repeated. "This is my final warning to leave this corridor."

I wasn't sure how I expected the three children to react to that statement, but it wasn't for all three of them to turn on us with shining eyes and excited expressions.

"You're invisible!" the girl said, at the same moment as her twin said, "Are you using a godmother object? Can we have a turn?"

"We need to discuss this elsewhere," the other boy said with a significant look at the guards.

Before the rest of us could protest, or even think of a reasonable response, each of the children had one of us by the arm and were towing us down the corridor. I couldn't imagine how it must have looked to the guards, but when I glanced back at them, they'd gone back to their earlier rigid postures. They were clearly so used to antics from these three that they weren't giving their strange behavior a second thought.

Xander and I exchanged looks and then shrugs as we allowed ourselves to be pulled along by the enthusiastic children. When we'd rounded a corner, the brown-eyed boy selected a door and pulled it open.

"It should be empty in here. Last time I checked it was—Yes, this will do."

He pulled the door the rest of the way open and held it while the three of us were ushered inside.

"Aren't you worried we might be a threat?" Xander asked. "We were lurking outside your royal vault, after all."

The twins stiffened at his words, exchanging perturbed looks.

"Are you a threat?" the girl asked, but she sounded more curious than worried.

"We are not a threat to you or Northhelm," I said firmly. "In fact, I'm—"

But before I could reveal my identity, the brown-eyed boy spoke over the top of me, cutting me off.

"He's right. We should get Danielle. Do either of you know where she is?"

I exchanged a bewildered look with Lori while Xander stared, slightly stupefied, at the twins' enthusiastic approval of this plan.

"She was with the dressmaker earlier," the girl said, "but I think she was going to the library after that. Give me a minute, and I'll get her."

She raced off, leaving us with the two boys.

"I'm Ben," the brown-eyed boy said after a moment of silence. "That's Andrew. And the girl who left is Arabella."

I opened my mouth to give my own name, only to decide I should wait for the two girls to return given that they were likely to be incredulous at my claimed identity.

Xander looked even more shocked at the boy's words than at their earlier comments. But before I could find a way to subtly ask him what was wrong, the door burst back open.

Arabella stormed in, a second girl following in her wake. I gasped at the sight of her, and then immediately felt foolish.

But there was no denying that this girl, who appeared similar in age to the other three, was also unlike them in a way that was hard to quantify. She was stunningly beautiful, despite her young age, but it was more than that. I had never seen someone so young carry themselves with so much poise, and something in her expression made me certain she was devastatingly intelligent as well.

But while I was held silent by surprise, Xander exploded into speech.

"You responded to a possible threat by fetching the *crown princess*? Alone!"

I gaped from the girls to Xander and then back to the girls, trying to make sense of his words.

"I'm not the crown princess until tomorrow when Grandfather abdicates and Father is crowned," the girl said calmly. "And they did quite right to fetch me." She gave Ben a look. "For once."

"I already apologized for that time," Ben said cheerily. "And I won't keep apologizing forever. You can't expect us to invite you every time given how often you've spoiled our fun."

"But we always have the best fun when Dani's with us," Arabella said reproachfully. "And no one ever catches us when she's with us either."

Danielle—apparently Princess Danielle—rolled her eyes. "Which is precisely why the boys never invite me along when they're doing something particularly foolish that's likely to fail. They know I'll stop them before they start. But what I want to know is what Prince Xander is doing in Northgate, and why you've stashed him in this room?"

"This is Prince Xander?" Andrew gave Xander a curious examination.

"Princess Danielle is the only one of you I met on my previous visit to Northgate," Xander said, "but I realized who the rest of you must be the moment you said your names. I really must advise you to exercise a little more caution in future."

I couldn't help laughing at that. "Like you and Xavier did at a similar age, I assume?"

His look turned rueful. "Oh dear. I'm turning into Rek, aren't I?"

"I've been assured that it eventually happens to the best of us," I said with a heavy sigh.

"Are you all princes and princesses, then?" Lori asked, clearly struggling to make sense of the situation.

"This is Princess Danielle, only child of Crown Prince William and Crown Princess Celeste," Xander said. "And the other three are her cousins. Prince Benjamin is the oldest child of Prince Rafael of Lanover and Princess Marie of Northhelm, and Andrew and Arabella are the children of Princess Cordelia of Lanover and Major Ferdinand of Northhelm."

"Emmett isn't here because he's only seven," Ben said. "He's always wanting to follow along with us, but thankfully his nanny keeps a close watch on him because he'd spoil all our fun otherwise."

"I feel sincerely sorry for both him and his nanny," Lori muttered.

"And how old are all of you?" I asked.

"We're eleven," Arabella said.

"But I'm about to turn twelve," Ben quickly added. "And Dani only just turned eleven."

"We're all aware you're nearly a year older than her." Arabella rolled her eyes. "But it doesn't change the fact that we listen to her when she's with us because she's the one who always gets us out of trouble while you just get us into it!"

I wasn't even trying to hide my grin now. Listening to them talk to each other was like seeing myself at their age if only I'd been surrounded by like-minded cousins. Basically they were my childhood dream.

"I'm still waiting for an answer to my question, Your Highness," Danielle said, looking at Xander. "And perhaps you could explain why my guards can't see you while you're at it."

"You just believed your cousin when she told you about that?" I asked curiously.

"Of course," Danielle said calmly. "My cousins might sometimes involve themselves in foolish escapades they haven't fully thought through, but they would never lie to me."

"Of course we wouldn't!" Ben glared at me as if I had outright accused him of lying. "Especially not with something that might actually be important."

"I'm back because I've been put under an enchantment," Xander said. "I believe the person who enchanted me has ill intentions toward Northhelm, so I'm here in an attempt to both stop her and release us from the enchantment."

Danielle's eyes flashed over Lori and me at his use of the word us, and I had the slightly uncomfortable feeling of being quickly weighed and measured. What would this unusual princess think when I told her my identity? Had she heard of the missing princess? Would she believe me?

"I don't suppose you're Princess Margaret?" Danielle asked after she'd finished examining Lori and returned her attention to me.

"I prefer Daisy," I said automatically before sputtering to a stop and staring at her. "Wait, how did you know who I am?"

She shrugged. "It was a fairly simple deduction. Prince Xander, who is searching Northhelm for a mysteriously vanished princess, shows up with a girl of the right age who just happens to be trapped under an enchantment of invisibility. Naturally, I assumed you must be the missing Daisy."

"When you put it like that, it does seem quite simple," I said, feeling a little dazed.

"I can see you're Aurora's daughter." Lori sounded impressed.

Her words made all four of the children tense, so I supplied a one-word explanation.

"Celine."

The original trio's eyes all lit up, and they exchanged excited looks.

"Have you seen Auntie Celine's fireballs?" Andrew asked.

"Did she make a wind to drive your boat along?" Ben added before I'd had time to answer the first question.

"Do you have your own godmother?" Arabella chimed in. "And if so, do you think *she'd* give us the gift of fire? Our godmother keeps saying no." She looked greatly downcast at this state of affairs.

I looked between them all and burst out laughing. "I'm utterly sure that no godmother would give all three of you fire power."

"Of course they would not," Danielle said briskly. "The question we need to be asking is why we can see you if you're supposed to be invisible."

"It's because of your age," I said. "I was only thirteen myself when I was enchanted, and for some reason that twisted the enchantment and made it so that anyone under the age of thirteen can still see and hear me like normal. But to anyone older, I'm not here. They can't see me, they can't hear me, I can't interact properly with any object in their sight. They can't even see something I write on a piece of paper and leave behind. I'm completely cut off from them. And since the other two got added to my enchantment, it follows the same rules for them."

"How fascinating," Danielle said. "What about someone who could see you and then turns thirteen?"

"On their thirteenth birthday, I suddenly turn invisible," I said, remembering Jayda and the other village youth with a pang.

"That village in the north!" Danielle looked at Xander. "So Daisy really was the girl in the tower then?"

He nodded. "One of the village girls took me to see her tower and was able to assist me in making contact with Daisy. Unfortunately, instead of freeing her, it merely absorbed me into the enchantment as well."

I flushed at the memory of what that contact had been. At the time I had been more shocked and indignant than anything else, but I would have a very different reaction if Xander ever tried to kiss me again.

"And I was in the enchantment nearly from the start," Lori said. "I accompanied Daisy from Trione."

"Yes," Danielle said absently. "The missing maid. We've been looking for you too."

Lori smiled, pleased not to have been forgotten.

"Mother won't be pleased that her agents dismissed the children's claims so easily," Danielle said. "She always wondered about the story. I think if the village wasn't so extremely remote, she would have gone there herself."

"I hope she isn't too harsh on them," I said. "I've been trying for a long time to find a way around the enchantment, and there really isn't one. Whatever happened with Xander, it isn't something I've ever managed to repeat."

I didn't look at him as I said the final sentence since I had an inkling of why that particular contact with Xander had been successful when no other attempts had. But it wasn't something I intended to discuss with this audience.

"So your abductor enchanted you not long after your delegation was attacked and then kept you captive in a tower for five years." Danielle's brow wrinkled. "We've already established you weren't taken by any of the group behind the initial attack in Arcadia—they were all dealt with long ago. But how did you end up in Northhelm? And why do you believe your captor is planning harm against the kingdom?"

Lori cleared her throat. "Northhelm was my fault, Your Highness. We didn't know who to trust, so we fled Arcadia, intending to find a ship home from one of your ports."

"You did a good job." Danielle sounded impressed. "Mother never managed to find so much as a trace of you."

"We started out well," Lori agreed. "But we didn't make it far over the border before we met Eulalie." She scowled.

"Eulalie?" Danielle frowned. "It's an unusual name, but it can't possibly be…" She trailed off, sounding like she was talking more to herself than to us.

"Have you heard of her?" I asked, surprised.

"I don't see how it can possibly be the same one," Danielle said. "After all, it's been centuries."

"Centuries?" Xander's eyes narrowed. "What do you mean?"

Danielle shrugged. "It's probably nothing. I was just struck by the unusual name—he had one, too, and I've never heard his anywhere else."

"By him, I don't suppose you mean that rebel from fifteen years ago?" Xander asked, and Danielle looked up sharply.

"That's precisely who I mean. He was born so long ago that his family's story had become a mere legend, but he had secretly found a way to prolong his life. Once I was old enough to be told about the rebellion, I studied every version of the tale I could find. Most versions focus on the three brothers, but I found one that mentioned a sister by the name of Eulalie."

"It can't be a coincidence," I said, looking at Xander.

"We don't know who she is for sure," Xander told Danielle. "But we did wonder if there could be a connection between her and the rebel of the tales. We think she got hold of some of the godmother objects he had collected."

"And unfortunately she seems to have the same obsession with her bloodline as he did."

"Another one who thinks she has more right to the throne than Grandfather." Danielle sighed. "I thought the jewel put a stop to all this nonsense."

"We think she might have found a way around the jewel," I said uneasily, glancing at Xander, who thankfully took over the story, outlining the extent of our theory.

Lori made several sounds of protest at our explaining the full details to a group of children, but neither Xander nor I paid her any heed. We had once been children just like these ones, and right now they were all we had.

When he reached the point of the story where we were left standing in front of the vault, Xander fixed Danielle with an intent look.

"Somehow I don't think your parents will dismiss your words as a fanciful tale of childhood. Can you go to them now and warn them? They need to make sure Eulalie doesn't get her hands on what's in that vault."

"My mother would certainly take me seriously," Danielle said soberly. "But unfortunately she's not currently in the capital. None of our parents are."

"What?" I stared at her. "But isn't the coronation tomorrow?"

"That's why they're absent," Ben said, jumping in. "The tour is timed to arrive back here tomorrow morning, and our parents all rode out to meet the tour outside the city. They'll all arrive tomorrow in a grand procession and wind their way through the streets of Northgate, waving to the cheering crowds, before they arrive at the palace for the ceremonies."

I paled, looking at Xander in fear. Had Eulalie timed her journey to arrive here so close before the coronation so that it would be too late for anyone to stop her?

"Eulalie only has tonight to try to get into the vault," Lori said, "and if she fails, she'll have lost her chance to usurp the handover of power. Do we really think she can get past those guards and those doors? It seems unlikely to me, in which case her plan will fall through even without our intervention."

"They'll be opening the doors tomorrow, though," Andrew said. "Do you think she'd have a chance to get in then, Dani?"

"I'm rather afraid she may find a way," Danielle said grimly.

"Why would they open the vault tomorrow?" I asked, horrified at the timing.

"They have to retrieve the official crown and scepter for the coronation," Ben said. "A whole group of honor guards do it, but if this Eulalie person has some sort of enchantment she could use, it won't matter how many guards they have."

I remembered the way she had slipped unnoticed through the palace gates, and my stomach sank.

Xander, however, still sounded cheery when he responded.

"In that case, we need to get inside and take the object in question ourselves before Eulalie can get it. And I suspect we have exactly the right group of people to help us steal something from the royal vault."

CHAPTER 21

"Aren't you invisible to adults?" Arabella asked. "Why would you need our help?"

"Unfortunately we're not invisible to Eulalie," I said. "And while we should be able to get into the vault fairly easily, we also need to make sure we can get back out, preferably with the object in question."

"And preferably without jumping out any windows," Lori muttered.

"That, at least, will be easy," Danielle said dryly, "since the vault doesn't have any windows."

"There's also the complication that we don't even know what we're looking for," Xander said. "We believe she's looking for something that will allow her to control your grandfather and father, but I'm not familiar with any such artifact. Have you heard of anything like it?"

"The jewelry set!" the twins said in unison.

"It's the reason the guards at the vault know us," Ben confided. "We went through a phase of trying to sneak in there so we could get our hands on it. The circlet lets you tell people what to think, and the necklace lets you tell them how to act."

I looked at Danielle, and she shrugged. "That's what the rumors say. Supposedly the set was a wedding gift to my mother from her godmother. I've never seen any of the pieces myself, but I've heard they're made with an elaborate design of gold and rubies, and there are three matching pieces—circlet, necklace, and bracelet."

"That sounds very promising," Xander said. "But given our limitations, we'll still need a clear doorway to get in and out, and we'll also need a chance to find and take the jewelry without being seen."

"But you're invisible!" Andrew said. "Surely being seen is the one thing you don't have to worry about?"

"It's not that they'll actually see us," I explained. "It's that the enchantment won't let us pick up anything in the room if a guard is looking in our direction. It will prevent us from doing anything that would result in someone seeing jewelry either disappear or go floating through the air. We'll only be able to pick them up if no one is looking our way. Given you said there will be a lot of guards, Xander is worried they may be watching every corner of the vault."

"Plus, of course, there's Eulalie." Xander rubbed the back of his neck. "I don't think we could manage the theft at all without the enchantment, but it will still be difficult, even with it."

"Thank you," Danielle said. "I'll pass on your compliments to our captain of the guard—along with a report on any weaknesses we do manage to exploit tomorrow."

"You'll help us?" I asked.

"Let's say instead that I'm going to help Northhelm," she said. "And that I have a burning desire to see this Eulalie for myself."

"You're going to come with us?" I asked doubtfully. "Won't the guards object? They seemed to have forceful opinions about the presence of the others."

Danielle gave a small, prim smile. "Naturally, the guards know to chase Ben and the twins away from anywhere even mildly sensitive. It's a different matter for me, however."

"Like I said, Dani never gets caught," Arabella said.

"Could you just collect the jewelry yourself, then?" Lori asked with her usual disappointingly practical approach.

"Unfortunately not," Dani said. "No one will cause a problem if I say I want to supervise the collection of the coronation jewels. But only my grandparents and parents are authorized to remove anything. I'll only be permitted to stand by the open door with one of the guards."

"That's unfortunate," Lori said heavily, but I couldn't help smiling.

"In that case," I said, "you can indicate which of the pieces we need to steal, while the other three distract the guards. We need something dramatic enough that they all look away from the vault's displays. We don't need them all to run off and leave it empty, or anything, we just need them to look the other way."

Ben cracked his knuckles and grinned disconcertingly widely. "That we can do." He glanced at Andrew, who was grinning back at him. "Our parents will have to understand a little destruction for such a worthy cause."

"Keep the actual destruction to a minimum," Danielle said with a hard look. "Tomorrow is the coronation, remember, and the palace will be filling with visitors. Don't embarrass our kingdom."

Ben gave a heavy sigh but seemed to accept her words without too much disappointment.

"Andrew," he said, "Arabella, I think the moment has come to test that powder we…requisitioned."

"What powder would that be?" Danielle asked suspiciously.

"I thought you knew everything that happens in the palace?" Ben asked in a superior voice.

"No, that's my mother." Danielle didn't appear in the least

disconcerted by his teasing. "But it's a good point. If she's let you hang onto it, it can't be too dangerous."

"We *think* it just creates a big bang and a lot of smoke," Arabella said. "But of course we need to test it to be sure."

"And here we have the perfect opportunity." Ben rubbed his hands together. "We can't even get in trouble for it! Well, not proper trouble. The cap will probably try to string us up before our parents arrive." He sounded perfectly cheerful about the possibility.

Danielle tipped her head to the side, considering. "No, you should be safe. The captain won't leave the coronation jewels just to deal with you three."

"Excellent." Andrew smiled at his sister. "None of the rest of them will do anything except get red-faced and quote rules and regulations at us until someone fetches our parents."

"It'll need to be timed right," Danielle said. "One of you will have to listen around the corner from the vault. When I say that the weather is perfect for the coronation, that will be the signal."

"What if it rains tomorrow?" Arabella protested.

I expected Danielle to show impatience with her quibbling, but she took the question seriously.

"It's been fine for more than a week now, and there are no reports of incoming bad weather, but if something unexpected does happen, I'll instead say that it's a pity the weather isn't nicer for the coronation. Is that clear enough?"

Arabella nodded, an expression of concentration on her face, as if she was carefully committing the code phrases to memory.

"What exactly have we gotten ourselves involved with?" Lori asked in a quiet aside.

"I think it's best not to ask too many questions." Xander was grinning, so he clearly didn't share Lori's concerns.

The two boys were in the middle of an ominous argument about exactly how much powder they should use and where it should be placed, so I turned back to the girls.

"I don't suppose you know somewhere out of the way where we could sleep tonight?" I asked. "Given the enchantment, we can't just book a room at an inn."

"Of course," Danielle said. "We can easily accommodate you here. Every guest room in the palace has been made ready given the number of guests coming for the coronation. But since many of them have timed their arrival to join the tour outside the city, there will be plenty of empty rooms tonight."

"Thank you!" I said with heartfelt fervor. It had been far too long since I'd slept in a proper bed.

"I can take you there now, if you like," she said. "It might save complications if you keep out of the way for the rest of the day. There are plenty of other children around the palace, and if they start making a fuss and telling their parents about invisible people, Eulalie might overhear something."

"Very sensible," Lori said approvingly.

I certainly had no objection to the plan, so we were soon installed in two out of the way guest rooms with a connecting door. Xander strolled through from his room to ours as soon as Danielle had left.

"We're fortunate with the ages of the royal children," he said. "If they were all a couple of years older, we would have been in trouble."

"I'm not convinced we aren't in trouble now," Lori muttered.

"I'm extremely glad we met them," I said. "And also that Arabella promised to come fetch us in the morning. I'm not sure I could find my way back to the vault without a guide. Although I suppose you spent some time in the palace on your recent visit, Xander. I'm surprised you didn't meet all the younger royals then."

"Princess Cordelia and Major Ferdinand had taken the three of them south to visit their relatives in Lanover. I imagine they traveled back north with a whole contingent of Lanoverians coming to attend the coronation."

"Well, now we know why the younger royals have been left out of this procession," Lori said.

I turned to give her a confused look.

"Just you imagine traveling with those three and tell me if you'd have any nerves left at the end of it," she said knowingly. "No one in their right mind would want to immediately set out on another trip with them—however short. Not when it was going to be a formal, political affair. They probably left Princess Danielle home to keep an eye on them. I can't imagine anyone else other than their parents managing the feat. At least I assume they must have parents in the same vein to have created those terrors."

"I thought they were delightful!" I protested.

"You would," she muttered. "Of course you would."

"They do seem a little outside the normal Northhelmian mold," Xander said with a chuckle. "I can well imagine the court must find them a challenge."

We all went to bed early after a supper delivered by the trio of young royals. They brought the food with the same furtive air they might have used to pass royal secrets to an enemy agent. But even Lori was grateful for the feast and shared the best delicacies with them before sending them off so we could have an early night.

Any nerves about the next day were easily overcome by the incredible comfort of the bed and pillow.

"Ahhh…" I stretched out, closing my eyes and reveling in the luxury. "I've missed this. My bed in the tower was better than the forest ground, but it wasn't like this."

"It's a fine room," Lori agreed. "And we'd best be getting what rest we can."

I agreed and fell quickly into a blissful sleep.

Lori woke me the next morning when she opened one of the curtains, letting light flood into the room.

"Mrghblgh," I groaned, covering my eyes with my arm.

"Princess Danielle said the coronation jewels will be removed from the vault early," Lori said crisply, pulling open the second curtain.

I sat straight up, my eyes flying open. "The coronation!"

We had saved some bread and cheese from the meal the night before, so we quickly completed a simple breakfast. Xander joined us halfway through, and we were all ready and waiting when the door opened.

I had been expecting Arabella, but it was Danielle who stood there, beckoning for us to come out.

"Ara was needed for whatever mischief they have planned," she said by way of explanation. "This makes more sense anyway, since I need to go to the vault too."

She led us unerringly through a series of corridors, eventually turning into one that held only a single, familiar set of double doors. Four new guards stood in the same arrangement as the guards the previous day, and two of their eyes flicked in our direction.

I had an unsettled moment when I thought they could see us, and then I remembered that the girl in the lead was perfectly visible to them.

She kept walking until she was standing directly in front of them.

"Lieutenant," she said respectfully.

"Your Highness." He gave a half-bow, looking clearly uneasy.

"I see I'm early," she said. "I'll wait for the captain."

The guard instantly relaxed, and Danielle stepped back to wait against the opposite wall of the corridor. She flicked her eyes down the corridor, and we obediently followed their direction to an alcove further down the hall. It was a tight fit to get the three of us behind the plinth that held a large, decorative vase, but at least we were out of obvious view for when Eulalie appeared.

I was so tense waiting to see if it would be the captain of the guards or Eulalie who arrived first that I barely noticed that our cramped quarters meant I was practically in Xander's arms. But I couldn't help but notice when his arms actively curved around me. It was a subtle movement, but when I looked up, I found him looking down at me with a warm expression that held a hint of mischief. I froze, heat rushing into my face as I forgot all about Lori pressed awkwardly against my other side.

Xander angled his head slightly to breathe words into my ear that were so quiet even Lori couldn't hear them.

"Would I be breaking my promise to avoid surprises if I kissed you now?"

My eyes flew back to his, a strange feeling washing over me. He'd spoken of surprises before—had that not been a dream? Had he really…The palm of my hand tingled while his eyes laughed at me.

I was saved from answering by sound and movement from the corridor. We all squirmed around as we tried to get a view of what was happening, and Xander's arms dropped away from me.

I told myself it was a relief and directed my brain to focus on the important happenings by the vault. Even so, it took me several seconds to absorb what I was seeing.

By the time I realized that it was a large collection of guards in formal uniforms with no sign of Eulalie, Xander was already looking down at me with both eyebrows raised. I shrugged.

I had no idea why she wasn't here yet, but her absence would certainly make our task a lot easier. The princess would be disappointed, though. She was ready to identify the correct jewels for us, but we weren't going to be able to identify Eulalie for her.

"Come on," Xander whispered. "We need to get closer."

We spilled out of the alcove, hurrying up to stand beside Danielle. She gave us a nod, followed by a significant look at the milling people in the corridor.

"She's not here," I said with an apologetic grimace. "Maybe she didn't know the vault was opening after all."

"Or maybe she already found a way in," the girl whispered darkly. "The four of us kept an extra watch on the vault all night, and we didn't see anyone approach it, but she may have had some other means of entry."

I winced. "I guess we're about to find out."

"Your Highness." The most elaborately dressed of the guards stopped in front of Danielle and bowed. "I wasn't expecting to see you here."

"My mother instructed me to observe the retrieval of the jewels," the princess said in a calm voice.

She offered no explanation about whether her presence was intended as training for her or oversight for him, but the captain didn't question it either way.

"Of course, Your Highness." He bowed again. "One of my men will keep you escort at the door."

Danielle nodded her approval of this plan, and the captain glanced back at his men. One immediately responded to the unspoken summons, striding forward to bow even lower to the princess before taking his place at her side.

Satisfied, the captain turned back to the doors and barked a series of orders. The four regular guards sprang away, taking up defensive positions in the corridor. Two stood on each side, their attention and spears pointing down the corridor, away from the vault door. If Eulalie did try to approach while the doors were open, I couldn't see how she would get anywhere near them.

Several of the guards worked together to lift the heavy bar and expose the keyhole behind. The captain ceremoniously produced an ornate key and fitted it in the lock. I suspected it wasn't an ordinary lock, but I didn't have a clear enough view to work out why it took him so long to open it.

As soon as he was finished, he stepped back and two more guards sprang forward to push open the doors. Just as Xander had predicted, the guards flooded into the vault, taking up positions that allowed them to surveil every corner of the large room.

Danielle moved forward herself, stopping one step inside the doorway with her hovering escort at her side. I could see why she wouldn't have a chance to take the necklace herself. The front of the room was taken up with large, sealed chests, while individual items of value were displayed on a series of tables and shelves at the back and side walls. The crown and scepter stood alone on a pedestal in the middle of the room, but that didn't stop the guards from paying equal attention to every corner.

"You don't need me in there," Lori said at the last minute. "It's quite full enough with people as it is. I'll wait in the alcove."

I waited to see if Xander would suggest I do the same, but he just grinned at me and followed the younger princess inside. I smiled and followed at his heels, stopping abruptly as soon as I was inside.

Just dodging the guards filling the room was going to be difficult enough, and I didn't dare leave it to the enchantment to shove them aside. In a situation like this, strange movement might be noticed by one of the other guards.

"Can you see the jewelry we need?" I asked Danielle. "You said rubies in a delicate gold setting, right?" I peered around, trying to find anything that matched that description.

Danielle gave the tiniest nod and threw her eyes toward the left wall. I moved in that direction, weaving my way carefully around the evenly spaced guards. I couldn't help getting distracted by the glittering beauty of the items on display until the guard assigned to watch Danielle shocked me back to attention.

"Excellent weather for the occasion, is it not, Your Highness?" He had apparently decided to ease the discomfort of his unexpected assignment with small talk.

I froze, looking back toward them. It was too soon for talk about the weather!

"**M**y parents have been most pleased at the run of fair weather lately," Danielle said without any hint of stress.

I stumbled forward, my ears straining for any loud noises and my eyes scanning the displays. A guard loomed in front of me, and I barely swerved in time to avoid him. I was moving too quickly, but I had to find the jewelry before the trio set off the distraction.

"We've been receiving weather reports from all corners of the kingdom," Danielle continued. "So we'll be well prepared for any approaching change."

The guard murmured something inconsequential, and I wondered why I hadn't yet heard a distant explosion. If the trio failed to come good on their promise, then the whole attempt would be useless.

I dodged another guard and froze, a flash of red catching my eye. I leaned forward to stare at the back of one of the display tables where a circlet sat beside a necklace and bracelet.

I looked up, waving frantically at both Xander and Danielle. Her eyes flashed my way once, and I pointed dramatically at the table. She gave no sign of seeing me, but instead turned to the guard beside her and spoke in a slightly louder voice.

"But it turned out all the preparations weren't necessary since *the weather is perfect for the coronation.*"

I now knew why the two cousins had been so specific about the code phrase. They had obviously been prepared for the subject to be raised by someone else. I marveled at their careful attention to detail, fairly certain it came from Danielle's training.

The seconds stretched on with no loud noise. I looked from Danielle to Xander, wondering how long we needed to wait. Whoever was listening in the corridor would need to signal the other two, so perhaps it was reasonable for it to take a minute, but the guards were already lifting the crown and scepter on their cushion and turning back toward the door.

A strangled shout from the corridor made all the guards inside the vault tense. Several of them lifted their noses and sniffed the air just as I detected the smell of smoke.

The captain barked out an order, and every guard in the room drew their sword. I was still staring at the door myself, so it was left to the enchantment to push me away from the closest blade. The force of it moved me backward, directly into the path of another drawn sword which caused the enchantment to thrust me back the other way again.

My feet stumbled, my balance gone, but an arm braced me from behind, ending my bouncing movement. I nodded gratefully at Xander and looked quickly around the room.

Tense guards were looking in every direction, still preventing us from taking action. But a new guard appeared in the doorway, shouting for the captain.

The smell of smoke intensified, and tendrils of gray drifted up from his shoulders and hair.

"Captain!" he cried again. "All the ceremonial uniforms!"

A gasp rippled through the guards in the room, and all of them turned to stare at the smoking newcomer.

"Now!" Xander cried, and we both leaped for the table.

I was positioned better and got there first. With one sweep of my hand, I scooped up circlet, necklace, and bracelet, thrusting them into my pocket.

"Come on!" Xander took my other hand and tugged me toward the door.

"Benjamin!" the captain said through gritted teeth, and the guards relaxed.

At a signal from their leader, they all returned their swords to their hips while Xander and I wove through the waving blades. We had nearly reached the exit when the captain and the guard carrying the cushion departed the room. Before we could slip out behind them, the other guards formed into a line and began to file out.

The enchantment immediately set in, causing both us and the guards to sway wildly as we jostled our way toward the door. Xander tried to pull me back, but I resisted, desperate not to be locked inside.

Danielle sent me a swift look, however, and I finally pulled back, letting the guards file out of the room. When the guard accompanying her gestured courteously for her to exit in front of him, she hesitated.

He frowned, but Xander and I leaped forward into the gap she'd created, colliding with each other in our haste to squeeze through the door ahead of the princess. She started moving the second we had passed, squeezing up behind us so as not to draw attention to the apparent space in front of her.

Her movements must have looked strange to the guard, but he didn't comment, merely following her out of the vault. The moment he was clear, two guards pulled the doors closed and the captain approached with the key. I ignored the laborious process of securing the vault and regarded the chaos in the corridor.

Even more guards had arrived, all of them milling around and exclaiming angrily while their fancy uniforms smoked. The odd effect gave the impression they were all wearing a layer of embers beneath the material.

"At least none of them look like they're in pain," I said dubiously as Xander burst out laughing.

"I guess that powder didn't create a bang after all," he said.

I looked around, trying to find the princess in the chaos of complaining soldiers.

"Keep the crown away from anyone wearing a smoking uniform!" bellowed the captain, obviously finished with securing the vault.

The guards all responded instinctively. The newcomers leaped for the far wall, lining up along it at attention. The vault guards were left facing them, varying degrees of dismay on their faces.

"What will we do about the coronation if all the ceremonial uniforms are damaged?" one of them asked, although I couldn't see any signs of actual damage, just the strange smoke.

I didn't catch the captain's reply, however, because the new state of order in the corridor had revealed that Danielle was gone.

"Where's the princess?" I whirled around to look in the other direction. "She was right here."

Xander frowned. "I'm surprised she didn't want to stay with the..." He trailed off, staring at me. "Daisy, where's the jewelry you picked up?"

"Right..." My words trailed off as I shoved my hand into my pocket and found it empty.

I looked back up at Xander with wide eyes. "She took them!"

He groaned. "Of course she did. Why would she allow virtual strangers to get their hands on dangerous items like that?"

"We have to catch up with her!" I gasped. I looked toward the alcove, shouting for Lori, but she was already approaching us. "We need to run!"

Thankfully, she didn't stop to ask questions, increasing her pace as we both turned and sprinted down the corridor in the direction of the empty meeting room Ben had found for us the day before.

We both almost slipped as we rounded the corner, grabbing at each other to keep our balance. Lori, moving at a safer pace, overtook us and pulled the door open, having guessed our destination.

We crowded behind her, peering into the room. Four children stood inside.

I immediately relaxed, stepping into the room behind the other two. But when Danielle turned to face us, she was wearing the circlet, necklace, and bracelet and looking downcast.

"They don't work," she said. "Unless you feel a strange compulsion to obey me?" She didn't sound hopeful.

I glanced at Xander and then shook my head. "I don't feel anything."

"Neither do we," Arabella said.

"Except elation!" Benjamin crowed. "I'm glad we worked out the powder wasn't going to explode because that was even better. Did you see their faces when they started getting dressed and then noticed each other smoking?"

He and Andrew went off into paroxysms of laughter, but I was focused on Danielle.

"What do you mean it doesn't work?" I asked. "You said they were a gift from your mother's godmother. They have to do something!"

"Do they, though?" Lori frowned. "Maybe they were just a gift. They're beautiful."

"Maybe they do something else," Xander suggested. "Their power might not be immediately obvious if you don't already know what it is."

"Perhaps," Danielle agreed, but I shook my head.

"If it does something else, then it isn't what we're after! No wonder Eulalie wasn't there this morning. We must have it completely wrong." I felt the blood draining out of my face. "In which case, where is Eulalie right now? And what was she actually looking for?"

Xander looked at me with an equally horrified expression. "We just let her go. We have no idea where she is right now."

"That design looks familiar." Arabella was staring at the necklace, ignoring our mutual panic. "Haven't you seen it before, Dani?"

"My parents took me into the vault a couple of years ago," Danielle said, but Arabella shook her head. "No, not those specific pieces. Don't they look like Aunt's earrings? The ones in the section of her jewelry box that she never lets us touch? I got curious and snuck a look once. You must have done the same."

Danielle gasped. "Yes, you're right! They look like they could be the same set."

"If there's a missing fourth piece, and it's the one with the power," Lori said, "why wouldn't it be stored securely?"

"Because someone wants to use it regularly." Xander's voice sounded grim, and he was staring accusingly at Danielle.

"Yes, you're right," she said calmly, removing the pieces she was wearing and placing them in a velvet bag. "But there's no need to look at me like that. My mother hasn't been using it for what you're imagining because those earrings don't allow you to control someone else. They just allow you to alter your appearance—a useful ability in my mother's line of work."

"They can make you look different!" I stared at her. "Are you sure?"

She nodded. "Of course I'm sure. Mother never lets me touch anything in that section of her box, but she explained it all to me last year."

"Then we were completely wrong about what Eulalie has been looking for," I said. "I should have realized that she can't use her current disguise enchantment as queen. It's designed to make people overlook and forget her, and once she's claimed the throne, she'll want everyone looking at her. But they'll never accept her as queen if they see her actual skin—especially since it's so much like her brother's was. She needs a new appearance —a queenly appearance. One that will stay the same all the time."

"Where is this jewelry box?" Xander asked Danielle.

"In my mother's chambers," she said.

"And your mother is currently out of the city." I took her arm. "You need to take us there now."

The boys had picked up on the urgency in the room, abandoning their discussion of their triumph.

"Eulalie might be there right now!" Ben said with something far too much like relish. "We should all go."

I didn't like his tone, but I wasn't going to stop to argue with him. We needed to find those earrings as quickly as possible.

Andrew charged out of the room first, and we all streamed behind him, moving as quickly through the palace as we could given the heavy traffic in the corridors. Servants seemed to be everywhere, preparing for the coming festivities.

Protests followed our swift progress, but we ignored them, focused on our goal. When we reached the right section of the palace, Danielle thrust her way ahead of the boys and was the first at her mother's door.

She pulled it open and led the way inside, Xander only a step behind. He had drawn his sword in anticipation, but the suite of rooms was empty.

Danielle moved straight to her mother's dressing room and produced a key from her pocket which she used to open a locked drawer. She drew out a heavy box and placed it on top of the dresser.

We all tried to crowd in behind her for a look, shoving against each other in our eagerness. But when she opened the box, extending out each of its sides, I could see no sign of ruby earrings. Before I could say anything, however, she ran her hands over the back in a particular pattern, making a second, hidden tray pop out of the bottom.

We leaned closer but there were still no ruby earrings. Danielle and Arabella exchanged a look, and Arabella put her finger on an empty section of green velvet.

"They were right here," she said.

We all fell back a step, even the boys looking serious now.

"Could your mother have taken them with her for the procession?" I asked, but Danielle was already shaking her head before she finished.

"It was only an overnight trip just outside the capital, and she was going as Princess Celeste, not Aurora. She won't have taken them."

"Then Eulalie already has them," Xander said slowly. "Which means she has everything she needs for her plan to take the throne."

"But how is she going to control the king and prince?" I asked. "There's a reason we thought she must be looking for something to do that."

"She must already have a way," Lori said. "Some sort of drug maybe, like that neyara stuff."

"It's nayera," Xander corrected absentmindedly, his brows knit as he considered the mess we'd made of everything.

A horrible thought occurred to me. If she waited until the king had passed authority to his son before enchanting them, there would be no need to keep the old king alive at all. One man would be easier to control than two. I couldn't say the thought aloud, though, not in front of the children.

"Dani," said Arabella, sounding uneasy, "we have to get going." She looked at her brother. "All four of us do. We're not dressed in our formal clothes yet, and if we're not there at the gates to welcome the procession with everyone else, we really will be in trouble."

"That's the life of a royal child," I muttered with a sigh. "Play whatever tricks you like, but don't you dare disrupt a formal event."

Danielle hesitated, looking at us. "We really do have to go. But we'll see our parents at least. We can warn them about what's going on. We'll stop the proceedings if we have to."

There was nothing we could do but agree as she closed the jewelry case and locked it away again. We followed the children out of Princess Celeste's suite, but they ran off once we reached the corridor, presumably heading for their own rooms and the very stressed maids that must be waiting there to assist them into their formal outfits.

"What do we do now?" Lori asked into the silence that followed their departure.

"We have to find Eulalie," Xander said with a return of his usual spirit. "We can't leave it to those children to save Northhelm on their own."

"We're not exactly leaving it to them alone given who their parents are," Lori said doubtfully.

"I agree with Xander," I said quickly. "We need to find Eulalie. We should split up."

Xander hesitated at that, but I glared at him. "It's a large palace, and we've lost her completely. We forgot to even ask where the handover of power is taking place. So we need to separate and search as much of the palace as we can."

He sighed. "I suppose that makes sense. Just remember we're looking only. No one should be confronting Eulalie on their own."

"Including you," I said sternly, and he nodded.

We divided up the levels of the palace and ran off in different directions. I kept to the edge of the corridor, dodging decorative plants and plinths rather than people. Everywhere I went there seemed to be activity, but nowhere did I see so much as a glimpse of leathery skin.

I was about to give up and circle back to the rooms we had

slept in—our agreed meeting place—when someone grabbed my wrist. Before I could see who it was, I was dragged through an open door into a small deserted sitting room.

I pulled my arm free as the door closed firmly behind us. Turning, my insides clenched as I saw who had attacked me.

"Eulalie," I said flatly, even while a detached part of me noticed that she wore elaborate ruby earrings I had never seen before.

"Daisy." She sounded far more surprised by my presence than I was by hers. "So you really are here. I thought I must have been dreaming when I saw you earlier. But this is much better."

"Better?" I asked, my heart speeding up until it was beating so fast I thought it might burst.

"I'm not going to ask why you disobeyed me and left the tower," she said in the tone of an indulgent parent. "It's all worked out for the best in the end. I was going to attempt to do this from afar, but I think it will be more successful with you here."

"What are you going to do?" I asked, trying not to shake.

I had lain awake so many nights, planning what I would do and say when I was finally free to stand up to her. But now that she was in front of me, it was hard to shake off years of habit.

"I'm going to remove your enchantment, of course," she said.

My thoughts stuttered to a halt. "What? You're going to remove it?"

She nodded, smiling with cold amusement. "I considered your words back in the tower, and you were quite right. The only way to ensure the success of today is to return the power I've wasted on you to the ring."

"You're...you're just going to release me," I said, too dazed to make sense of what was happening.

"That is correct." She raised the hand wearing the ring.

"I'll be free." My lips felt strangely numb.

She paused, her hand hovering in mid-air. "I don't think I can allow that." She sounded almost apologetic.

"What?" I stared at her, and my heart, which seemed to have stopped, began to beat too fast again.

"I've grown fond of you over the years," she said conversationally. "In a way, at least. You were so very compliant." She smiled but there was no true warmth in it. "But I can't possibly have you running around talking about me. There are some remarkably intelligent people in Northhelm, and I can't possibly get rid of all of them—not immediately, anyway."

I tried to make sense of what she was saying. She was going to free me only to kill me like she had her previous test subjects?

"I'm not saying I didn't learn anything from your test," she said conversationally. "It took me a full year to work out how to overcome the mistake I made regarding children."

"Only a year," I said slowly. "So my birthday never mattered. That's why you didn't care about being at the tower for it."

"Oh, did you think it was important this whole time?" She gave me a look of false sympathy. "I was merely inexperienced in triggering the enchantment when I captured you. It won't be a problem for future uses."

I considered telling her she was too late, that I had already told many people everything I knew about her and her plans. But I kept my mouth shut. I had to protect the young princes and princesses, as well as Xander and Lori.

At least if Eulalie removed the enchantment, they would be free. Xander's charade back in that distant market had served more than one purpose. She had no idea he was still caught up in the enchantment, let alone that he was here in Northgate with me.

The weak, trembling feeling of shock left me, replaced with a steady resolve. Eulalie might manage to kill me, but I would go down fighting. And I would make sure she lifted the enchantment first. I would be free, if only for a moment. And I would leave the people I loved free as well.

I felt the certainty of that thought hit me. Lori was like a favorite aunt, and I had loved her for years, but I was no less sure about my feelings for Xander.

I loved him, and not just because he was the one who had turned up to rescue me. I loved him because he included me but also everyone else. Because he was a royal, but he also cared about everyday people. Because he was intelligent, strong, and entertaining, and he was just as willing to run straight toward trouble as I was. The fact he was a royal from a kingdom my parents would want as allies was merely the gilding on top. No matter where I had met Xander, I would have fallen for him.

If my last act in this life was protecting the two of them, it wouldn't be a waste.

I felt myself straighten, but I tried to keep my expression cowed and off-balance.

"So, are you going to lift the enchantment or not?" I didn't have to fake the greedy look I gave the ring.

"Yes, that's the first step, certainly." She looked down at the ring, running a hand across the broken surface of the gem and muttering words I couldn't catch.

Nothing happened.

She frowned and stepped toward me. I backed up instinctively, and her eyes narrowed.

"I thought you wanted it removed?"

I nodded and forced myself to stand still as she approached. When she reached for me, I remembered the first time I had met her and the subtle way she had scratched me with the ring. This time she had no need for subterfuge, openly scraping the gem of the ring across the skin of my arm.

I half expected it not to work the second time either, but a strange sucking feeling started deep inside me. My hands flew to my chest, but it wasn't something I could touch. I felt something ripping free, and a rippling sensation ran through me.

I swallowed and stared at my arms, wondering if they were truly visible to everyone again.

"Yes!" Eulalie cried, making me look toward the ring.

There was no longer any sign of a crack on its surface, and it had also lost the light-sucking quality to its darkness. Staring at it, I thought I could even glimpse a touch of blue in the depths of the gem.

Seeing it, I realized my mistake. Lori and Xander were free, but the whole of Northhelm was now at risk in their place.

I looked from the ring to Eulalie herself and got another shock. Gone was the leathery skin, the familiar face, and even the ruby earrings. In its place stood a vaguely familiar stranger.

I stared at her long enough to realize why she looked familiar. She was a more beautiful, more feminine version of Prince William.

This was the queenly appearance Eulalie had chosen. This was the earrings at work.

"Do you like it?" she asked. The glow in her eyes showed how satisfied she was with the result. "Don't I look magnificent?"

She drew a dagger from her clothes, her expression turning regretful. "I really do feel bad about this. But at least you die knowing you helped implement what will be the greatest reign Northhelm has ever known."

CHAPTER 23

$\mathcal{I}$ backed away from her, wishing I had my own weapon to draw. My legs hit a small side table, and I picked it up, wielding it in front of me like a clumsy shield.

Eulalie's mask of civility fell away. "You dare to defy me after I cared for you all these years?" she screeched. "I could have stopped bringing you supplies years ago!"

I didn't point out that she had only visited the tower when it happened to be convenient, and she had never once considered that she wasn't providing me enough regular food to sustain life. I couldn't have stayed in the tower if it wasn't for Lori and the children.

Part of me wished I hadn't stayed in the tower all those years. But another part of me was thrillingly aware, even as she brandished her knife, that I was free of the enchantment. If I had escaped her and left Northhelm years ago, I would never have been truly free.

The table was successfully keeping me out of reach of her knife, but she was between me and the door. I kept backing up, hoping I wasn't going to hit a wall.

Instead, I ran into a second table. It was a low one, and when it hit the back of my knees, my legs crumpled. I twisted as I fell, instinctively throwing away my shield so I could catch myself with my hands.

I succeeded in breaking my fall, but when I rolled onto my back, Eulalie was advancing on me with a twisted smile on her face. I scooted backward, only to collide with a sofa that trapped me in place.

Eulalie stabbed down at me with the dagger, but I whipped a cushion off the sofa, thrusting it into the air. The blade sank through the fabric and into the stuffing. Eulalie grunted in frustration, ripping the cushion from my hands and throwing both it and the knife away.

Before I could get to my feet, she leaped on me, pinning me down with her knees, while her hands wrapped around my throat. I fought, kicking and thrashing as she tightened her hold, but my movement was hampered by the various pieces of furniture hemming me in.

I really did only get one minute of freedom, I thought sadly, even as I tried to peel her hands away.

But before everything went black, the door to the sitting room burst open and someone crashed into the room.

"It felt like it was coming from in here," Xander's voice said to someone over his shoulder, and then his eyes found us, locked together on the floor.

He shouted and drew his sword in a single, fluid movement, just as Lori appeared behind him.

Eulalie reacted by letting me go, scrambling desperately away from me as she reached for her ring. She made contact with it just as Xander leaped for her, but nothing happened.

She barely evaded his blade, horror on her face as she fled to the far corner of the room and huddled against the wall. Xander paused to look at me, concern all over his face.

"Are you all right, Daisy?"

I was too busy gasping for breath to reply with words, but I did my best to nod. My response seemed to worry him since he hovered beside me, blocking Eulalie's exit but not advancing toward her.

"I should have known the two of you were still in league with each other," she spat out.

"Yes, you should have." I finally recovered my voice and struggled to my knees. From there I made it to my feet, glaring defiantly at her. "I certainly was never your ally. You didn't own me then, and you don't own me now."

She threw her head back and laughed. "You think you're all grown up and so very clever." Her words dripped with poison.

Xander took a step toward her, his face dark.

Eulalie's eyes flashed, first with fear and then with something else. She drew herself up. "I can't afford to stay and play right now, prince, but I can assure you I won't allow you to have something that belongs to me."

She thrust out the hand with the ring toward us, and Xander gave an outraged shout.

I turned to look at him, worried she had hurt him somehow. But while he looked horrified, he didn't appear to be in pain. In fact, he was looking at me as if I was the one in—

My thoughts froze, cold creeping over me.

He was looking at me as if I wasn't here.

"What have you done to Daisy?" he shouted, trying to reach for me and not even seeming to notice when his hand swerved away at the last second.

When he couldn't find any sign of me, he leaped for Eulalie instead, his anger overpowering his good sense. But he was back inside her enchantment now, and when she lifted her ring hand, he was driven back.

She stood there regarding him with a satisfied expression, her skin once again leathery and unnatural.

"Nononononononononononononono!" I couldn't seem to make my mind work well enough to form proper words. She had put the enchantment back in place. How had she done that without touching me?

Obviously she had refined the method of enchantment in more ways than one. This must have been why she had thought she could remove the previous enchantment without physical contact. But in the end the original one had been bound by the original rules—just like with my ability to see children.

Another terrible thought washed over me. I was enchanted again, but this time without Xander and without children. Even Lori was excluded this time. I was truly cut off from everyone.

"Daisy's right there," said Lori, sounding confused.

I looked toward her, desperate hope filling me. "You can see me?"

"Of course I can. Xander, she's right there."

Xander froze, but he didn't look happy. He looked like he'd suddenly understood what was happening and was about to be sick.

"An enchantment to hide one person from only one other person shouldn't drain too much power." Eulalie glanced at her ring. "I got back more than I expected."

For a moment I felt relief until I realized what she had done. I might not be back under the full enchantment, but Eulalie had cut me off from the one person who I most wanted to see me— the one who had come looking for me and included me from the moment we met.

With one spiteful gesture, she had torn Xander and me apart forever.

When Eulalie slipped out the door, Xander was still frozen with shock. Lori glanced at the retreating woman and then hurried to my side instead.

"Are you all right?" she said. "Let me see your neck."

"My neck isn't the problem," I said in a quivering voice, and she gathered me into a hug.

My tears poured onto her shoulder, sobs shaking my body.

We had been so close to being free and then everything had been ruined.

"I assume you're not hugging the air right now," Xander said in a shaky voice.

"I'm hugging Daisy, poor lamb," Lori said. "Can you really not see or hear her? Just like the old enchantment?"

He shook his head silently, staring at the space in front of Lori, although I could tell from his unfocused look that he couldn't see me.

"I'm sorry Daisy," he said. "I should have—" He faltered, obviously unable to think of what he should have done.

I couldn't think of it either. Xander had done nothing wrong. He had saved my life, and I should be grateful to be alive instead of crying like the world was ending.

I straightened, wiping away my tears. "Lori, you'll have to be our interpreter. Please thank Xander for saving me. How did you both find me?"

"She says thank you for saving her life," Lori said to Xander, making his face twist even more. "As for finding you," she continued, "we both felt the enchantment lift—the shock of our lives that was and must have been for everyone around us too."

"I don't know how, but I just knew the enchantment had been lifted from this direction," Xander said. "I followed the sensation, and it led me here."

"Thank you for coming so quickly," I said. "If you hadn't…"

"She says thank you for coming so quickly," Lori repeated before sighing. "This is going to get tiresome."

"I agree," I said firmly, determined not to fall back into despair. "Which is why we need to find a way to get Eulalie to lift the enchantment again."

"And how do you propose doing that?" Lori asked doubtfully.

"Doing what?" Xander asked.

I waited while Lori repeated my words.

"I can't see you, Daisy, but both of us can now interact

normally with other people," Xander said. "So I think the first thing we need to do is go find the royals. The adult royals, I mean."

I nodded then remembered he couldn't see me. "I agree," I said aloud and then groaned when I remembered he couldn't hear me either.

"I think we can all agree on that suggestion," Lori said. "I don't suppose you'd know where to find them?"

Xander frowned. "From the activity in the corridors, I gather the procession has arrived at the palace and been formally greeted. Now everyone will be settling into their rooms and getting changed for the coronation. I'm sure the royals will gather together before the ceremony, and I think I know the most likely place. Follow me."

We hurried through the corridors behind him. I collided with two separate people before making the mental adjustment that I had to watch where I was going for myself now.

"It's almost enough to make you miss the enchantment," Lori joked, but I just shuddered.

"Never."

Xander led us confidently to a room in the back of the palace. It was a large sitting room but not formal in style, with tall windows overlooking ordered gardens. It was easy to imagine the extended royal family gathering here when they weren't engaged in official duties.

We strode in without knocking, causing everyone already in the room to stop what they were doing and look up. As soon as they saw Xander, there was a general outcry and several people hurried toward us.

"Xander!" A man in his thirties came over and clapped him on the back. "You made it back for the coronation. William will be pleased. He was disappointed that you disappeared like that, but I tried to soften the blow for you. I don't think William ever understood the lure of adventure in quite the way us younger sons do."

He smiled broadly, and it wasn't hard to guess this was Prince Rafael, better known as Rafe, the husband of Northhelm's Princess Marie. Sure enough, a fair-haired woman strolled over and put an arm around his waist, giving Xander a rueful smile.

"It's a pleasure to meet you, Your Highness. I've heard all about you from my husband. We're pleased to have you again, of course, but we may struggle to find a room to stash you in. Half of the Four Kingdoms have descended on us for the coronation."

"A room is the least of my worries," Xander said grimly, making them both frown.

Before they could question him further, however, the door opened and another woman walked in. She had a notable family resemblance to Rafe and hurried straight over to him with a harried expression.

"I think Ferdy has almost managed to placate the guards, and their uniforms have finally stopped smoking, but I can't find our children anywhere."

Rafe laughed, but Marie's face darkened. "I'm sure they went into hiding the minute the official greeting was finished. Even Emmett is missing, and I'm told he was eating breakfast when the incident happened."

"The children are missing?" Xander asked sharply. "You mean you haven't spoken to them yet today?"

All three of the older royals looked at him blankly. "We exchanged formal greetings on the steps," Marie said cautiously, "but that's all. I didn't realize you'd met our children."

"Who are you?" Cordelia asked, clearly too frazzled from the behavior of her children on the important coronation day to manage any niceties.

"This is Prince Xander of Kuralan," Marie said, and Cordelia flushed.

Dropping into a shallow curtsy, she smiled at Xander. "My apologies. It's been a long day and it isn't even midday yet." She glanced inquiringly at me and Lori who were lurking behind Xander, her fixed smile indicating she was ready to welcome us as well.

"Daisy!" The unfamiliar voice exclaiming my name in surprise made me start and look around the rest of the room.

A third woman was approaching from the far side, her eyes focused on me. I didn't need an introduction to know her, although I had no idea how she knew me.

I had thought Danielle startlingly beautiful only because I hadn't yet met her mother. There was no doubt in my mind that the dark-haired, golden-skinned woman in front of me was Princess Celeste, also known as the great spymaster Aurora.

I dropped instinctively into a curtsy. But when I straightened, I blurted out the first words that came to mind.

"How did you know it was me?"

"I requested a portrait from your family years ago," she said, finally reaching us. "You've grown up, but you're still recognizable."

"It's an honor to meet you."

"Don't tell me you really were the girl in the tower," she said in a voice that promised trouble for the agents who had been sent north to investigate the story.

I wanted to defend them, but Xander cut across our conversation.

"Apologies if I'm interrupting you, Daisy. You might already be telling them everything. But just in case you're not, we need to find out what's happened to the children."

I could see the thoughts chasing across Celeste's face far too fast for me to follow and felt sure she had noticed the oddness of Xander's words and had theories about it. But as expected, her reply focused on the most important part.

"What reason do you have to be concerned for our children?"

"They weren't just causing trouble this morning with the

smoke," he said. "They were helping me under Princess Danielle's direction."

All four of the parents stilled at that statement before exchanging a rapid series of concerned looks.

"We were only gone for a day!" Cordelia wailed.

Celeste held up a hand to silence her. "First we need to find the children. Then we need to hear what's been happening." The line between her eyes made it clear how unhappy she was that something of magnitude had been happening in her own palace without her knowledge.

She turned and signaled to someone I hadn't noticed before. The man was lounging in one of the furthest chairs, his attention on the riot of beautiful flowers outside the window. But he must have been watching us from the corner of his eye because he responded instantly to her silent summons.

Standing, he took a moment to straighten his clothes before strolling toward us. I watched him come in astonishment, blinking as I took in the magnificent splendor of his coronation outfit. I had never seen such an elaborately dressed noble. He outshone even the princesses in wardrobe.

He took Celeste's hand and bent over it. "Nothing short of your beauty could rouse me to such heights," he drawled. "But for the gift of your smile, I would dare far greater feats. I will find and retrieve the children."

He straightened, smiled at us all, and strolled out of the room with the same unhurried air.

"I can't say he's wrong," Rafe said into the silence that followed his departure. "I've always considered wrestling Ben into submission to be a feat."

"Rafe! That's our son you're talking about!" Marie frowned at him. "And he might be in trouble right now."

"If I believed that, I wouldn't still be standing here." Rafe gave her a beguiling smile, slipping an arm around her waist. "You should give the children some credit. And remember just how hard they are to catch when they're on familiar ground."

She relented, leaning against him for a moment.

"Who was that?" I asked in a dazed voice, struggling to understand what I'd just witnessed.

Rafe and Cordelia both chuckled.

"I always forget the effect Rivers has on the unwary," Cordelia said. "He's obsessed with beauty—his own and Celeste's in particular—but he's far more intelligent than he seems."

"He also knows every noble and courtier in Arcadia, Lanover, and Northhelm," Celeste added. "And not one of those nobles takes him seriously. In short, he's one of my most valued agents."

Marie's eyes shot up, but Celeste just shrugged. "Thanks to Celine, everyone in this room already knows all about Aurora." She glanced at Lori. "You are Lori, I assume?"

Lori nodded, eyes wide, and Celeste smiled at her. "A lady-in-waiting with loyalty like yours no doubt shares all your mistress's secrets."

"Of course she does," I said fiercely. "But is that man, Rivers, really one of your agents?"

"He was Arcadian originally, but he followed me to Lanover after our first meeting. When he insisted on following me again after my marriage to William, he proved as adept at inserting himself into the Northhelmian court as he had been into the Lanoverian one. That's when I knew I had to recruit him."

"Your husband doesn't mind him following you around the kingdoms?" Lori asked.

"Of course not," Rafe said. "Rivers considers Celeste's beauty to be a gift from the godmothers—a gift not just to her but to all the kingdoms. He believes it's only natural that he should want to gaze upon their marvelous work. He's not interested in Celeste as a person."

"Not romantically interested anyway," Cordelia hurried to add. "He's proved to be very loyal to his spymaster."

"Rivers wants a queen to adore, not a woman to love," Celeste said crisply, "so the arrangement works to everyone's advantage. So since we can trust that he will uncover the children 'and deliver them here, can we please hear the story?"

Xander and I looked at Lori who held up her hands and took a step back.

"Don't both go looking at me!" she exclaimed. "Just because you can't see Daisy doesn't mean I have to tell the story. These Northhelmians can hear the both of you just fine."

"Xander should tell it," I said quickly.

"She wants you to do it," Lori repeated, making Celeste narrow her eyes.

"I suppose whatever is happening here is part of the story?" she asked.

"I'm afraid so." Xander sighed. "I'll tell it as quickly as possible, but I'd better start at the beginning, or it won't make any sense."

He outlined everything that had happened since Charli first led him to my tower. Only as he reached the end of the tale did a dreadful thought occur to me.

"Where are King Richard and Prince William?" I asked. "They haven't left for their private ceremony, have they?"

"I'm afraid they have," Celeste replied, looking drawn and pale, but still more beautiful than I looked on my best day.

"I'm sure they'll be all right," Cordelia murmured, putting her hand on her sister's arm. She didn't seem certain of her own words, though.

The door opened, and I was so on edge that I jumped. But it was the children who came spilling into the room. Ben was first, followed by a younger boy who had to be his brother. The twins came after with Rivers following.

"Where's Danielle?" Celeste asked sharply at the same moment as Xander spoke to Ben.

"You were supposed to tell your parents about Eulalie!"

"No," he said with none of his usual boisterous cheer. "Dani was supposed to tell them. But she disappeared as soon as the greeting was over. We've been looking for her everywhere." He turned to Celeste. "I'm sorry Aunt, but she isn't in any of her usual haunts."

Celeste's face was frozen, her back rigid. "We need to alert the guard and send out—"

"No!" I said so loudly that she went silent. "I know what's happened."

I felt sick to my stomach, but I had to push on. "Eulalie's first test subjects were adult men, and when they proved too difficult to handle, she chose a small girl for her next victim because a child would be easier to control. I should have realized that when she said that, she didn't just mean for the test. We thought Eulalie must be looking for a way to keep the king and prince under control because it seemed unlikely she could keep two grown men safely chained to her side. It occurred to me earlier that it would make her task simpler if she killed King Richard and just kept one man, but I should have taken the extra step to realize the full truth. If she kills them both, then the next heir is an eleven-year-old girl who would be far easier to control than even one grown man."

Cordelia let out a moan and sat down on the nearest chair. Marie rushed to her side and put an arm around her shoulders.

"She won't find Dani easy to control," Celeste said through her teeth.

"No," I agreed. "From what I've seen, she has no idea who she's dealing with. But she's not going to realize that until it's too late for the king and prince."

"What's Daisy saying?" Xander asked urgently and Lori began to murmur to him in the background.

"I'm afraid this is partially my fault," I said miserably. "I never properly understood Eulalie's test—not the full extent of it anyway. I always thought she didn't know who I really was, but I think at some point in the five years she must have discovered my identity. And I fooled her into thinking that even a spirited princess, if taken young enough, can be cowed into docility and compliance. So now she thinks she can do the same thing with Princess Danielle."

"We have to go after them at once!" Celeste said.

I darted forward and grabbed her arm, my desperation overriding my earlier awe. "Let Xander and me go!"

"Why would—" She cut off her own request, her mind clearly working through every angle of my plea. "You want the chance to undo your own enchantment. That's understandable but not enough on its own. But you're right on the other counts too. This isn't a battle that will be fought with swords, and you know Eulalie far better than any of us. And you're the only two immune to her enchantments."

"We are?" Xander asked, clearly bewildered.

Celeste looked to me. "That's what you were going to say, wasn't it?"

I nodded.

She looked around at the others and said only, "The earrings."

"I'm afraid I still don't understand," Lori said, so Celeste continued.

"When Daisy was under the enchantment, she saw Eulalie's true face and she was wearing my stolen earrings. When the enchantment was lifted, she saw only the earring's facade. When the enchantment was renewed, she saw her true face again. Anyone connected to Eulalie by the ring's enchantment—this bubble that Xander spoke of—is immune to the effects of any other objects she wields. Plus, if they arrive after she casts the enchantment on my husband and daughter, they will still be able to see and speak to them. Eulalie made a fatal mistake when she reconnected Daisy and Xander to herself and her ring. So that means they're the two with the best chance of stopping her."

We all stood in silence, absorbing her words. She looked pointedly at me and then Xander.

"So go!" she exclaimed. "Quickly!"

CHAPTER 24

We lurched into movement, turning toward the door.

"I'll show you the way." She picked up her heavy, formal skirts and sprinted out into the corridor.

We followed, and I was soon panting. Celeste was clearly in far better shape than she appeared.

I expected us to be heading to the throne room or somewhere else equally important, but Celeste led us outside of the palace altogether. She slowed her pace considerably once we were free of the building, leading us through a thicket of trees.

"Thankfully, they will have taken a long time to get here," she said. "Earlier, this whole space was full of cheering crowds come to see them make their way to the pavilion. It will be full of crowds again to see them emerge, but this whole area is supposed to be clear for the actual ceremony save for a few guards."

"So we need to make sure no one sees us go in or out," Xander said, picking up on the significance of her words. "Or it could jeopardize the validity of the handover."

She nodded. "Which is another reason I can't go myself. Marie, Rafe, Cordelia, Ferdy, and the children are expected to lead the crowds' return, along with my mother-in-law and me, of course. If any of us are missing, there will be questions. And as a princess of Lanover, I am particularly suspect. I will be their queen, but not until they have assured themselves that the jewel glows around my husband's neck."

"We understand," Xander said. "We'll deal with the situation and get ourselves, Eulalie, and Danielle out as discreetly as possible."

A guard appeared in front of us, and both Xander and I stopped. Celeste kept going, however, merely nodding to the man and beckoning for us to continue.

"One of your agents?" I guessed.

She gave me a tight smile. "Let's just say that he can be trusted not to breathe a word of us having been here."

"I'm glad you work for the good of all the kingdoms these days," I said in an awed tone.

She smiled again. "Just don't let a Northhelmian hear you say that. When there aren't any issues of succession in the mix, they're very proud to have me as their own."

A small building appeared on the other side of the trees, presumably the pavilion she had mentioned. It looked like a gazebo with enclosed sides, and I guessed there was only one room inside.

Two guards stood at attention in front of the closed door, and Celeste led us back into the trees so we could circle around to the rear. Windows ringed the building, so it was easy to locate one out of sight of the door guards.

We all crouched beneath the chosen window, and Celeste carefully raised her head high enough to look inside.

"What can you see?" I asked. "Is Eulalie in there?"

"As far as I can see, she's the only one in there." Celeste didn't have to say more for us to know what that meant. Eulalie had already enchanted the others.

But had she done anything else to them?

"I'm trusting you," Celeste said fiercely. "Save my daughter and my husband. No matter what it takes."

"We will," Xander said equally firmly.

Celeste nodded once, stood up, and punched her fist through the glass of the window. She had wrapped her fist in her thick skirts, which muffled the sound, but it was still a shock. By the time I had absorbed what was happening, she had unlatched it from the inside and pushed it open.

I stood as well, and she immediately offered me her cupped hands. When I dazedly put my foot into them, she catapulted me through the window head first.

I retained just enough sense to roll on landing, springing to my feet just as Xander bounded through the window and landed behind me.

"The broken window might look suspicious later," he said in a cheerful tone.

"I suspect she'll have her guard cover that up," I replied before remembering with yet another pang that he couldn't hear me.

"You again!" Eulalie screeched, her eyes on Xander.

"Yes, it's me." He smiled even more broadly before looking around the room.

Celeste might have seen Eulalie standing alone, but just as she'd predicted, I could see three other people. The king and prince had both been bound and were sitting together against one of the walls. It was easy to see how she had subdued them given she held a dagger in one hand and Danielle in the other.

Danielle's eyes were fixed on us with a hopeful expression while the two men had no room on their faces for anything but anger.

"Your Majesty, Prince William." Xander bowed in their direction. "I apologize for leaving so abruptly, but you have now experienced the enchantment I fell afoul of."

"You claim no one can see or hear us," King Richard spat at Eulalie, "but neither of them are having any trouble."

"I'm afraid she's telling the truth," I said. "We can see you because we're inside the enchantment with you. I've been inside it for five years in fact. I'm Princess Daisy of Trione."

"So you found her!" William said to Xander. "I'll confess I didn't think you would."

"Never doubt the godmothers," Xander said. "No matter how cryptic their guidance. Their words gave me confidence I would find her—even though my own brother didn't believe. I'm going to enjoy telling Xavier I interpreted their words correctly."

Eulalie screamed again, the strident sound cutting through the conversation. She was enraged by Xander's attitude, as he had no doubt intended.

"Don't think your presence here makes any difference," she hissed. "There will merely be four to die in this pavilion instead of two. And no one shall ever find your bodies. Northhelm cannot claim I killed their king when they saw him enter this pavilion with their own eyes, just as they will see me emerge with no sign of any bodies left behind. They will have to believe that the High King intervened directly as was promised with this jewel as seal."

She stroked the glowing sapphire that now lay around her own neck.

"She is not the true ruler," King Richard said when he saw our eyes linger on the gem. "It glows only because my son and granddaughter are so close."

"Yes, we know how it works." Xander sounded a little guilty. "And we apologize for disturbing your sleep. But we really needed to know if it would glow when not around your neck."

"What?" the king asked, clearly confused.

"Let's save our confessions for another time," I said. "Eulalie, you must realize that my presence here shows you will never be able to control Danielle for any length of time. Your plan can't possibly work."

Her eyes narrowed. "I didn't wait four hundred years to fail now!"

"You've really waited four hundred years for a plan this flawed?" I asked skeptically. "Are you sure you haven't been waiting only fifteen years since your brother died and you got your hands on the godmother objects he collected—the ones he was much better at controlling than you?"

"Don't you speak of him!" she snapped. "Those beasts killed him!"

"He brought his death upon himself," the king said coldly.

To my surprise, Eulalie seemed to accept that statement. "He was always interfering and unpleasant," she said. "So I'm not surprised."

I stared at her, shocked by her complete turnaround.

"He was jealous of me is the truth of it," she said. "He knew all three of my brothers liked me best, and I always preferred my middle brother. I think that's why Rumpel chose to freeze me."

"To do what?" I asked.

"It was one of the first godmother objects he found," she explained, seeming to warm to the topic now that she had started her reminiscences. "He froze me under a sleeping spell so that I slept for four hundred years. He promised he would wake me once he'd wrested the kingdom back from our younger brother, but I woke cold and alone to a strange world I no longer recognized."

For a brief moment, I felt a pang of sympathy for the young Eulalie, and then I remembered what she was currently trying to do. At least I now knew why she had such an unstable mental state, and why it had only been deteriorating as the years passed. It couldn't possibly have been healthy to be under an enchantment for centuries with her life unnaturally prolonged. Was that the real reason for her strange skin?

"So now it is up to me to reclaim Northhelm from our

younger brother's descendants." She shook Danielle. "That makes me a very great aunt of yours. You should show more respect."

"Don't touch my daughter," William said in a dangerous voice.

"It's time I dealt with you." Eulalie raised her knife and stalked toward William, dragging Danielle with her.

I prepared to throw myself between them, but Danielle planted her feet, pulling back on Eulalie so hard that she stopped just short of the men and stared back at the girl. Danielle gave her a chilling stare.

"If you harm my father or grandfather, you will never have a moment's peace. I will hound you every second until I break free and prove your fraud."

Eulalie scoffed. "Do you think I need these two to act in the role of hostages? Hardly. I'm going to be queen, remember? I'll have control over every person you care about and will be able to keep you as compliant as I need."

Danielle didn't flinch. "My mother is a princess of Lanover, so if you want to keep Northhelm intact, you can't touch her. She's also more intelligent than anyone you've ever met and has an army of agents more loyal to her than any crown. I trust her to keep everyone I love safe—even if you're queen. At least, everyone she can see. These two are mine to save."

Her impassioned words were somehow more impactful because of her young age, and I could see Eulalie falter. Her gaze shifted sideways and landed on me and Xander.

"You two, at least, aren't needed," she said, latching onto a different outlet for her anger.

But Xander drew his sword and stepped in front of me—or at least where he thought I was. He was wrong about my position, but it was a sweet gesture. Eulalie glared at the sword, tightening her hold on Danielle until the girl winced.

Apparently she didn't think our bond with the Northhelmian was strong enough to use her as leverage, though, because she put down the dagger and withdrew a small mirror from her pocket in its place.

"Whatever that is, don't waste your time," I said in as scathing a tone as I could manage. "You bound us to you again, and I can see your true, four-hundred-year-old face despite those baubles you've got on your ears. Whatever that object is won't work against us either. The only thing that will work is the ring, but I'm guessing you've drained that dry now that you have five of us bound in your enchantment."

"What?" She held the mirror toward us, shaking it when nothing happened. "That can't be right!"

"You've tied us to you and to your other victims," I taunted. "We can see your true self as well as them, and we can talk to anyone we want. Soon all of Northhelm will know the truth about you."

Danielle chimed in, shaking her head. "How foolish to have them in the same enchantment as us. I can see you didn't think that through."

She was fighting for us to be freed, even though it wouldn't help her or her family.

"Be quiet!" Eulalie panted, clearly driven close to the edge by the disruption of all her plans. "I can fix this," she muttered. "I can still fix this."

I was looking at Danielle as Eulalie stretched her ring toward me, and I was hit with a memory—one even Eulalie didn't know about. When she had extended my enchantment to cover my tower, Lori had been touching it and had been sucked into the enchantment along with the building. And when Xander managed to connect with my lips, he had been sucked in too.

What if it worked the same way in the other direction as well?

As Eulalie began to murmur under her breath, I threw myself forward, stretching my arms as far as they would reach. I fell heavily on the ground, outstretched, but as Eulalie said the final word, I had one foot hooked around Danielle's ankle, and one hand resting on both the king and the prince.

I scrunched my eyes shut as the same sucking sensation hit my insides, followed by the tearing feeling and the ripple that ran from my fingers to my toes. For two breaths I kept my eyes closed, not ready to see if my desperate ploy had worked. Then I opened them.

Eulalie had become a beautiful, queenly figure, but the expression on her face was one of horror as she gazed at the five people around her. People I could still see. Contact with me had been enough. When she lifted the enchantment off me and Xander, she had lifted it off them as well.

I turned my head to look at Xander and found him staring straight at me, wonder in his eyes. He didn't even seem to have noticed the others.

Eulalie recovered from her shock quickly, however, and once again thrust out her hand.

"The ring!" Danielle cried, transforming suddenly into a hissing, spitting, clawing wildcat.

Caught totally off guard, Eulalie's words faltered and her hand dropped as she attempted to control the girl she was holding.

The king cheered his granddaughter on, while Prince William repeated her words, his eyes on me. "The ring! The ring!"

I let them go and scrambled inelegantly to my feet. There was no one in the enchantment now, which meant this was our chance to destroy the ring forever without killing anyone in the process.

I rushed forward and tried to grasp Eulalie's hand. She realized my intention and pulled it away from me, letting go of Danielle at the same time.

But the tables had now turned. Instead of fighting to free herself, Danielle latched onto Eulalie and wouldn't let go, her dead weight anchoring one of her arms.

As Eulalie tried to pry the girl free with the other hand, I grabbed her arm. Pulling with all my strength, I stretched it away from Danielle.

"Xander!" I screamed. "Xander!"

He rushed forward and seized Eulalie's forcibly outstretched hand. For a second he struggled with her writhing fingers and then he managed to pull the ring free.

He fell back panting as Eulalie began to convulse. Danielle and I both dropped her and backed away. We watched with wide eyes as she gave one final shake and fell to the ground.

William, having finally worked free of his bonds, leaped to his feet. Rushing over, he turned his daughter's face into his jacket, shielding her from the sight of what had become of Eulalie.

We were all silent for a long moment, although I could see Danielle's shoulders shaking as she quietly sobbed—a natural reaction to the release of tension.

Xander was the first to move, walking carefully forward and retrieving the earrings that could no longer disguise the reality of the dead woman. He also picked up the jewel of the true ruler, its blue still glowing brightly. I gulped and turned away from the little that was left of a person after four hundred years. I didn't have my father there to shield my eyes, so I would have to do it myself.

Xander crossed to William and handed him the earrings and the jewel. He took them with a quiet thanks and glanced at his father who was still bound.

"I'll do it," Xander said equally quietly and hurried over to help the king extract himself from the ropes.

As soon as he was free, I addressed him.

"Did you complete the ceremony before Eulalie arrived, Your Majesty?"

"She was waiting in here with Danielle when we arrived," King Richard said. "We couldn't see Danielle at first, but she did something with that ring, and then we could."

"She had us complete the handover before we tied ourselves up," William said. "It didn't happen in the way it was supposed to, but this is mine now." He put the chain around his neck, the sapphire settling against his chest where it glowed a steady blue.

"She was trying to get Father to transfer his authority to me so she could kill them both when you arrived," Danielle said, apparently having recovered herself, although I noticed she was carefully not looking at what remained of Eulalie's body.

"The crowds are coming back," I said. "I can hear a distant roar which must be them."

"That means we need to get out of here," Xander said urgently. "And we need to get Danielle to the front of that crowd to join her mother."

"Quick, out the window." I hurried back over to it, holding it high as William easily lifted his daughter through the opening.

"We'll be together again in just a moment," he promised her.

"Father, I'm fine," she said in her usual voice.

I was about to hoist myself through the window when Xander's hands wrapped around my waist, easily boosting me high enough to get through. Once I was standing outside, I turned back to help him, but he had already climbed through on his own.

William closed the window frame, carefully avoiding the broken glass, and turned toward the door.

"Come on." Xander took my hand and pulled on it. "We have to go."

We snuck back through the trees, the same way we had come with Celeste, but with Danielle at our side this time.

"I'll join the crowd from here," she said, "and work my way through to the front. That way it will look like I'm joining them from the palace. I may be the crown princess now, but I'm still young enough that they'll forgive me being a little late. Better that than have anyone guess I was inside the pavilion."

She had barely finished speaking when she darted out and

plunged into the middle of a group of people walking past the trees. I took one step to join her, but Xander stood firm and still, pulling back on my hand.

I stopped and looked back at him. One glimpse of his blazing eyes, and I forgot all about the crowd only feet away beyond the trees.

I let him pull me gently back toward him, not stopping until there was only a hair's breadth of space between us. My breath hitched as I looked up at him.

"I can see you again." His voice was full of wonder.

I smiled, feeling warmth creep up my cheeks, and angled my face toward him.

Somehow the light in his eyes grew even stronger, burning now as it reached out to consume me too.

"Are you sure?" he whispered in low, teasing tones, as his arms came around me and he pulled me against him. "I wouldn't want to surprise you."

I shivered. "I'm sure."

He lowered his head toward mine, pausing just before our lips made contact. "You have no idea how I've been holding myself back."

I reached my arms around his neck, pushing onto tiptoes and staring into his eyes. "If you don't hurry up and stop talking, I think I'll know exactly how hard it was."

He chuckled, the rumble in his chest flowing into me as he finally pressed his lips against mine in the most delicious second first kiss I could have imagined.

CHAPTER 25

$\mathcal{B}$y the time we joined the festivities, the crowds were already flowing back toward the main palace. William was leading them, the jewel glowing brightly on his chest and his wife and daughter at his side.

I'd managed a glimpse of the new queen's face, but I was probably imagining the joy and relief in her eyes. The spymaster Aurora was an expert at hiding her true feelings.

I wasn't attempting to hide my own overflowing joy, however. I wasn't even bothered by the crowds pressing me on all sides, the total opposite to my years of isolation. After everything that had just happened with Eulalie, I reveled in the contact and the new future it represented. I had spent so long cut off from the world, but now I was swept into the center of it, caught up in the celebrations of the Northhelmian people.

And at my side was the man who had rescued me. Not from the tower—I had climbed out of that myself—but he had reached into my solitary life and made me part of a team. And I never wanted to lose that connection.

Xander's hand rested in mine, solid and warm—like a promise that he intended to hold on just as hard as I did. He turned his head and smiled down at me, his eyes twinkling, and the rest of the people faded away.

A strident neighing brought me straight back to reality, though. I rose onto my toes to peer over the crowd.

"Is that a horse?" I asked. "Over there by the doors to the throne room?"

A strange sense of familiarity gripped me at the sight of the animal's golden coat. He appeared to have a strange, pale-colored saddle, but he had no bridle or halter, and there didn't seem to be a groom in attendance.

A fanciful thought drifted through my head. It was like he was here as a guest instead of someone's mount. And he was accompanied, of all things, by a large cat. The ginger feline sat upright on the horse's back, surveying the crowd with an expression I could only describe as displeased.

"Where?" Xander asked, following the direction of my pointing finger. As soon as his eyes reached the animals, he stopped, pulling me to a halt with him and forcing the people behind us to dodge out of the way with muttered complaints.

"Puss!" he exclaimed and started moving again, this time tugging me forward with him.

"Puss?" I cried. "You mean Kali's cat? The one from my dreams?"

Xander snorted. "I wouldn't let him catch you suggesting he's a pet. He has strong feelings on the matter."

I grinned, caught up in the magic of finding myself in the world of my dreams. While asleep, I had watched the adventures of a talking cat, and now I was about to actually meet him.

"But what's he doing here?" I asked. "And with Arvin too." I had finally remembered why the horse looked familiar. "Why is Giselle's horse in Northgate?"

"That's Arvin?" Xander increased our pace. "I've heard a lot about him."

"You have?" I gave him a sideways look. "Why have you heard a lot about Giselle's horse?"

Xander grinned. "I understand he has an interesting personality."

I chuckled as we finally reached the two animals, remembering some of Arvin's strange behavior back when I'd traveled with Giselle. "I suppose you could say that. I'd forgotten what he looked like but seeing him brings it all rushing back."

So the missing girl really is here, Arvin whinnied. *I was starting to think it was yet another elaborate scheme from those gray-haired women.*

I nearly tripped over my feet, and I wasn't even moving.

"Did he just talk?" I whispered, afraid all the extreme emotions of the last few hours had affected my brain.

Of course I talked. Did you think I was a regular horse? Must I constantly remind people that I come from the Palace of Light?

His nostrils flared, and the mound on his back began to move. The cat leaped down with an outraged growl, and the remaining dregs of the crowd called out in alarm, scattering away from us as large wings unfurled from Arvin's sides.

I gasped, my hand jumping to my mouth as I stared at his wings. He had always been an unusual horse, but this transformation was a lot to absorb. How had I ever taken the folded wings to be a saddle? He must be able to fold them unnaturally small, but even so…

"So it's true!" Xander sounded delighted. "I can't wait to tell Xavier that I've seen you for myself."

He turned to the cat. "It's a pleasure to meet you again, Sir Puss." He gave the animal a half bow.

The cat looked up at him with no obvious lightening of his displeasure. *One of you really was enough, you know. Two can only be considered a surfeit.*

Xander just laughed, not appearing offended at this insult to him and his twin.

Sometimes one is a surfeit, Arvin whinnied in a tone that was somehow dark. *Take Celine, for instance.*

"Is she here?" I asked, struck by an excited thought. "Did she come to see her sister crowned queen?"

Thankfully not, Arvin neighed. *There are far too many of you as it is.*

"Too many of us?" Xander's eyes jumped from Arvin to Puss. "When you said two was surfeit, did you mean that Xavier is here now?"

Of course he's here, Arvin said in long-suffering tones. *Those* women *have been keeping themselves busy gathering anyone they could lay their hands on. Which would be well and good if they hadn't insisted that we attend as well. As if creatures from the Palace of Light are worried about human coronations!*

"Xavier's here in Northgate!" Xander looked so elated by the idea that I couldn't help smiling too.

"What about Daisy's family?" Xander asked, making me forget all about the possibility of meeting his beloved twin.

"My family?" I whispered. "Is that possible? They have no particular tie to Northhelm, do they?"

Don't you have ears? Puss asked. *Arvin said it was the godmothers' doing. They love big reunions.* He sounded contemptuous of such sentimentality. *Of course they would make sure your family came.*

My knees nearly buckled, and Xander slipped a hand around my waist, steadying me.

"Are you all right?" he asked.

"My mother and father are here right now." I repeated the words in a daze, trying to take them in. "I'm going to get to see them now instead of waiting for weeks while we travel—"

"Come on!" Xander slid his hand down my arm to take my hand, his smile lighting up his face. "Let's go find them."

We turned for the doors together as Arvin folded his wings back into position and Puss leaped up to take his original place.

And the godmothers claim I *lack gratitude,* the horse grumbled as we sped away.

I threw an apology over my shoulder, but the two had already lost interest in us. At any other time, I would have been utterly fascinated by them both, but all I could think about was my family. Had Teddy and Millie come too? What about Isla and Ray?

My feverish anticipation fizzled as we reached the doors and discovered them blocked by a solid mass of people. Desperate, I tried to push through, but the crowd was packed too densely to allow any movement.

Xander pulled me back with an apologetic expression. "It looks like they've allowed the general public to fill up the standing room behind the rows of seats, and they've packed in as many people as possible. Our families will all have seats of honor near the front of the room, so I don't think we'll be able to get to them until the ceremony is over."

Disappointment burned through me, but I forced myself to smile. I had expected to have to wait for much longer than the length of one coronation.

Other members of the crowd had also failed to secure a place inside, and they were slowly spreading across the palace grounds, waiting for the celebrations that would occur once the coronation was complete.

I stayed by the door, though, too wound up to move away or wait patiently. Faint sounds of the ceremony drifted above the crowd, and I caught the deep tones of the new king uttering the traditional words of commitment and respect for the crown and kingdom.

I could picture him up there with his eyes glowing as blue as his jewel, his expression earnest and steadfast. And crowned at his side would be someone who shone even more brightly. The populace might not know Celeste's hidden identity, but they recognized her beauty and intelligence. Northhelm couldn't be in better hands.

The cheering that shook the room told us when it was all over. Xander pulled me against the wall beside the doors just in time to avoid being flattened by the wave of people pouring outside.

I was almost dancing with anticipation as I watched them stream past, chattering and laughing with bright, eager faces. The crowd seemed to thin, and I tried to pull away, but Xander held me back.

Sure enough, there was another surge of people, many of these ones dressed in more elaborate outfits, dotted with jewels.

As soon as their numbers diminished, Xander let me go, and I plunged into the river of people, moving upstream. People grumbled as we pushed our way through, but I ignored them.

My eyes scanned the remaining clumps of people scattered among the chairs while my feet carried me toward the front of the room. William and Celeste were still there, with Danielle beside them and their family clustered around.

But my eyes skipped on to another group of people who stood close to the Northhelmian royals. I gasped and sped up. My family.

I had nearly reached them when someone grabbed my arm, pulling me to an abrupt stop. I turned, ready to growl at Xander, but instead I found myself facing a grim guard in Northhelmian livery.

"The public celebrations will be held in the palace grounds," he told me in warning tones.

I glanced down at my outfit, remembering I had chosen it to blend in with the general populace. I didn't look like I belonged here.

"Let her go." Xander's voice held just as much warning as the guard's had done, and the man stiffened in response.

I gave Xander a quelling look. There was no need to threaten a man who was just doing his job.

"Actually," I said in my brightest tone, "I'm—"

"Princess Daisy." The compelling voice cut across the room, making the guard come instantly to attention.

He took one look at his new queen's face and dropped my arm, bowing low in her direction. I turned as well, intending to give her my thanks and instead was engulfed by a mob of people.

"Daisy!"

"Daisy!"

"Daisy!"

Their glad cries overlapped as they all tried to reach me at once, their arms stretching toward me from all directions. I had no idea who I was hugging at any particular moment, passed from arm to arm in a whirl of beautiful, familiar faces.

Tears were streaming down my cheeks, and I didn't seem to be the only one crying, given the sniffles and the damp cheeks being pressed against mine. They had all come. My mother and father. Teddy and Isla. Millie and Ray.

Even two small bundles of squirming limbs and cute button noses whose chuckles suggested they found the group hug a delightful experience. I had dreamed about a new niece and nephew, and fresh tears ran down my cheeks to know they had been more than a figment of my imagination.

The family had grown without me, but they clearly hadn't forgotten me. My heart swelled so full, I thought it might burst under the pressure.

When the chaos subsided somewhat, I found myself wrapped in my mother's firm embrace. The seconds ticked by, but she didn't lighten her hold, apparently unconcerned about her dignity as a queen.

I hugged her back until my eyes lifted above her shoulder and I saw another familiar figure hanging back from the group.

"Lori!" I pulled away from my mother's embrace, but kept hold of her arm. "Did you see Lori, Mother?"

"Yes, we met before the ceremony," Lori said calmly. "Her Majesty was most gracious."

"Our family will always be indebted to you," my mother said, sounding like she was going to start crying again.

"I promised her lots of gold," I said cheerfully, provoking a scandalized response from Millie.

"That sort of loyalty can't be bought with mere gold, Daisy! I hope you've been treating her with proper gratitude."

I grinned. "I'm not thirteen anymore, Millie."

Teddy rolled his eyes. "You don't seem to have changed all that much. She's teasing you, Mill."

Millie gave a soft sigh. "Of course she's teasing. I should have known that." She looked at me. "I'm glad you're still you, Daisy. But we've missed so many years. You have to tell us everything that happened, but even so, it isn't the same as being there."

"I've missed a lot too." I looked at the two toddlers, one held in Isla's arms and one in Ray's. "So tell me the most important thing right now—do my niece and nephew get mer-tails when they go in the water? And if they do, why am I the only one to have missed out?"

They all laughed, their faces displaying their relief at finding me still a familiar version of myself.

I sensed Xander behind me and turned to smile at him. He stepped up to join me in response.

"Mother, Father, everyone, allow me to introduce Prince Xander of Kuralan. He's the one who rescued me."

Xander swept into his most elaborate bow.

"Actually, Daisy rescued herself. I was merely permitted to assist."

Teddy snorted. "That sounds right."

"It's a very great pleasure to meet you all," Xander said. "Daisy has told me a lot about you. She missed you all greatly."

I smiled at him, overwhelmed with love and gratitude to have him standing by my side.

"Prince Xander," my father said in a thoughtful tone, his eyes flitting between my face and Xander's. "So you're the youngest of Sultan Khalil's sons. We were most grateful when we heard you were searching for our daughter, and you must allow us to offer our deepest thanks for the assistance you've rendered her. Once the coronation celebrations are complete, we'll have a proper discussion of terms and settlements. I'm confident we can come to an arrangement that will satisfy your father."

I blinked, trying to understand what he was talking about.

Xander, however, seemed to understand immediately. He stiffened for a brief moment before a smile spread over his face.

"I'm quite sure we can come to a mutually agreeable arrangement." His hand found mine, squeezing it.

I blinked, looking from him to my father and finally to my mother's beaming face. Her focus was on Xander and my entwined hands and seeing her made it all finally click into place.

My father was talking about an alliance—a *marriage* alliance. My pulse raced. He was talking as if a marriage between Xander and me was a forgone conclusion.

I had no objection to the idea. I loved Xander. I would love nothing more than to remain a team with him for the rest of my life. And Xander had kissed me. But he hadn't yet said he loved me. He hadn't talked of marriage.

My family was getting completely ahead of themselves.

I opened my mouth to protest, but Xander squeezed my hand again, warning me to stay silent. I complied, but concern filled me as I gazed up at him. Was he being pressured into agreeing because of my father's rank? Did he think he owed me something after what we'd been through together?

My niece began to wail, distracting the family's attention, and Xander stepped back, gently drawing me with him.

"I'm sorry," I whispered in a rushed undertone. "You don't have to agree—"

"Daisy." He silenced me with my name, looking down at me with eyes full of warmth and amusement. "My father made it clear a long time ago that he expects me to marry to the advantage of Kuralan. Did your family never say similar things?"

"Not outright, perhaps, but…"

He nodded. "We're younger royals. I'm sure we both grew up knowing what was expected of us. And if I'd known there was a princess like you across the ocean, I wouldn't even have minded."

I held my breath. "Do you really mean it? Are you sure? I don't want you to feel pressured."

"Daisy." He turned fully toward me, cupping my face with his hands. "I didn't want to rush you, but I'm certainly not going to fight our families' expectations on this. I'm far too grateful to have met someone so advantageous to Kuralan who also happens to be so very lovable."

I went pink, blood rushing to my cheeks at the light in his eyes and the warmth in his smile.

"I love you too," I whispered. "And I will happily marry you as soon as our families can arrange it. I'll even move to Kuralan—just as long as I can visit Trione first."

"We can visit for as long as you'd like," he promised.

His face moved toward mine, as if he couldn't resist stealing a kiss, despite our surroundings. But before our lips made contact, a new voice shouted my name.

I jerked back in time to be swept up into yet another hug. I threw an apologetic look at Xander, but he looked amused rather than offended, so I leaned into the embrace.

When the young woman pulled back, I beamed at her. "Giselle!"

She shook her head, one hand resting on her bulging belly. "You have no idea how worried I was when no one could find you! Are you really all right? If it wasn't for the godmothers' reassurances…"

"Yes, about those." I peered around the nearly empty room. "Are any of them in attendance? Because I have a bone to pick with them."

"I haven't seen any yet," she said sounding half amused and half concerned. "But there are some other people who will be just as glad to see you as I am."

She waved at a huddle of people behind her, and two other young women stepped forward.

"Cassie!" I cried. "And Daria! I heard you went back across the ocean."

"I did," she said in her usual calm way, although something about her had changed.

I decided it was the air of confidence and contentment that hung about her. It suited her.

"The godmothers were very insistent we all come," Cassie said with a smile. "I live across the Great Desert these days, but I can't say I minded the excuse to visit Northhelm." Her eyes traveled to Celeste, reminding me that Cassie had been even more fascinated by the idea of the spymaster than I had been.

"Cassie is a spymaster herself now," Xander murmured in my ear, making my eyes widen.

"I hope you aren't spilling all our secrets, Xander," Cassie said with a look of amused reproof.

"I don't have any secrets from Daisy." He slid his arms around me from behind.

All three girls exclaimed in delight.

"I see we're going to steal you across the desert," Cassie said in a satisfied tone.

"I knew it all along," a new arrival said. "There had to be a reason the godmothers kept giving their clues to you, Xander."

I turned to see a familiar face, although I'd never met the dark-haired young woman before.

"Kali!" I cried, delighted.

She blinked, clearly taken aback. "You're obviously Daisy, but how do you know me? Don't try to tell me Xander carries portraits of all his family around with him because I won't believe you."

A laugh from behind her drew my eyes to another new face. This one made me suck in my breath. It was Xander. But it also wasn't.

"Xav!" Xander released me to go to his brother.

I watched their enthusiastic greeting with amazement. They really did look alike, but there was an indefinable something that made me certain I would never mistake Xavier for Xander, or vice versa.

"But really," Kali said, not to be deterred, "how do you know me?"

"Actually," I said, "the godmothers didn't entirely abandon me." I explained about the dreams, and they all wanted to know which parts of their stories I'd seen.

"You even dreamed of me?" asked another young woman who had been lingering at the back of the group. She had large eyes and an elegant air, and I would have recognized her anywhere.

"Of course, Zaria! I loved your adventures. Is Rek here?"

She nodded, clearly bemused. "How unexpected. He's over there congratulating the new king."

She pointed to where a tall, handsome man was conducting a serious conversation with King William.

"Good to see Rek is as responsible as ever," Xander said with a grin.

"He's been attempting to reform me," Xavier said with an exaggerated shudder, his eyes gleaming. "He seems to think I might be a weaker target alone."

"That shows how much he knows," Kali muttered under her breath, but the look she threw him was full of love.

"Please tell me you're coming home to rescue me soon,"

Xavier said, and I could sense a serious vein beneath his light-hearted air.

Xander shot me a quick look. "We're going to Trione first. Daisy hasn't been back in five years. But that will just be a visit. I'll be bringing her home to Kuralan after that." He looked at Kali and Zaria. "You'll have to help her learn everything she needs to know about our kingdom."

"Of course," Kali said promptly, looping her arm through mine. She grinned at me. "You couldn't ask for better sisters-in-law than Zaria and me. I promise!"

I smiled back at her, delighted. These girls didn't know me like I knew them, but they were willing to embrace me all the same. I had longed to be their friends for real, and now I would be.

"You'll be very welcome there, Daisy," Zaria said with a welcoming smile of her own. "And don't listen to Xander. The rest of us aren't half as dull as he paints us."

"I would never believe you were in the least dull," I assured her. I looked around at the cluster of women. "I can't believe we're all here! In one place!" A sudden thought occurred to me. "Did you all know Arvin can talk?"

Giselle and Daria both burst into laughter.

"Oh, we are all too aware," Giselle said mopping her eyes. "I suppose that means he's arrived?"

"Could you always hear him?" I asked her. "You did used to act oddly around him."

"The wretched creature acted like I was the only one he could talk to," she said. "And then suddenly he develops the ability to talk to everyone." She shook her head.

"And wings," Daria added. "He also got those."

"I saw that too," I said, remembering my shock. "But did you really marry Percy, Daria?"

She nodded, a gentle smile on her face. "Falling in love with a prince took me by far greater surprise than it can have taken any of you. But I'm extremely happy."

She smiled across the room at a dark-haired man who was still recognizable as the boy who had once trailed around behind the older royal children like I did. From the way he smiled back at Daria, he was just as happy with his choice as she was.

"And you live here now, Giselle?" I asked. "Well, not here in Northhelm, but here in the Four Kingdoms? In Arcadia? And you're having a baby? Congratulations!"

She rubbed her belly again. "Yes to the baby part, but I'm actually based back home in Eldon now."

My brow furrowed. "Didn't you marry an Arcadian?"

She chuckled. "It's a little complicated. I met Philip in Arcadia, but he's actually a noble from Lanover. And we decided to base ourselves in Eldon."

"Celine must be happy about that," I said, and she nodded.

"I really am relieved you're safe," she said. "And your maid too." She nodded a greeting at Lori who still stood a short distance away.

"I owe everything to Lori," I said sincerely, beckoning for her to come closer.

As she approached, Giselle glanced at Daria. "Have you seen Arvin yet?"

Daria shook her head, and I described where I had seen him. When I added that Puss had been with him, Kali joined the other two as they headed toward the outside doors.

I took the chance to pull Lori aside. "Did you hear?" I asked in a quiet voice. "My father wants to make a marriage alliance for me with Xander."

"Congratulations," she said, as if the news was entirely to be expected—which it probably was for her.

"How long have you been expecting this?" I asked accusingly.

She shrugged. "I'm not saying it was love at first sight, but the enchantment must have recognized the potential for true love at least."

"What do you mean?" I asked.

"It let him through, didn't it? For that first kiss. I don't know if it was the enchantment itself or the work of the godmothers, but no one else ever managed to touch us, and yet it let him through."

I laughed. "I suppose you can think of it that way. If you choose to."

"Do you have another explanation?"

"I don't! And so I will choose to believe you completely." I grinned at her, thinking of all the times she was the one rejecting my wild theories.

The familiar feeling of joking with her sent a sudden worry sweeping over me. "You'll come with us to Kuralan, won't you?"

I had decided on the road that I was willing to leave my family, but it hadn't occurred to me to picture a future that didn't involve Lori busy somewhere nearby.

"That depends on what I decide to do with all my gold," she said with a totally straight face. "I might get a maid of my own and live a life of luxury from now on."

"Of course you should." Xander reappeared at my side. "In Kuralan, you'll have an army of maids to wait on you hand and foot."

I laughed. "Are you trying to bribe her to come?"

"I think we Kuralanis can match anything Trione might be able to offer," Xavier said, joining the cause.

"Well, how could I say no to an offer like that?" Lori said in a serious tone, but I caught the affectionate look she gave me.

I threw my arms around her and sniffed. "I can't believe you're teasing me over something like this!" I cried.

She patted me on the back. "Don't worry, I'll come with you. I agreed to accompany you on that delegation five years ago because I had no family in Trione. But after all these years, I suppose I got into the habit of thinking of you as my family. And

I'd rather be with family than alone in a familiar place. I'm sure I'll get used to all the sand soon enough." She said the last sentence in a way that suggested she didn't really believe it but was being polite.

Xander laughed. "Don't worry, the desert doesn't extend right up to the gates of the city."

"If you say so," she said in the same polite voice, making me laugh as well.

"I can promise you your own sand-free suite in the palace," Xander said. "My father will consider it a light price to pay for my unexpected good behavior in my choice of bride."

"We have to invite Charli to visit, too!" I exclaimed. "We should send her a message as soon as possible. Surely her parents will let her come when they learn my real identity?"

Everyone wanted to know who Charli was, including my family who had drifted over to join us. The Northhelmian royals appeared as well, and I told them all about the girl I had befriended.

When I finished my tale, Celeste pulled me aside to thank me for saving her husband and daughter. Afterward, she assured me that she would personally handle getting a message to Charli—and anything else I wanted by way of thanks.

But when her agent returned two weeks later, it was with bad news.

"Her family were gone before my agent got there, I'm afraid," Celeste told me. "She had left you a letter and package, though."

She handed them over to me with the promise that if I wanted, she could have her agents track the family down. I thanked her, but after reading the letter, I declined the offer.

Charli and her parents and sisters had moved into the remote mountains—off to join extended family who had left several years before. From the sound of it, her parents weren't likely to let her go jaunting off across the kingdoms, so there was no point asking Celeste's agent to make such a long journey.

At least Charli had been vindicated before she left. When the enchantment was lifted off me, it had also been lifted off the tower. And with such solid evidence before them, the adults of the village had finally believed their children's tales.

And in her usual kind and thoughtful way, Charli had sent me a final gift. After my departure, she must have returned to the clearing and climbed the tower. Because neatly folded into the package she sent was every one of the gowns I had so carefully embroidered.

I cried at the sight of them, sobbing over the material for too many reasons to explain, even to myself. But the tears eventually dried, and when Kali and Zaria arrived, I was ready to show them the results of my years of labor.

They had both taken Xander's request seriously, taking me under their wing and regaling me with stories of their home. And they were equally enthusiastic about the dresses, especially the odd design I had struggled over which turned out to be an ancient design from Kali's mother's people.

I was soon laughing with them and making plans for the future. My parents were already planning the wedding, having sent an invitation to the Sultan and Sultana to join us in Trione. And most of my friends, new and old, were planning to come. I suspected at least half of them of accepting the invitation because they wanted to meet merfolk, but I didn't mind.

Northhelm was safe, and I was finally free. I had left the tower behind, and I was ready for the wide world still in front of me. And best of all, I had my friends around me and Xander at my side. Whatever adventures still lay ahead of us, none of us had to face them alone anymore.

NOTE FROM THE AUTHOR

Find out what fairytale adventures await Charli in the Four Kingdoms duology, a retelling of East of the Sun and West of the Moon, starting with To Ride the Wind.

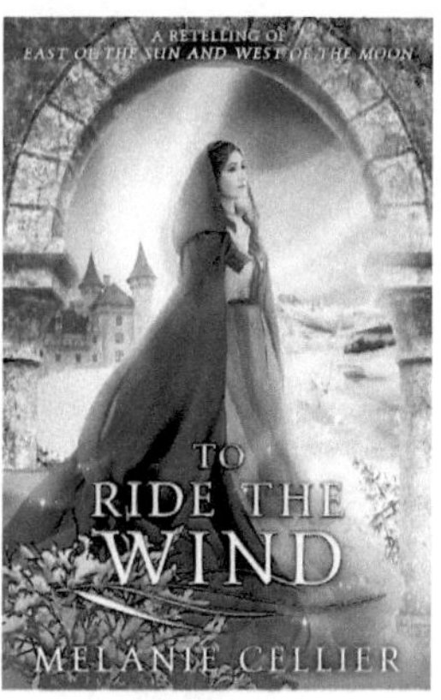

Or if you missed first meeting Daisy as a child, read Beyond the Four Kingdoms, starting with her first introduction in A Dance of Silver and Shadow: A Retelling of The Twelve Dancing Princesses.

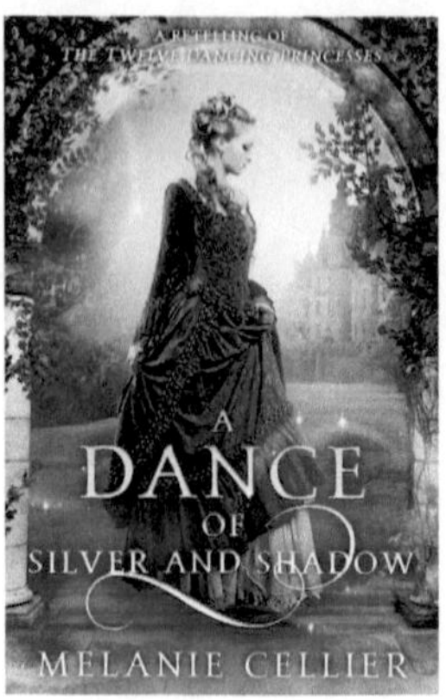

To be informed of my new releases, as well as new bonus shorts, please sign up to my mailing list at www.melaniecelli er.com. At my website, you'll also find an array of free extra content in my Four Kingdoms world.

Thank you for taking the time to read my book. I hope you enjoyed it. If you did, please spread the word! You could start by leaving a review on Amazon or Goodreads or Facebook or any other social media site. Your review would be very much appreciated and would make a big difference!

ACKNOWLEDGMENTS

It's been a long journey since Daisy first appeared as Teddy and Millie's younger sister in A Dance of Silver and Shadow. And for years now, probably the most frequent question I get asked by readers is when Daisy's story will be coming. I can only hope this story has met the expectations of all those who have been waiting for her adventure for so long.

Although I'm still planning a duology set in the Four Kingdoms world, it won't be set in any of the existing kingdoms, and so, in many ways, this book has felt like the final book of not just this series but of three series. Because of this, it has more links back to previous books than most of my fairy tales, and I hope my readers can forgive the indulgence on my part. My first Four Kingdoms book (The Princess Companion) was the very first book I published eight years ago, and the Four Kingdoms will always have a special place in my heart. This fairy tale world has been with me for my whole publishing journey, and it feels daunting to think of saying goodbye to so many well-loved characters.

I would like to give an enormous thank you to all the readers who have loved these books—whether you read them or listen to them, I have so appreciated hearing about your enjoyment of the stories. You have taken these kingdoms and characters into your hearts in a way I couldn't have dreamed when I first started writing them, and I couldn't be more grateful.

And, of course, I'm also incredibly grateful to my team. Many of them have been with me since that first book, or joined me very soon after, and I couldn't possibly maintain my publishing pace without their expertise, flexibility and dedication.

For my beta readers and editors: Mary, Dad, James, Rachel, Greg, Ber, Priya, Katie, and Deborah—I feel so blessed to have such a wealth of expertise and interest in my circle.

And as always, a big thank you to Karri. Daisy's cover is one of my favorites, and that's saying a lot after the number of fairy tale covers we've done together.

And I'm sure I couldn't thrive in the author world without my supportive network of author friends. Thank you Marina, Kenley, Shari, Brittany, Aya, and Kitty for being your fantastic selves. And to all the others—whether we were exchanging a short message or I was introducing you to the wonders of vegemite, thank you for being part of my author community. It's thanks to you that what could be a solitary career has become one that includes colleagues all across the world.

To Marc and my three kidlets—you bear the day-to-day burden of living with a struggling creative, so you deserve a whole extra level of thanks. Thank you for all the hugs when I finally step out of my office for some real life interaction.

And as always, the final thank you goes to God. He is the one who always sees us, who knows us most deeply, and who loves us most completely. May we all give to those around us a measure of the love and connection that He gives to us.

Melanie Cellier grew up on a staple diet of books, books and more books. And although she got older, she never stopped loving children's and young adult novels.

She always wanted to write one herself, but it took three careers and three different continents before she actually managed it.

She now feels incredibly fortunate to spend her time writing from her home in Adelaide, Australia where she keeps an eye out for koalas in her backyard. Her staple diet hasn't changed much, although she's added choc mint Rooibos tea and Chicken Crimpies to the list.

She writes young adult fantasy including books in her *Spoken Mage* world, her *Mage's Influence* world, and her various *Four Kingdoms* and *Kingdoms of Legacy* series that are made up of linked stand-alone stories that retell classic fairy tales.

www.ingramcontent.com/pod-product-compliance
Lightning Source LLC
Chambersburg PA
CBHW051249210726
48287CB00002B/419